A Dream Before Dying

— The Initiation

by
Tony Scott Macauley

A Dream Before Dying — The Initiation
by Tony Scott Macauley

Dancing House Publishing
Atlanta, Georgia

Published by
Dancing House Publishing
PO Box 10566, Atlanta, Georgia 30310

Printed in United States of America

10 9 8 7 6 5 4 3 2 1

The book has been set in Palatino Linotype. Body is 10 pt.

A Dream Before Dying
— *The Initiation*

by
Tony Scott Macauley

"Truths are easy to understand once
they are discovered; the point is to
discover them."

Galileo Galilei

Thank you,

Tony Crawley

1 Cor 10: 11

PROLOGUE

Vincent J. Christopher is, in a word, unique. He belongs to an elite group of men focused on the journey toward the age of enlightenment. Up to a point, their journey resembles that of other men. Traveling the pathway toward their truth, these elite learn about life as any other male child does. As with other young men, those chosen of God attain a certain age at which they learn the truth of who they are.

Followers of Christ, who remain faithful until the end of their journeys, receive the reward of eternal life, living forever in the presence of God. However, not all followers enter triumphantly through the gates of Heaven. Those like Vincent J. Christopher, whose paths take a distinctive U-turn, travel separately from mere mortals. These devoted souls, destined for God's glory, unwillingly return to Earth to once again grow from boys to men, continuing to fulfill God's divine plan.

Charged with an assignment from On High, God's chosen are held in the highest esteem. God destines each of these proud warriors to bear the burden of this painful, yet rewarding, commission. They seek and protect God's elect, preparing them for the battle that will precede the return of Christ. They will bring the deceived out of darkness, warning them about the false Christ. This is Vincent J. Christopher's commission.

He is one of God's Immortal Keepers.

But first, there's 1967, Detroit...

.

Episode One

November 7–November 30

What can I tell you about my graduation day? Like every other morning, I lay in bed, searching my room until my eyes settled on the image that had kept me focused for so long. I only had Vanessa's high school and college graduation pictures to remember her by, but, after today, I'll be one step closer to finding her.

I awoke to church bells ringing and, as usual, counted them while stretching in bed. I thought of the six morning chimes as "first hour." Those bells have been part of my life for twenty-one years, marking many memorable events of my entire family.

"Besides everyone else, I think I will miss you most of all, ol' faithful," I said to myself later, as I listened for my row to be called at the graduation ceremony.

"One step down; one step to go," I said to myself, thinking about my upcoming commission in the U.S. Army and my orders to serve in Vietnam. Finally graduating gave me a sense of accomplishment, like getting my driver's license and driving home for the first time.

They announced my row and I stood, thinking about my mother and how much she had supported me during my college days. She helped me stay focused through the ups and downs—including some tough ones. For four years, I climbed up a mountain called the University of Detroit with my mother on belay, proving, in more ways than one, that she was my support. I leaned on her when my professor rejected my final paper, written on the theological interpretation of Matthew 24. The

Episode One

rejection left me so disgruntled that I wanted to drop out of school, give up on my military commission and take my chances by joining the army as an enlisted soldier.

"You stand in there and fight it out, son," she said then. "It's your right to defend it. And if you have to, go over his head. You have come too far to give up now."

Waiting in line at graduation, I spotted Dino, my seven-year-old half-brother, sitting in the audience next to my mother. He had mixed emotions about today—I couldn't blame him. I could see his feelings as clearly as picturing the unbalanced scales of Justice. His sadness over me leaving home for the war in Vietnam outweighed his joy at my graduation from college. As young as he was, he was old enough to understand that graduating meant that I would leave home, possibly for good. I had gone through the same thing when Vanessa left, so I knew exactly what it felt like.

I would miss being here to watch him grow up over the next few years. God forbid, I might never make it back at all. Dino didn't know what it was like to truly miss someone. He never had the chance to meet his father, so he had no idea how painful losing a loved one can be.

What would it be like for a kid like him? Maybe like rushing home every day to play with his best friend, the family's golden retriever, then, one day, finding that she had to be put down while he was in school and he never got a chance to say goodbye.

That's it, I joked to myself. Guess that makes me the family dog, and Dino's best friend. He'll understand one day that I had to do this for me. I hoped.

The graduate in front of me climbed the platform steps. I heard my name. "Vincent Joseph Christopher III." The announcement echoed in my ears as I stepped onto the stage. Okay, here I go, I'm graduating. Finally! I can start living the life. And I'm ready.

I had distracted myself pretty well to this point, but, suddenly, my fears overwhelmed me. I needed to walk across this stage without incident.

Shoelaces, shoelaces, shoelaces. I looked down at my shoes. Three steps up, pause, look right, turn right, seven steps forward, shake right, receive left, seven steps forward, pause, look right, turn right, three steps down and it's over. I repeated these instructions in my mind, envisioning myself succeeding. I felt like someone with a fear of heights walking across a swaying plank, with stairs, thirty-five feet in the air.

My six-foot frame had proven capable of making quite a scene when I toppled over onto the floor at my high school graduation. Some of my crueler acquaintances never let me forget tripping over my shoelaces and crashing to the stage floor four years ago. I certainly don't want that to happen again. As I walked across the stage, I thought I heard voices saying, "Fall, Lurch, fall."

"…Chaplain, U.S. Army," added the announcer, as I arrived safely. The R.O.T.C. commander and I shook hands, then he proudly reached for my jacket.

Getting my degree in theology was great, but I really looked forward to getting pinned. I glanced down towards my left collar to glimpse what I had contemplated seeing for four years. It took that long, but I finally earned my lapel cross. This pinning ceremony marked the beginning. My thoughts, the new insignia, and the sparkle from the cross caused what can only be explained as a sort of spiritual hiccup.

"I'm finally a U.S. Army chaplain and through me the Holy Spirit will make a difference for all those lost souls in battle. Amen!" I shouted proudly, at the same time hoping I didn't embarrass myself.

Once the shine of my lapel pin blinded me, I felt even more convinced. The walking instructions I had frantically tried to remember no longer mattered. I just seemed to float across the stage with no problem at all. I finally reached the top of that mountain, looked down to see just how far I came, and then danced a jig.

"Vincent Joseph Christopher III." As I received my diploma, my name rang out the second time, echoing throughout the auditorium like a timpani drum roll, for some reason reminding me of how my friend, Rick, had teased me without mercy. My friend from a very early age, he imagined himself to be a Comedy Club headliner act. In reality, most of Rick's rants were as comfortable as a daily wedgie. During the week of my graduation, he had been nothing but a jerk.

"Let the trumpets sound, St. Peter! It's Vincent Joseph Christopher III, Chaplain Extraordinaire," taunted Rick. "Yo! Brother Christo"— as I was known to my neighborhood friends — "Tell me something. You gonna finally get a girlfriend before you go and save all those lost souls in combat? I mean, man—I just don't see how you do it. You just gonna go over there and die a virgin? Man! That is too sad for words. I mean, man, I can't even joke about that. I mean, it ain't even funny. Ha! Come on now, you gotta get lucky at least once before you go and get your damn brains blowed out." Rick punctuated his taunts by grabbing his private parts.

Derrick, another lifelong friend, joined Rick in his foolishness. "Yeah, man, why don't you just get married like the rest of those fools going to war? At least they gettin' busy one last time. Man, you really missing out.

Episode One

Who knows, one good night with a sweet fine young thang could make the whole dying-for-your-country thing seem more worth it—or not. Ah-ha. At least you'll have something to think about while you laying there, dying all over the place. Yeah, that's what you should do, get yourself married before you go off and become a hero. Oh—and don't worry, I'll check in on her while you saving souls." Derrick wrapped his arms around himself in a mocking fake hug.

As usual, Big Lump, my only true friend, came to the rescue. "Y'all need to chill out," he growled.

Isaac Lumpkin and I had been friends since fifth grade elementary. We didn't live in the same neighborhood, but did attend the same elementary school and high school, St. Martin de Porres. Now we were graduating from the same university on the same day, and with orders for Vietnam. At six-feet two inches, I had always been tall for my age, but at six-feet-four, Lump was a giant. I had my mother's lankiness, but Lump looked like a thick side of beef, solid in proportion to his height and a top athlete. His skin was just as dark as his body was large. Lump's friends joked that he was so black that he glowed purple in the dark. Due to our similar heights, we could be walking together at night and his darkness literally made him look like my shadow. Gentle as a puppy, yet frightfully large in appearance, he remained my best friend.

"One day y'all gonna wish you lived a life as sweet as our boy here, instead of ending up in jail where you probably on your way to, any day now," quipped Lump.

"What do you know? You just a big ol' lump," laughed Rick as he sprinted across the street out of Lump's daunting reach.

I don't want to think about those chuckleheads today, I reflected, refusing to let their negativity dampen my spirits.

I prided myself on having matured beyond such superficiality. I thought about Isaac. He especially wanted to see me receive my diploma and second lieutenant's bars and I was just as excited for him.

Returning to my seat, I listened for Lump's name. My flash of nervousness about walking across the stage past, my thoughts drifted toward my mother and our most recent conversation. She had recently admitted to keeping a few secrets from me. As I recalled our talk, I felt just as confused as I did the day we talked. The things she told me about the day I was born left me feeling more like an orphan than the beloved son of James and Lilly Christopher.

4

A Dream Before Dying

My mother, Mrs. Lilly Christopher, had a face as bright as the sun. Most people would agree that she always made them feel welcome. To them, Miss Lilly always seemed calm and in perfect spiritual harmony. Taller and slimmer than most of the people who knew her, she stood at five feet, eleven inches and extremely slender. Whatever she lacked in girth, she made up for in character, honesty, and faith. After being widowed twice, her personal life had been an emotional battle. She focused on Dino and me to keep from feeling sorry for herself. She would never allow others pity her.

"I have all the love I need," she would say, referring to us.

"I was so afraid on the day you were born, son," she said as we sat in the kitchen. "At first, I was afraid that you didn't survive the delivery…oh, it took you so long to cry out your first breath," she said sighing. "It seemed like minutes passed. The doctor couldn't get a peep out of you. It was like you refused to cry. Baby, that freezing night of December 31, 1946. It just seemed like you didn't want to be born."

"What are you trying to tell me, Mom?" I asked, attempting to pry more information out of her, but not sure if I wanted to hear. "What are you saying?"

"Son, I love you, but there is something, well," as she hesitated, carefully choosing her words, "different about you. I think God has something special for you to do here on earth."

Relieved, I sighed. "I know, Mom, don't you think I'm doing it?" I asked, still feeling that she hadn't quite told me everything.

"I'm proud of you for graduating from the College of Theology, and going off to do the Lord's work in the war, but I'm pretty sure that's only part of it," she explained, "and I knew it from the beginning. The nine months I carried you seemed more than just a gift from God. Lord knows, every woman who carries a child probably feels the same, but there was something especially different about carrying you," she said, touching her stomach absently.

"After you were born, I watched you sleep and I thought that God might take you from me. It looked like you remembered things from another life while you slumbered. You seemed held captive, only released when your eyes opened. That whole first year you seemed to be haunted by your dreams, but every time you woke up, your face would shine with joy."

"I don't remember any of that, Mom," I said, witnessing the concern in her eyes.

"The expressions on your face while you slept made me feel like you were asking God why you had to be born—again."

Episode One

"Born again—what do you mean?" I had a difficult time grasping how 'born again' related to me as an infant.

"This is hard for me to say, Vincey, but the whole time I carried you, I couldn't help feeling like your soul had been to earth many times before and that, for some reason, God chose me to carry you this time. It frightened me to think that you might have been handpicked and sent from heaven, but at the same time, it helped me understand things about you."

"I had no idea you ever felt this way, Mom," I said, sensing her inner pain. I closed my eyes for a moment, feeling dizzy from the brightness in my head. I expected it to go when I opened my eyes, but still felt somewhat woozy. As I wiped the sweat from my face, my stomach felt like a volcano erupting.

"My life totally changed when you grew inside me," she said, laying her hand on top of mine. "My cravings, as strange as they are in every pregnancy, were also extremely odd."

During the nine months my mother nurtured me in her womb, she felt compelled to read the Holy Bible more than ever before. She felt as though this yearning came from my soul, urging her to study more and more each day. The intensity of study increased as her delivery date drew near. She spent hours reading the books of Jeremiah, Isaiah, and Matthew out loud to me, her unborn child. Her quest for understanding the words of the prophets overwhelmed her. She felt a never-ending hunger for God's knowledge, and she consumed for two, spiritually.

"But I had a happy childhood, Mom, didn't I?"

"Yes, son, you were very happy, but the first time I laid my eyes on you, I didn't know what to think. You seemed so sad—like you were being haunted by shadows of past memories left behind from some other life."

She also told me that, while pregnant with me, she became obsessed with the number forty. Searching through the scriptures, she discovered that, in the biblical numbering system, the number forty meant probation. She found plenty of instances in the Holy Bible. These probationary examples were God's way of preparing each subject, before they fulfilled their parts in the completion of His plan. She believed that having me had more to do with God's plan than hers and that, although she wanted a family, her pregnancy was the beginning of a preparation or probation period for her child.

"Honey, it wasn't just me," she said. "Even the doctors and nurses that delivered you called you the baby with the mournful tears, wise beyond your years. They called you an 'old soul'."

With that conversation still fresh on my mind, I sat pensively in my seat, slowly raising my head to watch Lump receive his commission and diploma. Then I waited for the remainder of my graduating class to walk across the stage.

"Congratulations," I said when I caught up with Lump after the ceremony.

"It's time to go change the world," said Lump. We shook hands and hugged.

"We got orders to do just that." I pointed to Lump's second lieutenant's bars. "I'll see you in Vietnam, then." I felt slightly puffed up as we both saluted each other.

Episode Two

December 1—December 25

Three weeks later, on my last day in the U.S. before reporting to duty in Vietnam, I went to Mercy Medical Center to see my best friend. Lump was hospitalized, partially paralyzed, comatose, and unable to fulfill his commission with the U.S. Army. All of his dreams and aspirations had been stolen in one chaotic, tragic instant. It was like witnessing Charles Atlas, the world's strongest man, failing at his attempt to hold the world upon his shoulders and plummeting headlong, defeated by the worst of earth's violent emotions, fear and anger.

"I'm here to see Isaac Lumpkin," I told the receptionist.

"You here again?" she replied, without ever looking up at me. "You know the room number—271. You can go right on in, sir."

Making my way down the hall, I remembered how much of our free time Lump and I had spent visiting here. During high school and college, we had visited the children's wards. I was a pretty good amateur magician and Lump, always popular, would wear his football jersey and brag not about himself but how the kids were much braver than he could ever be.

This time was different. I couldn't find anything to be joyous or happy about. The night before we were supposed to go overseas, my friend, instead of helping others to be brave, lay in bed fighting for his life. No magic could replace what had been taken from him. In my heart, I felt it was my fault. If I had only been more humble and less proud, we would be leaving together.

Together, we felt unstoppable. Lump had hoped to apply for chaplain's assistant, which, to him, meant he would be my armed bodyguard. But now yin and yang had to go separate ways, leaving the world out of sync.

"Pride," I whispered, "it's because of my pride that you're lying here, my friend, and I'm so sorry." I was guilty of the very same character flaw I preached against, had warned Dino against, over and over.

"Wow!" I said, looking around Lump's room. The former football and basketball star of St. Martin De Porres High school was still popular. "Wow!" I said again, as I admired the gifts placed throughout the room.

"I guess I'll just put these flowers over here for you," I said, walking toward the window.

I had something far more meaningful to give my closest friend. I reached into the pocket of my dress green uniform and pulled out a photo of Lump and myself taken when we were in the seventh grade.

My father, who died while serving during the early part of the U.S. involvement in the Vietnam War, had been a military recorder and photographer. Even stateside, we never saw him without his photographic 'third eye'. He had taken this photo of us on the church steps after service one Sunday morning.

At times I would stay so long after church that my parents and Vanessa would begin slowly walking home, hoping that Lump and I would catch up. Lump, however, never left my side, shadowing me until I finished talking to everyone about God's word. Jokingly, the priests would chide me for making them look bad, then shoo us both away from the steps of the church porch. On this particular day things went as usual. Following church service, Holy Bible in hand, I explained my understanding of the scriptures and verses read by the priest earlier.

But I'll never forget what happened on the Sunday when this picture was taken. The regular parish priest had been away that day and another priest had taken his place. I was explaining verses to the Houston family when the visiting priest, apparently disturbed by my revelations, came down from the porch and snatched the Bible from my hands. Raising it high over his head, he prepared to swat me on my backside. Anticipating the priest's next move, Lump leaped between us and—always an accident waiting to happen—surged forward, tripping over a crack in the pavement, sending all three of us falling to the lawn beside the pavement. As the Bible flew skyward, I stretched as far as I could to catch it before it hit the ground. My body flipped over in midair, then landed face-up on top of the pile.

The whole scrimmage resembled the famous Hail Mary pass with me catching the holy football. In the end, Lump lay sandwiched between the facedown priest, with me lying sprawled face-up on top of them both.

Episode Two

Lump, usually quite agile for his height and size, sometimes missed a step or two while walking. Like missing a beat or skipping over a loose shoelace, he would stumble slightly or, in the worst-case scenario actually fall down. He tripped and fell over somebody so often that his football coach, who thought of it as a hidden talent, put him right at the center of the offensive line.

Vanessa and my parents had just started walking. Something told my dad to turn around. Dashing back toward the church, camera set on zoom, he stopped just in time to take a once in a lifetime photograph.

"Nice catch!" exclaimed my dad.

To this day I'm not sure if he was complimenting himself for capturing the picture, or me for my clutching reception.

I had been promising to give a copy of the picture to Lump for over ten years, but could never find the negative. Lump cherished that photo, one of the funniest reminders of our childhood, as much as I did.

"Here's the original," I said to my unresponsive friend. "It will probably outlive us both."

Looking back on that Sunday, I realized that Lump had always been there for me as a friend, and sometimes as a protector. "You always were, and will continue to be, Superman, my friend," I said, pretending to show off my muscles.

Now he lay there unconscious. I tried to find a way to say goodbye. I thought about how hurt I had felt on the day that Vanessa finally left. I remembered my dad dying in the war, when I never got the chance to say goodbye.

"God forbid that you should die," I thought, touching him on the shoulder. Another wave of guilt swept over me. "It's my fault you're in here," I said, trying to hold back my tears. "Please forgive me, brother."

I said a prayer and felt myself wanting to ask God to let me take Lump's place. I wasn't sure whether I actually asked or not, but if I did ask, I'm sure that God heard me.

With my plane due to leave in a few hours, I couldn't visit for very long. I used a safety pin to attach the photo, along with a copy of my duty orders, to Lump's hospital gown, then kissed him on the forehead. Before leaving I took one last peek at the photo and read my standing orders out loud.

"Attention to orders: 'Second Lieutenant, Christopher, Vincent Joseph. III, Army Chaplain, social security number, 374755550 Duty Station - Replacement Center - Nah Trang, Republic of Vietnam'.

My hand shook uncontrollably as I wrote the address a little larger on a separate sheet of paper. I wanted Lump to be able to read it easily, immediately after recovering from his coma. The actual orders were mostly a gift for Lump.

"Goodbye, my friend. I'll send you a postcard," I promised, backing out of Lump's room.

Actually saying goodbye only took a few moments, but afterward, hearing the words repeat in my mind, the moment lingered for what seemed like a lifetime. Saying goodbye to everyone was hard, but never being able to say goodbye was painful.

———————————————

During the long flight, too many distractions plagued my mind. Thoughts about my upcoming birthday, Christmas just around the corner, and winter all over the world kept me awake. But my reasons for volunteering to go to Vietnam interrupted most.

The Vietnam War, a mysterious, guerilla-fueled conflict had raged for close to ten years, ending countless thousands of Vietnamese and American lives, including my own father's life. Ever since I grew old enough to understand about the war in Vietnam, I had felt compelled to teach God's word to the soldiers sacrificing their lives for freedom of religion in that communist-led country.

Growing up, no one understood where such an aspiration came from, but I did. The moment I saw the first posthumously honored soldier returned home, I felt my spirit awakened.

"They don't need God over there," my friends would say. They mocked my dedication to soldiers fighting for freedom and their need to understand God's plan. "And they ain't over there fighting so people can be free—don't you watch the news?"

"They need to be free so they can worship God," I argued, never really insisting that they understand.

Even church and family members who opposed the war couldn't figure out why I felt it necessary to put my life on the line in combat just to teach God's word. For some reason I felt born to do exactly that and wouldn't have peace of mind until my fate, destiny, or God's will looked me straight in the eye.

All that being said, it seemed I would never truly rest until I found Vanessa.

"Can I get you anything?" asked the stewardess.

"No thanks," I said. "But thank you."

"You're welcome. You should get some rest then—we've got about ten more hours to go."

Episode Two

My eyes grew heavy. The roar of the engines faded into dreams of Christmas holidays gone by. Seeing her face, I wanted to close my eyes and think of Vanessa, and the years she spent with us. Thinking about her always calmed me down when I felt restless.

My mother and Vanessa met at church one day during service. Overhearing them talking one day I heard Vanessa saying that her step dad sexually abused, then abandoned her and their family when she was nine years old. Secretly listening, I overheard other things but couldn't understand any of it. One thing I did understand, my mom saying, 'the devil this and the devil that', Satan had a lot to do with it. After her dad left, something about her being passed around like party favorites, her mother looking the other way the whole time. When I was older my mother told me the story, that Vanessa's mother sobered up but could not afford to raise her. Rather than run out on her, Vanessa's mother asked the church to help find her a home. After a short stay in the convent one of the nuns introduced them and Vanessa became the daughter my mom never had but always wanted.

Even if I had understood what they were talking about it would not have changed how I felt. As far as I was concerned, she was just right for me, even if she was ten years older. At six years old, I was crazy about her.

"You want to study with me, Vincey?" she would ask knowing I would always say yes.

She studied with me, helped with my homework, and insisted that I read the Bible each day. At first, Vanessa seemed like my appointed guardian. As I grew older and more mature, she became that perfect masterpiece eluding the grasp of the most fervent art lover. Describing her now, as an adult, I wondered if I conjured my rendering from years of dreaming of the day we'd finally meet again.

In the picture in my mind, Vanessa's hairstyle matched her personality—neatly shaped, perfectly placed, and hanging just above her shoulder, hiding half of her face. She wore her hair like a veil, protecting onlookers from accidental hypnosis during truly awkward moments. She often caught men being scolded by their wives and girlfriends for staring too long in hopes of getting a better look. Concealing half of her face was her way of saving the world.

Simply catching a glimpse of Vanessa's Aphrodite like features would induce a fit of excitement that most mortal men were unable to handle, leaving them intrigued beyond the point of reason.

In order to see both sides of her face, a person had to know exactly when to look. With certain words, her face would push through her bangs, parting her lips into a smile that, in my mind, she intended just for me. Every once in a while, she brushed her hair away just so she could put a smile on my face. It was her way of playing peek-a-boo, and I loved playing it with her.

Whenever we talked, I found myself searching her face as if it held clues to the meaning of life. I looked straight into her eyes as her lashes batted my way, revealing a blue shadow that made my skin tingle. Like a sculptor molding a masterpiece, my gaze made its way down to the small dimple on the tip of her nose, to the dent in her top lip, and, finally, to the soft depression in her chin. I noticed how perfectly they all lined up together when she spoke. Entranced, there were often moments when I couldn't hear a single word she was saying.

She asked me to recite verse after verse.

"Ask me another one?" I would say, hoping to prolong our study together. I was more than happy to oblige her and studied even harder if I thought it would make her happy.

In truth, unbeknownst to me or Vanessa, I had been blessed with a remarkable ability for memorizing verses from the Holy Bible, and applying them to the second coming of Christ. Friends of the family used to call my talent a miracle. I not only possessed a photographic memory, but also had an inexhaustible hunger to understand the word of God.

"Vincey, how can you remember all of those verses the way you do?" she would say, teasing me with her hair. Then, when she made eye contact with me, "You're the best little brother in the world."

I kept busy counting the years between us. At six, I loved being thought of as her little brother, but, as I got older, that changed. When I was seven years old, she was seventeen. When I was sixteen, she would be twenty-six. And when I was twenty-one—well, she'd be perfect all over again. In my heart I knew that we would get married just as soon as I grew up; and at six years old I was counting down the days.

Back then, Vanessa influenced more then the way I studied. She also had a lot to do with the way I felt about the war and what it meant to be a hero. She constantly talked about the lives of the soldiers serving, more than the actual war itself. She decided to volunteer after finishing college, where she studied music. She signed up as a music specialist for the U.S. Armed Forces and was stationed in Vietnam.

So my reasons kept me restless during the flight. Was it Vanessa? Was I enticed by desires yet unfulfilled? Was it because of my dad, or was it truly because I thought I could make a difference? What difference did it make anyway? I'd become what God wanted, an Army Chaplain on a mission. I had kept my promise to God and Vanessa, made the right decision, and, in my heart, I knew I had been thoroughly prepared for the next part of my life. I looked forward to whatever adventure lay ahead.

The over sixteen-hour flight from Ft. Lewis, Washington to South Vietnam left me exhausted, yet exhilarated as I reported to the replacement center at Nha Trang, a coastal city in the south known for its beaches. Bearable temperatures during the day and cool nights, even during the winter months, made this city a great place to visit during more peaceful times.

While settling in, I saw others like myself just arriving 'in country'. There were new soldiers everywhere. They called us 'N.F.G.s'—new freaking guys—and I was proud to be one.

I also saw the men who were heading back to the world. These combat veterans looked as though they had been taken right out of the middle of a combat zone. Physically, they waited in the out-process area, but mentally they were still engaged in their most recent firefight somewhere. The wear and tear of combat life sank into their weather-beaten faces, which seemed completely detached from their present reality. From the top of their heads to the bottom of their boots, each soldier bore witness to his struggle to staying alive in the deep bushes of combat.

Cold eyes stared blankly into space, as they sat in the out-processing section, aimlessly searching for parts of their soul eternally lost in combat. As I passed by them, I felt their eyes piercing right through me, as if looking beyond death.

"This is the reason that God has me here," I said, clenching the Holy Bible closer. "This is why I'm needed here."

I don't know how it happened, but I soon found myself becoming sort of a shoulder to cry on. Though they shed no actual tears, I could hear their souls crying for spiritual help. Normally, seasoned warriors like these men would have nothing to do with N.F.G.s like me—and they were older than I was.

It's the collar. I thought of it as a spiritual type of truth serum.

Shortly after my arrival, a young army private about my age singled me out and privately confessed his sins to me, a rookie chaplain.

His declarations sounded like a series of war stories, but were confessions all the same. He talked about the firefights, the fields stained with blood of both friend and foe, and his friends who would return dead, dying or dismembered. The desperate veteran talked about how, at times, he went without sleeping. He feared that he would never know what resting with his eyes closed felt like again. The fear in his heart, the exposure to everyday violence, and his will to survive, had desensitized him so that he came to enjoy the killing. After months of killing and running from death, he feared he would never truly find peace.

How could a child of God be subjected to such evils? My heart cried in anguish for him.

My job would be much more than visiting the wounded and delivering last rites. Everything that the N.F.G.s, the old soldiers, and I experienced during the war would affect us for the rest of our earthly lives. I prayed that, through faith, the grace of God, and the power of the Holy Spirit, I would be able to make a difference in their eternal lives.

"Jesus Christ will give you the rest you seek," I counseled him. "Anyone with a heavy burden, a tormented soul, or an empty heart, need only draw closer to Him, and their souls will find rest. His comfort means knowing you'll never have to look over your shoulder again."

As I reassured him, I noticed his two buddies listening intently to the conversation. They had the faces of men who expected to be jailed for some horrendous crime.

I wasn't sure if I was saying the right things; being in the presence of true warriors made me stammer as I spoke. I only hoped that they wouldn't see through my inexperience.

"But how?" questioned one soldier. "Just finding Jesus doesn't seem like enough."

Another solider insisted that he had already found Jesus, but it didn't seem to help. I calmed their fears by explaining that just finding Jesus only promised eternal life. Living life on earth with peace of mind meant finding much more.

I instructed them, "Find Jesus and then keep searching for the rewards and blessings of God's Spirit. They can be gained through wisdom and understanding."

"Find yourself a wise Bible teacher," I advised, "Your soul will know when a true teacher of God's word is speaking. Develop an understanding and you'll find the rest you need. Don't settle for being preached to—ask questions. The true rewards lie in the answers to the mysteries that God has waiting for you. Don't look for what makes your flesh happy, or simply comforts you emotionally, but instead let your soul do the searching."

Episode Two

"Lieutenant Christopher?"

The clerk was addressing me, so I excused myself from the out-processing soldiers until later.

"You're all set, sir. You'll just be hanging around here for about three weeks getting acclimated, waiting for your orders. The P.T. is at 0600, sir."

Time moved quickly for me. I was busier than I could ever have imagined, but bored with my daily routine. I would never see any real action while remaining attached to the processing center. I had been assigned to, but not attached to, a company-sized field unit, but was not given the chance to join them.

I wanted to get my feet wet, so I put in a request to be attached to the field unit. They granted my request and, on Christmas Eve, about three weeks after reporting for duty, I landed by helicopter in Saigon, about three hundred miles from Nah Trang.

After the temperate climate in Nah Trang, I found Saigon's environment to be dry, though the soldiers who had been there through the summer had plenty of stories to tell about monsoon season. I enjoyed the climate, but missed the winter snow of Detroit.

I felt more involved in the war effort now. As I off-loaded from the helicopter I heard a voice saying, "Merry Christmas, Father." I looked up. Two men, waiting to depart for the out-processing center, were going home for Christmas. Yet, as I took a good long look at them, I recognized that same piercing look of death. To them, as combat veterans, it was business as usual.

"God bless you, men," I said, "and when you get home, before you look for anything else, look for Jesus. He is your only true way out of this place."

"Amen! Holy man," the second soldier shouted, "Jesus must be at home 'cause He sure as hell ain't in this place!"

During my first few days I exhausted myself by touring every military base camp and medical facility located in the south end of Saigon. Standing next to a soldier who had been in battle made the hair on my arms rise. I couldn't help wondering what it was really like for them in combat. I had seen enough to know that, by the time the men were brought back to the rear medical units, it was usually too late. I was sure that I could serve God and the unit better by joining the men out on patrol.

A Dream Before Dying

Most of the action occurred on the Ho Chi Minh Trail, and I thought I would be able to do my best work there. More of a transport system than an actual trail, it ran from North Vietnam, or the Democratic Republic, to South Vietnam, also called the Republic of Vietnam. An intricate network of truck routes, paths for foot and bicycle traffic, and river transportation ran through the neighboring kingdoms of Laos and Cambodia, providing manpower and materials to the enemy Viet Cong troops.

I put in a request to join a patrol mission, and found out that a small team was currently out on patrol. I wouldn't be able to link up with them until they returned. I remained patient and, in the meantime, planned a Christmas service for the men and women in the rear detachment.

My private living quarters consisted of my bunk in one corner with a stand-up locker behind the headboard. For a person as tall as me, it should have felt a little cramped, but I was quite comfortable. My footlocker rested at the end of the bunk. Next to my bed, my battery-powered radio sat on the desk. The radio made me feel at home.

The war in Vietnam launched the Motown sound globally and, at times, the music made all U.S. soldiers feel welcomed. The Temptations' "My Girl" played on the radio my first night in the field, and I thought about the day Vanessa bought a copy for me from the record store. I just knew that Vanessa was my girl and the Temptations wrote a song about it just for me. Now, although I was over nine thousand miles from Detroit, that sweet sound on the radio was all it took to make me forget how far from home I really was.

I sorted through the mail, searching for a letter from Lump, who I hoped was doing well by now. I smiled when I found a letter from Dino. As I read, the smell of fish filled my nostrils. I thought the odor came from the letter. Dino loved fried fish; maybe he had been eating some while drawing pictures of me in my uniform. But the odor hung in the air everywhere, and I realized that I had been smelling fish since stepping off the helicopter in Saigon

Is that death? Is that what death smells like? It's bad enough to have death surrounding you all day, but to have it smell like rotten fish makes it worse.

Over the years, the land of Vietnam had been laid waste. The once beautiful countryside had become an enormously overflowing toilet bowl, clogged with daily violence and scheming political corruption, but, most of all, the countless dead and dying. The stench flowed through the air like a tsunami of death.

Episode Two

I dwelt on the death surrounding me and the way no one could escape its toxic fumes. Like people who lived near a factory, forced to breathe in its fumes, we inhaled death, which had become as prevalent as life.

In an effort to combat the pervasiveness of death, the Lord impressed on me that I should continue with the Christmas service for the soldiers. It was easier to gather the troops than I expected. I had anticipated rejection, but the opposite was true. These soldiers seemed hungry for the word of God.

I opened the Holy Bible, read through Matthew, and delivered my first sermon on the birth of Jesus Christ. As I looked around the base camp congregation, mostly administrative teams and medical staff, joy and compassion filled me. Yet I understood that they would much rather be at home with their families.

Teaching about the Christmas story reminded me of the many times I had taught it at my church at home. I always introduced the idea that Christ was born in the fall rather than winter, and that Christmas celebrated the date of Christ's conception, plus or minus a few days. John the Baptist was six months older than Christ, and I would prove it while teaching from the book of Matthew.

At home, the churchgoers weren't so sure they wanted to believe my version, although some admitted that it made much more sense. It seemed logical that Christ be born during the Feast of Tabernacle, especially since the mandatory census took place during the fall of that year. I had often explained how Mary, the mother of Christ, conceived six months after the course of Abijah, a religious event that happened in the middle of June each year.

At home, I discussed how Zechariah, the priest responsible for this particular course, received a message from an angel while performing his priestly duties. He fathered a child who became the forerunner for the Messiah. His wife Elizabeth conceived in late June of that year and then, six months later, Christ's miraculous conception made Him exactly six months younger then His cousin, John.

I planned on telling this same story to the soldiers sitting in front of me, but suddenly knew that they needed to hear something more personal, that what they were doing over here was right. They needed a much bigger picture than the earthly power struggles of corporate and political interests. This was part of God's plan. Everyone across the globe who wished to celebrate the birth of Christ should have the freedom to do so. They needed a Christmas message about the God who commissioned them to help bring about the completion of His plan. I knew it was much easier believing in the spiritual freedom of mankind than the furthering of diplomacy, democracy and capitalism.

"Ladies and gentlemen!" I said sharply. "This war is much bigger than economics or politics. It's the war between God and the enemies of God. It's a war between good and evil. It's the war between Jacob and Esau. God loved Jacob, but He hated Esau, and for some reason that dislike was established before they came to earth."

I continued preaching, teaching the troops that any communist system angers God because communism does not allow Him. I emphasized over and over that God didn't hate the communist people, but hated a communist system that denies the children of God the right to worship Him.

Prophecies foretold that Rebecca, the mother of Jacob and Esau, would carry two warring nations in her womb, one favored by God and one hated by God. As much as God dislikes civil war, he still placed them both in her womb. Twin brothers of the same bloodline placed in the womb, growing up together, only to feud with each other till the end of time.

Why would God allow this? A better question, which partly answers the first one, is: why would God allow something that He hates to happen? In a way, God, by placing those two warring nations in the same womb and knowing the outcome ahead of time, caused it. But why did He? I compared that ancient biblical civil war to the war in Vietnam.

"There is another civil war that exists right here, and we are in the middle of it," I said, closing the Bible.

"Unfortunately, as with most wars, the soldiers have no choice in the matter. The decision to go to war is made for us, even before we have a chance to pray about it. We can only pray for the success of God's will, which is to bring freedom to the children who wish to serve Him. Ladies and gentleman, this is our mission. We are here, and not in the comfort of our homeland, because we have been chosen to sacrifice everything in order to help God complete His plan."

I told them to make the completion of God's plan their main focus; it would keep them mentally alert during battle. I told them that nonstop prayer would reinforce their spirit. I told them that, in order to stay focused, especially during battle, they must talk with God daily, nightly, and even minute-by-minute. I said, "In wars of old, soldiers were successful in battle because they convinced God of their sincerity and desire to do His will.

"Tell yourself each and every day, while you are here in this country, that God sanctioned you to bring about the completion of His plan. It's not about you or the enemy. It's about God. We are doing this for Him. We are here for the children of God who are denied their rightful heritage—God. Our worst enemy over here is not the Viet Cong. It's our own minds. Don't focus on the bad. Stay positive by knowing God has chosen you to help Him, and how honorable that is.

"Keep your head to the sky. Keep your focus on God's plan and repeat it to yourself over and over, minute by minute. You will convince yourself and, more importantly, you'll convince God. He will search your heart, and what's better, he will know your heart.

I couldn't believe I said all that. I had never spoken positively about the actual war in the past. I didn't know where those words came from. I had just attempted to persuade a group of soldiers that the war was right, and it left me unsettled. I felt dizzy, and wondered if I accidentally inhaled smoke from the nearby reefer hut. I had never thought about God being part of the war effort in Vietnam. It sounded as if I was promoting the war. I needed to take inventory of my true feelings. How could I have said these things?

I grew up believing and practicing Colossians 3:23, 'and whatsoever ye do, do it heartily, as to the Lord, and not unto men; knowing that of the Lord ye shall receive the reward of the inheritance: for ye serve the Lord Christ'. Serve God wherever you are and be thankful that you've been chosen. That was my golden rule. I reckoned that the soldiers needed to hear it, and the Holy Spirit put those words in my mouth.

As the Christmas sermon ended someone asked me to finish the story about Jacob and Esau. What was the lesson in God placing one He loved against one He hated in a civil war?

"That's a great question." I turned to answer, pleased to notice that no one had left. "Most of the Bible, when applied with understanding, refers to the second coming of Christ," I added.

I could picture each major event in the Holy Bible as an announcing trumpet, heralding the return of Christ. The entire Old and New Testaments held warnings and lessons for the children of God who will be here in the end.

"The ongoing feud between two brothers represents the type of civil war that will take place in the end times among Christians who love the Lord and are waiting for His return."

"The two sides of the war," I continued, "will be made up of those waiting for the true Christ and those who are deceived into following the false one. It will be a war fought over the soul and spirit, and it is a civil war—because we are all one family in Christ."

That night, I rested in my tent, trying to adjust my senses to the elements surrounding me, natural and unnatural. I had been in Vietnam for only a few short weeks now, and it wasn't getting any easier. I still needed to figure out my sudden support for the war and why I said those things during the sermon. I knew the soldiers needed reassurance, but, for some strange reason, I had been swayed toward the war effort as well. What would I become if I continued to think that way? I supported our soldiers one hundred percent and always had, but I had never actually confessed support for the war.

During the night, after studying in my quarters, I realized I did not fear for myself. I had volunteered feeling fully prepared to die for my county. I feared for the ones who were not spiritually prepared for death. They would have to remain here to fight, to kill, and possibly be killed. I had to let them know there was forgiveness for them, that killing in war was not the same as murdering someone. I prayed that the Holy Spirit would touch each one of them before the end, and save each of their souls.

Early the next morning, a medevac helicopter landed. The wounded soldier lying on the stretcher stared straight into my eyes. As if I were the angel of death, his expression seemed to say, "I hope you don't see me."

From my point of view, it felt like death was staring at me. I shook off a chill.

His boots had been removed, and fresh blood pooled near his ankles. Apparently he had triggered a booby trap that took off both his feet. As the surgeons rushed him to the emergency unit, I noticed a black bag covered in blood just above the skid of the Huey. I went to retrieve it, but one of the medics beat me to it.

"You don't want to see that, holy man." The medic ran off to join the team carrying the stretcher. I could just make out what looked like boot laces hanging from the bag as he ran away.

"Besides," the medic called over his shoulder, "We need to ID him."

I remembered that infantry soldiers always attached one ID tag to their boots while on patrol. I ran to the emergency room behind the medic. I wanted to be there, just in case I had to administer the last rites. If this soldier had to die, I would make sure that he spent eternity much better than his last moments on earth. Unfortunately, the wounded soldier didn't make it. After giving the last rites, I looked at his boots for a long time.

"Well, you'll be made whole again in heaven."

I thought about how the soldier stared at me. Before he died, I had felt death as a physical presence. I wondered: if I had acted sooner, maybe I could have taken it by surprise and, through prayer, sent it back to hell. I ran outside and gazed upward. If heaven opened up to receive God's newest slain hero, I did not see it. The stench of death still filled the air, but I was sure that PFC Wesley met God that day.

Hour by hour, the images of war became more and more real. When we were younger, Lump and I spent hours staring at photographs taken during the early part of the war. Now I began to put all the images together. My father had sent large envelopes home from the war, sealed with official labels warning of the content. He instructed my mother to lock them, unopened, in a footlocker in the third floor attic of our house.

Painfully, I remembered the last envelope that came. It wasn't delivered by mail. Early one evening, I watched from my bedroom window as an official government vehicle pulled up in front of our house. I had seen it stop at other homes in the neighborhood. In my naïve curiosity, I had hoped that it would stop in front of our house one day, too. Two soldiers, in U.S. Army dress uniforms, stepped out of the vehicle and, keeping step, solemnly marched up the pathway to our porch. One of the men slowly reached forward to knock on the door. The reach for the door looked like a slow motion salute, and the three ceremonial knocks on the door lingered like taps performed by a passionate bugler.

Vanessa, as if she already knew what the visit meant, tried to stop me from greeting them. She did not succeed; excited, I ran down the stairs, trying to beat my mother to the door.

"Let me answer it!" I pulled the door open, only to have my mother step in front, blocking my view. "Let me see, Mom." I managed to squirm my way to where I could see the two spit-shined soldiers.

She held her breath tightly as she pressed her hand over my left ear, and my right ear to her apron. I couldn't hear a word, but, from Vanessa and my mother's reactions, I began to understand that this wasn't a happy visit. The other official handed over an envelope while reciting a verbal apology from the President of the United States. Vincent Christopher II—known as Jr. to friends, had honorably given his life in service to his country.

A Dream Before Dying

My mom never let me read the letter from the president. Yet, as much as I tried to comply with her wishes, the visit from the soldiers forever haunted me. I had never cared to see what was in the previous envelopes from my father, but I felt compelled to read that last mysterious document from the president.

My mother refused to open it. In her rejection, she stored the letter, forever unopened, with the rest of my father's correspondence. I figured out that my father wouldn't be returning home, but wanted to read the words for myself.

I was forbidden to enter the attic, but, disobeying my mother, I began sneaking into the attic after school. While looking for the letter from the president, Lump and I spent hours discovering the truth about the war. Hundreds of images of brutality both sickened and saddened us.

Despite the images, I came to think of dying in battle, in all its gruesomeness, as heroic, honorable, sanctified and, in a way, holy unto God. I didn't feel that way at first, but, during my search, I found a verse from the Holy Bible written on the back of a photo that showed the graphic death of a soldier. I recognized my father's handwriting, so I looked at the backs of the other photos.

I found written and, at times, scribbled, the verse 2 Timothy 2: 3-4, "Thou therefore endure hardness, as a good soldier of Jesus Christ. No man that warreth entangleth himself with the affairs of this life; that he may please Him who hath chosen him to be a soldier."

I was convinced that my father's final words to me were written on the backs of those photos. In my heart, I felt as if he found a way to say goodbye after all. These messages from beyond helped to convince me of my destiny to serve God and country. In a way, this repeating verse, attached to the pictures of those who had died in battle, seemed like an attempt to send each soul back to God with an honorable farewell.

Now that I was serving in Vietnam, I realized that the black, white, and gray images from the attic footlocker softened the truth. On one hand, the emotionally packed black-and-white television footage that Vanessa and I watched on the local news channels years ago inspired in us loyalty, pride, and unconditional allegiance to the men and women in uniform. For impressionable viewers, the footage became a type of recruitment, bringing out heroic aspirations in prospective warriors. Young boys, filled with adventure and not truly understanding the meaning of death crowded around their TV sets and watched flag-covered coffins off-loaded from cargo planes, hoping that they would one day be G.I. Joe, returning home a hero.

Episode Two

But on the other hand, these same colorless images brought out fear, anger, and irrational hysteria in others toward the troops placed in harm's way every day. The truth is, all the TV footage and pictures collected in books could not compare with the images I saw daily, in living color. My father's camera captured still figures, some of men scared for their lives, some of dead men, and others of the dying, but the medium hid the full impact of their true emotions. As I looked around, I found myself laying real life footage over images from the past, like adding color to an old black-and-white silent movie—once a slide show, now playing in real time.

Each event that unfolded formed part of my destiny. I didn't know it, but I would soon experience a different sort of movie, one where I would be the leading actor. December 31, the day of my twenty-first birthday, would arrive in a day or two, and God had a front-row ticket for me.

Episode Three

December 25—December 27

I met more of the soldiers. It was Christmas day and early that morning each platoon returned from the field one by one. One of those soldiers was a man I had dreamt of meeting since I studied about him in my college R.O.T.C program. Like most Christian men, I contemplated walking in the footsteps of Christ, and I thought that following the jungle boots of Colonel Franklin Preston Harris would be a good start. One of the few black colonels in the whole U.S. Army, he was also one of the greatest, black or white. Well on his way to becoming a brigadier general, he was Ranger qualified, Airborne qualified, and—what I considered his highest qualification—a Christian warrior.

Weary from coordinating no less then seven ongoing missions from an adjacent command post, but alert and exuding leadership, he passed within arm's reach of me as he marched toward the command tent.

Unable to resist the urge to meet him, I moved respectfully toward Colonel Harris, only to be signaled to stop. He was transmitting and receiving an urgent message by radio. One of the squads from Charlie Company was pinned down, surrounded by enemy troops with no way out. In a flat area with no helpful cover or identifiable terrain features by which to navigate, they were sitting targets.

A lieutenant reminded Colonel Harris about radio silence. Colonel Harris was acutely aware that the Viet Cong monitored the daily radio frequencies, and even knew the secret codes for that day. The enemy would overhear any message he got across to the squad. As if swayed by a powerful spiritual connection, Colonel Harris put the squad's radio operator on hold and motioned to me for help. He took hold of my elbow and moved off to the side of the command tent.

"Need some help here, Preacher," he said sharply.

"I need to set up a holy play option. I need my men to see the vision in my head so we can get them out of that hellhole, alive. We're gonna call this Zerubbabel, 'cause we be comin' out of confusion. Can you be with me on this one?"

"Absolutely, sir," I said, making a mental note that my initial conversation with Colonel Harris made me feel like an infant uttering its first words.

As Colonel Harris and I huddled over the radio, it looked as if we had entered into prayer. The colonel grabbed the microphone and spoke to the trapped squad's radiotelephone operator. "Private, were you in that Bible study class that I gave last week?"

"Yes, sir," said the RTO firmly.

"I want you to picture Moses' tabernacle," said the colonel, setting the stage.

"Roger that, sir."

"Do you remember the direction of the Mount of Olives in relation to the altar of sacrifice?"

"Um, that's a big negative, sir," answered the RTO hesitantly.

"Well, I suggest you pay attention next time, son," said the colonel, looking at me and shrugging his shoulders.

"Yes, sir," the RTO whispered into the hand microphone.

"Don't worry, son," said the colonel in a fatherly tone. Then, speaking deliberately, he said, "I'll give you another chance. Think about the city of Jerusalem. Do you remember the direction to the Mount of Olives from the Holy of Holies? If you do, I want you to squelch your mic, twice, over."

"I can't mention the direction over the air, son, so I gotta trust you on this one," said the colonel. "You with me?" Colonel Harris listened as the RTO squelched his hand microphone twice.

"You're gonna be surrounded by cannon fire from every direction. Son, for about thirty seconds it's gonna feel like you died and gone to hell. Instruct your squad leader that we're gonna continue firing artillery into your area from all directions and then cease firing in one direction only. That will be the way out, understand me, son?" The RTO replied again by squelching his mic twice.

"We're gonna create an invisible corridor for you and, son, your squad better haul butt like you love life more than anything else, 'cause you gonna have about thirty seconds before we close that door and start lighting it up again."

The RTO replied again by squelching his mic twice.

"Direction is as follows," said the colonel. "Your position right now is, I say again, your current position is the Mount of Olives, squelch twice, over. After thirty seconds the cease-fire will begin for your departure. Leave the Mount of Olives, head one thousand meters toward the Holy of Holies, and then turn ninety degrees to the left and then head for the pick up zone. That's your exodus. It's a holy riddle, son, you follow me?"

"Roger that, sir," said the RTO, confidently. "Mission Exodus."

"At 0735 hours, you wait for the initial bang, and we will pour out the lake-of-fire on top of your heads, over."

"Roger that, sir. Over and out," said the RTO.

The colonel ended his transmission with the RTO and returned the radio to the lieutenant. "Lieutenant, take these coordinates and call for artillery fire from every direction, and then cease firing only from the west. We need to create a seam for our men to thread through on the west end," instructed the colonel.

"Roger that, sir," said the lieutenant, taking over the radio.

"Inform them that this fire mission is danger close, Lieutenant, and that our boys are in the kill zone," said the colonel. "And get those birds to the pick up point, pronto-like."

Once the artillery knew that the target area was in very close proximity to friendly personnel, the colonel issued orders for the helicopters to pick the squad up at the alternate pick up site.

I trembled inside. In the presence of Colonel Harris, the hair on my arms stand at attention.

Wow, I reflected. One of these days God will surely reward him. When Jesus returns to earth to reclaim His church, I'm sure that Colonel Harris will be with Him, fighting alongside Him amidst the heavenly army.

"Don't worry, Preacher," he said. "They'll get out of this alright 'cause you can't go wrong when you follow Jesus, and the Commies don't know enough about Jesus to shoot their way out of a dead rice paddy, follow me?"

"Yes, sir."

"I appreciate your being here with me today, Preacher. The Bible teaches us that where two are gathered in His name, He'll be in the midst."

"Amen, sir," I said, feeling my first sense of achievement.

"Amen, Preacher. So, I understand you volunteered for this unit. Got tired of that plush job near the beach, huh? Want to see some action,

Episode Three

huh? Well, my men need you. For some reason a lot of them know Christ, maybe that's why I got this command, and with you here our faith will grow even stronger. Any time you want to beat the bush with the men, you let me know. We don't meet much resistance usually. Charlie Company was out on a different mission, but they'll make it back. Christopher, huh? I believe that means follower of Christ, in the Greek language?"

"Yes, sir," I confirmed, pleased by the colonel's knowledge. "Christopher is Greek for follower of Christ."

"Friends call you Christo for short?"

"Um, sometimes my really close friends do, but mostly my dad called me that, sir," I said as visions of Rick, Derrick and Lump flashed through my mind.

Colonel Harris had a way of making all the men feel like family—like he was a father and we were his sons. His men were fortunate to have such a reassuring figure as their leader. Over the next three days, I accompanied Colonel Harris in and around the base camp. By then, most of the soldiers had seen or at least heard of me, as Colonel Harris had given me credit for Charlie Company's successful escape mission. I felt like I was beginning to realize my calling.

———————————

Base Camp Alpha, a smaller company made up of special operation teams, was due for their command inspection. Colonel Harris had invited me to accompany him, and I gladly accepted.

The special operations teams infiltrated enemy territory, extracted 'hot targeted personal', and initiated offensive engagements with the enemy.

"These teams are my Michaels—you know, my archangels," boasted the colonel.

I stood next to the colonel as the driver removed the top hood of the Jeep. I had been surprised when I first met him —at nearly six feet, seven inches tall, the colonel was much taller than I had expected and built like a professional athlete.

According to military protocol, I crawled into the back of the Jeep on the passenger side before the colonel entered, while the colonel sat in the front on the passenger side. The colonel, the driver, and I proceeded out of Base Camp Charlie and headed toward Alpha.

I could see the colonel's face by looking into the side view mirror. The image of Malcolm X, the celebrated black liberation advocate, flashed in my mind, especially his most famous photograph. Colonel Harris's broad chin had the same chiseled dimple and, like Malcolm X, his punctuated speech seemed to hypnotize listeners. The colonel's military-issue sunglasses had the same type rim worn by the slain leader. I could barely make out his eyes through the tinted glasses, but noticed how the wrinkles around them made him appear more distinguished than old. Although he kept his scalp clean-shaven, his face revealed a subtle shadow of red stubble across it.

Unbeknownst to me the Colonel was also observing me through the same side-view mirror and gave an approving nod, sensing that a greater light had joined his command team.

The driver intuitively maneuvered the Jeep as it skidded, weaved, and bounced along paths worn by frequent travel. Strangely, I felt perfectly balanced in my seat. A single passenger in the back seat was usually tossed around uncontrollably because of the rough terrain. The colonel raised an eyebrow as I calmly rode over a large bump.

The colonel looked over his right shoulder, then back just as I leaned forward to my left and around his left shoulder. We both ended up speaking at the same time, but missing each other. Realizing that the colonel was about to speak, I immediately switched to his right—just as the colonel switched to his left to hear me speak. Again, we both ended up speaking at the same time, missing each other again.

"What's that, son?

"Say again, sir?"

We chuckled, clearing our throats. Returning to our original positions, we tried again.

The driver must have noticed also, as he made an awkward attempt at clearing his throat—probably to cover a laugh. I looked into the side view mirror again and asked the colonel to speak first. Colonel Harris looked over his left shoulder, turned sideways in his seat and initiated the conversation.

"The trails between the base camps are laced with landmines," he said, pointing out over the front and back of the Jeep. "We know where all of them are, but we just leave them. You know why, son?" asked the colonel.

"No, sir," I answered, following the direction of Colonel Harris's hand.

"Cause if we move 'em, Charlie will replace the ones we moved and add some we don't know about."

"That makes a lot of sense, sir," I said, hoping that there weren't any new mines that the Jeep's driver didn't know about.

Episode Three

"That's right, son, and remember this: in war, sometimes it's better to do nothing than to do something and get killed for it."

I would have never learned that back in R.O.T.C.

Colonel Harris left that tidbit as quickly as he started it, finished with the small talk. Apparently, in Vietnam, helpful advice about how to stay alive was nothing more than water cooler conversation.

"Look here, son," he said, with a calm authority "I want you to keep pumping the Gospel of John to my men. It's my favorite gospel of all."

"May I ask why?" I inquired; seeking to gain a clearer understanding of the colonel's spiritual leaning.

"Why? I'll tell you why, son, but you already know the answer."

"Yes, sir, I believe I do, but I would like to hear you tell me, if that's alright, sir."

"If that's alright! If that's alright? Son, you can ask any one of my men. Of course I don't mind telling you or anyone else how I feel about the Gospel of John. It's the one Gospel that specifically says, point blank, no ifs, ands, or buts about it, that Jesus was the Messiah, and the only begotten Son of God."

The colonel had truly done his homework. I had conversed with many people who were convinced that the Holy Bible never referred to Jesus as God's only begotten Son. I would point out that the Gospel of John mentioned it more than once. John, the disciples of John the Baptist, Andrew and Nathaniel, specifically called Jesus the Son of God.

"Sir?" I began. "Knowing that Jesus and John the Baptist were cousins, why do you think that, in Chapter 1, John the Baptist says that he doesn't know Jesus, but identifies Him as the Lamb of God?"

"Well, son, this sounds like a test question to me. Are you asking me as a test of my knowledge? Because, around here, debts are paid in full, one push-up at a time. How many can you do? I'm beginning to feel a holy wager coming on. What do you say, son? How many push-ups can your triceps handle? You think you can beat the old man?"

"Well, sir, I was just—a... just a..." I thought about the size of the colonel's triceps and knew I couldn't cover that bet.

"Quit your stuttering, Preacher. Stick to your guns. You never know. I might not know the answer. We got a bet?"

"Well, sir. I'm not really a betting man, sir, but I'd like to hear your opinion. I'm sure it will prove to be of great value."

"Not a betting man?" repeated the colonel, shaking his head. "Well, that's good because I actually have a pretty good answer for that question."

"The Holy Bible never mentions a meeting between John and Jesus prior to His baptism," the colonel answered. "The earliest report of Jesus, after His birth and exile to Egypt, is when, at the age of twelve, He traveled with His parents to Jerusalem. Cousin John did not know him, but had no problem identifying Him as the Son of God, the Lamb of God, and even the Messiah because he had been told what to look for."

"'Whomever the Spirit descended upon and remained upon, that same person would baptize others with the Holy Spirit'. If that wasn't enough proof for John, then the voice of God also spoke to him, saying, 'This is my beloved Son, in whom I am well pleased'," quoted Colonel Harris.

I was quite impressed with the colonel's scholarly yet simple opinion.

Colonel Harris seemed proud of his interpretation. "Well, son, what do you think? That's a pretty good answer, huh?"

"Yes, sir, that is a very convincing answer. You're saying that John recognized Christ as the Son of God, but didn't personally recognize Him. And in fact, believed he didn't know Him at all. He's saying, and these are my words, mind you, 'See that man coming this way, I don't know Him, personally, but I know for a certainty that He is the Messiah.' We, of course, know from reading the book, that John and Jesus are actually cousins. Yes, sir. That's worth teaching. Do you mind if I use that sometime?"

"Don't mind at all, Preacher. I respect a man, a professional, like yourself that can be humble enough to learn from others. Since I've given you something to think about, and it didn't cost you your triceps, you need to give me something to think about. I blessed you with some words of wisdom, now you can return the favor. I'd like something from the Gospel of John. Bless me with some wisdom, son. Go ahead and take a few minutes to think. No pressure, but let me warn you—I done heard it all, and don't want to hear nothin' they taught you in that fancy seminary school you went to, either. I want something that has foundational impact. You understand me, son? Do you understand what the Holy Bible means when it mentions, 'foundation of the world'?"

"Yes, sir. I understand you clearly, sir. You're referring to the 'Mysteries of God', the very foundation of this earth age and the earth age to come. Is that correct, sir?"

"That's right on, son. And I know you didn't learn that in no Sunday school. So, lay it on me."

While Colonel Harris was talking, I prayed silently about the significance of someone who should know Christ but not able to recognize him. Deep in thought, my mind analyzing at full speed, I wanted to make sure that my answer would be clear and easy to understand.

"Sir, the fact that the Gospel records that John does not recognize Christ should cause followers of Christ to ask why. Why it is even mentioned? Not everything that happened is recorded. What is the hidden meaning, and what is the practical application of it? Will this type of event take place again in the future?"

"That's exactly what I'm talking about, Preacher, the future. Now I know why God sent you to me. Do you mean that, sometime in the future, folks will not be able to identify Christ?"

"Yes, sir." I began explaining the future.

Competing with the noise of the Jeep's engine, I spoke at the top of my voice explaining how someone who should know Christ but not recognize Him gave any student, strong in the word of God, a lesson to learn. What lesson could those present in the end times learn from this example? God called John to preach about the coming of our Savior. Ironically, although he preached this message for years, he was unable to identify Him as He approached. It's the template for an event that will take place in the future where spiritual leaders will find themselves facing the same dilemma of trying to identify the true Christ.

"Switching topics, sir, I mentioned Nathaniel earlier. Along with John and Andrew, he claimed that Jesus was the Son of God. But the story leading up to his proclamation is very enlightening," I said, shifting my weight in the seat.

"You talking about how Jesus picked His disciples?"

"Yes, sir," I answered, leaning forward.

"Well, get to preaching it, son," said the colonel, wrapping his left arm around the seat.

"Nathaniel asked, 'When did you see me or how do you know me?' Christ's answer convinced him of His authority. 'Before that Philip called thee, when thou wast under the fig tree, I saw thee.'

"Prior to being chosen, Nathaniel had been sitting under a fig tree. He wanted to know how it was possible for Christ to have seen him. It doesn't sound impressive when we read it, but apparently Christ's ability to see him under the fig tree was some sort of a miracle."

"Don't sound like much though, does it?" said the colonel, smacking himself on the thigh.

"No, sir, not at first glance. That's exactly what made me wonder why it's even mentioned. What impressed Nathaniel so much? And what is Christ teaching us? What is the lesson from this example, and how can it be applied to His second coming?"

Professionally, I felt my students learned the most when I picked a topic, then led them into asking the right questions. If they asked questions, then I knew they were learning something. It seemed to work with the colonel, too.

"I'll tell you what," said the colonel. "Have you ever seen the size of some of them trees? They can be wider than a barn door."

"Yes, sir, fig trees are quite large and can be impossible to see around. Anything under it or behind it might well be hidden from sight." I emphasized the word hidden to see if he could catch it.

"I understand something miraculous must have happened, but it's hard to see what that is," said Colonel Harris. "But from the way you answered, I'm guessing there's a deeper meaning, so what is it?"

"Sir, I'm not sure just how deep, but I've prayed over this for some time and I do believe that God blesses us with understanding if we pray for it."

"Well, you certainly have been blessed with that," said Colonel Harris. "Continue."

"We know that Nathaniel was one of God's elect because Christ chose him that day. God is telling us in this lesson that His elect are never hidden from Him.

"Hot damn," said the colonel, smacking his leg again.

"God's elect are chosen to explain the truth," I said. "Nathaniel, one of God's elect, stated that Jesus must be the Son of God and the King of Israel. With these words, Nathaniel uncovered the truth, which had been hidden up to that point. He identified the true Christ. In the future, God's elect will reveal the truth and then teach others how to do the same. This follows the commanding order of God's plan."

"Commanding order—son, are you talking 'bout God's chain of command?" asked the colonel.

"Yes, sir, I am. Christ receives the word from God and brings it to earth. He seeks out His elect and reveals the words to them. Christ uncovers the secrets hidden from the foundations of this age and explains them to the disciples, who reveal them to the followers of Christ."

"That is quite profound, Preacher," said Colonel Harris. "I'd like my men to know that. It's what we need over here. When all else fails, we will always have our understanding. They can never take that away. Do you know what I'm saying?"

The colonel seemed to hang onto every word I spoke. Feeling confident that I had the Colonel's full attention, I concluded my mini-sermon with a wrap-around thought.

Episode Three

"Yes, sir. Remember, Christ knows who His elect are. In the book of Jeremiah, God refers to His children as good and bad figs. He knows exactly where to find the good figs, even when they are hidden amongst the bad ones. They remain in the world until found by Christ, and most times are hidden in plain sight. Just as Jesus found Nathaniel, God knows exactly where His elect are."

"Well, son," said the colonel, "you have certainly given me a thorough biblical study today. I am looking forward to my men receiving this type of enlightenment, but now I have to be about this war business."

Feeling content with the opportunity to discuss the word of God with a man like the colonel, made me anticipate teaching it to the soldiers. I shared God's word to show my love for God. I felt a spiritual reward was rendered to me when sharing this good news. However, I would soon find out just how much God loved me. My reward waited just a few days away.

Episode Four

December 27—December 28

Colonel Harris and I fell silent.

I found myself thinking about my days attending Saint Philomena Catholic elementary school. I grew up a non-denominational Christian, but attended the neighborhood Catholic school, and my family attended its church. Overtly, I was treated just like the other non-Catholics. As a non-Catholic, I had to sit in the back of the classroom during school hours—a place the nuns referred to as purgatory. During church services, my mother and I sat in the back of the church — not allowed to receive communion.

Covertly, I was treated differently. One of the older priests, in opposition to the ruling of the Archdiocese and against the strict adherence of the parish priest, clandestinely made sure that I was treated just like the Catholic kids and, at times, even better. My First Holy Communion, one of the seven sacraments, was celebrated in secret. Only my family and Vanessa attended. Every week, this mysterious priest would perform the holy oblation in secret, after Mass, for my family and me. As a child, it made me feel brand new, invincible, and, for a moment, free of sin, every time.

With my mother's permission, he tutored me privately. He taught a doctrine contrary to everything I learned during school hours. I caught on very quickly and he sometimes commented that it seemed like I must have heard all of this before.

I was even baptized differently than most Catholics, who were merely sprinkled with holy water. The defiant priest, after much prayer, and with permission from my mother, insisted that I be properly

35

Episode Four

baptized. Roman Catholics do not commonly practice fully submerged baptisms, but this particular priest felt inexplicably compelled to make sure that I was made totally new.

At the age of eight, while underwater, I wanted my thoughts to stay submerged and never come up for air. Father Shelly seemed to agree with me. I recall him bringing me up after I ran out of air. I didn't mind, though—I felt that the longer he left me underwater, the cleaner my soul would become.

Before the baptism, he told me that the word 'baptize' meant to dye, or to change the color of something while being submerged, as in dyeing a piece of fabric. Spiritually, it meant to have one's soul dyed and made new. He seemed convinced that the soul of someone like me had to be brought as close to the brink of death as possible to be cleansed. He could have been reading my mind because I was disappointed with the resurrection part of the baptism. I was looking for more; I wanted to taste death. He knew it, and insisted that desire be fulfilled.

When he referred to "someone like me," I scratched my head in confusion. I thought he meant a non-Catholic, but he corrected me. That wasn't it at all. "There's something different about you," he told me.

I just chalked him up as a loony old priest, but other than nearly drowning me that one time, he was okay. Father Shelly had a knack for bucking the rules and a lackadaisical attitude toward his order. I liked most that he seemed to understand why I wanted to tempt death. And so I spent time with him, helping him on the grounds once or twice a week. During chores I would listen to his wonderfully wild tales of secret realms existing here on earth.

"Young Keeper," I assumed he was referring to me as the grounds keeper, "move the trash can closer, so you don't have to take so many steps."

"Okay," I said, happy to help especially after seeing all the boys hanging around the outside of the schoolyard fence hoping I would try and make a run for it.

"Sure you don't want to go and play with your buddies?" Father Shelly asked.

"No, I'm sure." I never confessed that they were not friends but in fact bullies daring me to step off school property.

One day he started telling me stories about the legendary Immortal Keepers, special souls who lived forever, serving God on earth until the second coming of Christ.

"Why are they called immortal?" I asked knowing that people didn't really live forever.

"It's not the same as living forever," he said as we moved toward the fence. "These special warriors, chosen by God, are not immortal in the common sense. They live forever in spirit and soul, but their human forms, like those of any mortal person, succumb to death and must be replaced."

He explained that the immortal elect of God and mortal men experience death differently. With mortal man, the flesh dies, but the spirit and soul return to heaven to have eternal life with God. They wait patiently or impatiently in heaven for the Day of Judgment, to receive their just reward, good or bad, from God the Father.

The closer we came to the fence the more the wind began to gust and the harder for me to chase the litter. Focusing on the litter, when I looked up I found myself within three feet of the fence. The boys on the other side were trying their best to reach through the fencing to grab me. As the wind blew harder I was also blown towards them and unable to resist. The gust blew me around to notice Father Shelly standing behind me as if he were in control of the force, his cincture and cassock fluttering. It seemed like everything that wasn't fastened down went hurling toward the fence. Trash cans, lids, brooms, leaves and litter flew right passed me causing all the boys pressed against the fence to jump back in fear.

"That was really weird, did you see that? What just happened?" I asked running back to his side.

"Not sure, seemed like a mini tornado or something," said Father Shelly, then continued telling about the Immortal Keepers. "When God's immortal elect achieve death, their soul and spirit return to earth to become reborn. As they are raised again through childhood, they have no memories of previous lives, angelic visits, or dreams, and serve God reluctantly, but with extreme loyalty."

"No memories about their families?"

"None at all," he answered.

As if to fascinate me even more, Father Shelley would hint that I might be one of them. I wasn't sure if I wanted to be an Immortal Keeper. It was right around my eighth birthday, I began to feel emotionally drained and I didn't know why. I was sure it had something to do with my dad dying in the war. Pretending to be one of the beings from Father Shelly's enchanting stories helped with my emotional pain. He said that God's Immortal Keepers experienced life's ups and downs the same as any mortal boy until initiated at the age of twenty-one. I could think of all my ups and downs as part of my service to God.

Episode Four

Every time I listened to his vivid stories, he almost had me believing that I could be one.

"When will I find out if I'm one of them?" I asked, pretending, but also wishing, as young boys do, that it were possible.

"On the night of your twenty-first birthday, you'll have one or two divine dreams and you may even get a visit from the angel Gabriel. During these dreams, you'll find out how long you have served as one of God's soul gatherers. And, at that time, the feeling of reluctance will begin."

"The Angel Gabriel will visit me in my dreams?" I asked, hoping it was true but knew it was just a story.

"That's right. They call it the Jesus dream, and as your spiritual eyes open for the first time you'll see detailed visions of your original divine commission."

"What does that mean?" I asked.

"You get to dream about the very first time you were commissioned by God," said Father Shelly as he repositioned the trashcans. "You and others receive your new commissions, swearing fealty as one of God's Immortal Keepers. But until that night, shielded in secrecy, you live unaware of your true destiny."

I looked around the yard, all the trash that we had picked up was all over the playground again.

"Looks like you're going to be busy for awhile longer," he said as I saw a few bullies still waiting to be picked up by their parents.

I never asked him about the Jesus dream but he went on about it enough.

"In the 'Jesus dream', God rewards each immortal for their work. Through the dream He gives every one of His supernatural elect a dream about the three-year ministry of Christ. Every time they are initiated, they dream about Jesus from His baptism through His crucifixion."

"What happens after that?" I asked, half listening collecting as much trash as I could.

"The day after the Jesus dream, the work begins."

"But why are they reluctant?" I asked, thinking that everyone would want to live forever serving God.

He told me that prior to their initiation, Immortal Keepers shared the pain and sorrow common to us all. In addition, within them, their souls remained in constant agony over repeatedly being denied entry into heaven and God's presence. They felt this pain, but remained unaware of its cause. He chalked up the dreams they had during their infancy, and the hidden emotional pain of separation, as a sort of side effect of being sent back to earth.

"God loves His immortals and needs their service but they pay the price in their exile from Him."

I thought I could relate to what he was saying. After all, growing up I felt the sorrow and pain of hearing my mother crying herself to sleep at night after my father passed.

While acknowledging my pain, Father Shelly called that earthly pain, which couldn't compare to the spiritual sorrow felt by an Immortal Keeper. Chosen because God loves them, they want only to return to heaven and remain, but they are continually denied.

Father Shelly preached to me like he was passing the torch, as if his own light would soon expire. I'm not sure if he was one of these beings, but he also assured me that sharing these stories broke Immortal Keeper protocol.

"I have a feeling about you," he said.

Sometimes this felt like part of the fun of the pretend world, other times it felt chillingly real.

As I got older, I wrote off the stories as his way of trying to make me feel better. When Father Shelly passed on, I pushed everything he told me to the back of my mind, forever.

Now, staring out the window of the Jeep, I thought, They'll be great to tell my kids one day.

During the silence, the rhythm of the Jeep's engine put me into a type of trance. The colonel pondered John the Baptist, while the Jeep driver kept his eyes on the road.

"Help me clear up something, Preacher. You called the acknowledgment of Nathaniel the first miracle. I thought the changing of water to wine was Christ's first miracle?"

"Yes, sir, changing the water to wine was definitely the first recorded miracle. I was saying that Nathaniel felt as though a miracle had happened. Christ even said something like, 'well, if you think that was something, wait until you see what else is to come'."

We both chuckled at that answer.

"Tell me about the wedding celebration. What was really going on there? I know it has to mean a lot more than Jesus getting the opportunity to perform His first miracle. What was the lesson there?"

Episode Four

"Roger that, sir!" I said. "The wedding feast symbolizes the wedding that will occur during the end times. Certain words of Christ should alert the wise to investigate for hidden messages concerning His return to earth.

"Jesus specifically told His mother that this wedding was not His wedding," I said, hoping the colonel would pick up on my implication.

Colonel Harris was sharp and figured out what I was suggesting right away.

"You sound like you're implying that, since it was not Jesus' wedding, that it was the wrong wedding. This is another one of those example types you keep talking about," said the colonel, nodding his head.

I love it when others pick up on what I'm explaining. They don't have to agree or believe me, but as long as they understand and find it interesting, I've achieved something. At times, talking with others about the future felt like struggling to breathe, then finally getting a second wind during the halfway mark of a marathon.

"There are other great examples in the wedding story, sir," I said, noticing the driver staring at me in the rearview mirror. "The wedding feast is recorded first because it's the most important, among a long list of important lessons in the Holy Bible."

"I agree," said the colonel, still nodding his head. "Even the wine is significant."

"Yes, sir, even there you have a reference to the end time. The host of the wedding serves the bad wine first, but saves the best wine for last." I added, "In the end times the children of God will either be sober or intoxicated."

"They have a choice—they can be intoxicated by the corrupted wine of Satan or wait to drink the pure wine of Christ," added Colonel Harris.

"Roger that, sir," I agreed. Still competing with the engine noise I finished my point, speaking faster as if that would help. Apparently the driver was just as interested as the colonel. It seemed like the faster I talked, the slower we traveled. I waited for the colonel to scold him for driving too slowly, but he never mentioned a word about it the whole time. For a while the Jeep had been moving so obviously slow that I thought we were going to stop and park.

"Son, you been talking my ears off, but don't forget we fighting a war over here. Time is precious, and we need to get back to work. But, if I thought it would work, I'd make a phone call and stop this war for as long it takes, just so I could keep listening," the colonel joked.

"That would be awesome, sir," I said adjusting my pistol belt.

"We're here," said the colonel. "Let's go and get you acquainted."

"Yes, sir. Thank you, sir," I said.

The Jeep driver rushed over to hold the door for Colonel Harris, but he wouldn't move. Instead, he motioned for me to exit first. The driver helped me unravel and squeeze out of the back seat, while Colonel Harris remained seated, breaking military protocol.

In total, we had probably only gone about half a mile, passing Base Camp Alpha about three times. None of us had commented on the fact that we had been driving in circles the whole time.

Colonel Harris sat in the front seat as the driver and I waited by his door. He had a regular routine when arriving at a base camp for inspection. He would get out and stand with the passenger door held open, his back to the base camp. He would stand there, pull out a cigar, reach for his lighter, and wait to signal the company commander. Never actually lighting the cigar, he would flick the lighter case open and shut while chewing away at the cigar tip. Some days he would get back into the Jeep, canceling the inspection. "Uncle Sam needs you to be flexible," he would say. That was one of his ways of keeping the troops on their toes.

If he got back in the Jeep, there would be no inspection. If he closed the door and turned his attention toward the camp, it meant that the company commander should approach. The camp's company commander would receive the colonel according to protocol. Together they would proceed to the barracks or assembly area. Then he would inspect, looking for spit-shined boots, polished brass, and well-maintained weapons.

This time, however, the colonel never got out of the Jeep. He just sat there, flicking his lighter and chewing the cigar.

I could tell he had something on his mind. Pretty sure what it might be, I waited for the colonel to speak. The driver and I stood alongside of the passenger door. The driver focused opposite the base camp, as if posting security. I stood next to the door, where I could look slightly over the colonel's sunglasses and into his eyes. I placed my hand on the open window seal to be prepared to reopen the door when prompted.

"Preacher," said the colonel, "You know this whole wedding story's got me thinking about a parable I've heard much about. Isn't the parable of the ten virgins related to this wedding at the end of days? If I'm not mistaken, didn't five of the virgins miss out on the wedding because they left in search of something and returned too late?"

"Yes, sir," I answered, smiling from ear to ear.

Episode Four

I hoped he would come up with that conclusion on his own. The parable of the ten bridesmaids explicitly shows how painful it will be for those who love the Lord, but are deceived in the end and, thus, shut out of the wedding. Spiritually speaking, the five foolish bridesmaids were found not watching and waiting for the arrival of the true Christ. But the five wise bridesmaids faithfully remained, watching for the enemy and waiting for their Lord. Their lamps stayed lit because the true oil filled them. To have the true oil, or seal of God, means that His elect, His true bride, prepare to receive the true Bridegroom and ultimately reject the false one, while also revealing him for the evil imposter he truly is.

Spiritually speaking, those not attending the wedding with the true Christ have been deceived and have taken part in the first wedding with the fake Christ.

"They been served the bad wine, huh?" added the colonel.

I could see that he felt a sense of joy deep within, the kind of joy that felt good all over. Christ prayed that each of His elect would experience that joy whenever divine messages were revealed with meaning, and related to His return. I always knew when one of God's elect felt that joy. I could see it in their eyes. Both humbling and inspiring, it happened whenever a deeper truth about the second coming was made clear. It was how God proved His love. The joy of understanding can never be taken away, even when everything else is falling apart everywhere else.

I looked at Colonel Harris as he exited the Jeep. "Kind a like a light being turned on in a dark room, huh?" said the colonel as he watched the reception team marching toward him.

"Just like a light, sir," I agreed, standing at attention.

"Good afternoon, Colonel," announced the confused Base Camp Alpha commander, saluting as he approached the Jeep.

42

Episode Five
December 28—December 31

"God bless the U.S. Army," said one of the soldiers as First Squad walked into the operations tent. After returning from Base Camp Alpha, I finally met the squad that I would accompany on their upcoming mission. I sat in on the briefing, which brought back good memories of Ranger school. I wished Lump were here now.

Most of the men in the squad liked the idea of me coming along on the mission, except Private First Class Jinx from Baton Rouge.

"Holy man, huh!" Jinx quirked his eyebrow. "Well, you can just stay as far away from me as possible, and we'll get along just fine. Just bad luck is all."

"At ease, Jinx!" said Staff Sergeant Matthias, the squad leader from Indiana, while making the crazy sign with his finger circling his ear. "Pay him no mind, Preacher. He's got a few problems."

"And he's a know-nothing smart-mouth too," said Corporal Peterson from Chicago. "Good to meet you, sir. I'm Eric, Eric Peterson."

I held a Bible study a day or two before the next mission. Corporal Peterson seemed to be very interested in the first Apostles. He wanted to know who they were, what they were like, and why they were picked.

Raised in a Catholic family and the youngest of ten children, Peterson had asked nonstop questions about the apostles John, Paul, and Matthew when he was younger. Because of an early childhood speech problem, whenever he said the word 'apostles', it sounded like 'impossibles'. His constant questions annoyed his older brothers so much that they decided to pull a trick on him. Peterson's older brothers convinced him that there was a lost 'impossible' and together they made up John, Paul, Matthew and Peter, the famous 'impossibles'.

Their cruelest, yet most ridiculous joke began on the day that he made his First Holy Communion. The oldest brother persuaded Peterson that he wasn't their real brother, that they had found him on the street as a baby with a note attached saying, 'Long lost son of the impossible Peter. Please protect him'. They told him that he had to keep his true identity a secret from family and friends. Peterson, young and naïve, believed that he was a direct descendant of a famous apostle until he was nine years old.

I listened attentively while Peterson told this heart-wrenching story. Peterson's brothers had him completely fooled. It was a cruel trick to play on a vulnerable child, but older brothers often did that. I was close to bursting from holding back the laughter. I wanted to laugh so hard that I belched from trying to hold it in. I waited to make sure it was okay to laugh and, when Peterson finished with his story, we both sounded off with hysterical laughter.

"Ah, man, you really had me going there," I gasped. "And you're not pulling my leg? That is a true story?"

"Yes, sir, that's a true story," said Peterson, catching his breath. "Seriously, Chaplain Christopher—" Peterson tried to get control of his laughter. "—why was it so easy for the disciples to follow Christ? I mean, all he said was 'follow me', right?"

Drying my eyes after laughing so hard, I answered Peterson by explaining how the descendants of Judah expected a Messiah. They expected someone to save them from Roman oppression. They knew the Savior would be divine and was prophesied to be the Son of God, but were expecting a warrior.

"They weren't expecting Jesus to offer eternal salvation," I said. "The disciples were ready to fight alongside Christ as He ushered in His new kingdom. Many followed Him eagerly, hoping for a high position in His Empire, but they thought it would be a realm of earthly power. As far as they knew, Jesus was handpicking the soldiers that He planned to lead into battle."

I reminded Peterson that it was prophesied that He would come as Savior and would perform miracles, and that's exactly what He did. "It's kind of easy to follow someone who performs miracles, especially when that person invites you personally."

"Oh. That makes sense." Peterson continued helping me pack for the upcoming routine mission, lightening the mood.

Imitating a TV commercial, in his best pitchman portrayal, Peterson announced, "Although the ALICE lightweight backpack, which fits snuggly to your back, can, when made heavy enough, conveniently cut into your shoulders and back, drawing blood with only minor discomfort, is made to carry large amounts of gear and ammunition. It is also just as handy for those short trips where you only get to kill a few people along the way to your favorite vacation rice field under the sun." We both laughed.

"Two pair of sock?" said Peterson, purposely not pronouncing the S.

"Check," I said, holding them up for display, as if part of the mock advertisement, then dropped them into my open backpack.

"Portable shovel?" said Peterson, laughing at my reaction.

"Check," I answered, holding it up, and then attaching it to the side.

Peterson continued with the checklist, "…short-sleeved shirt; poncho liner or waterproof tarp; bivouac sack; gloves, heavy socks, knit cap, wet weather pants and thermal underwear; mess kit; waterproof bag with two to three days' worth of provisions and snacks, and a dead partridge in a dying pear tree."

"This mission will be a breeze, sir," Peterson promised. "We're just going out to reposition our claymore mines around the camp's perimeter—oh, and there's one or two small villages we have to escort back to safety."

This particular team didn't usually take on defensive missions, but it was possible to run into spontaneous firefights and ambush attempts when escorting friendly villagers from hostile territory.

"Of course you can use your ammo pockets to carry your good book," said Peterson, pointing to the large side pocket on the backpack.

"Exactly," I said grabbing my Bible.

———————————————————

I wasn't issued a weapon. I would just clutch my Holy Bible and hold it as a weapon of peace. I was a soldier, but, as a preacher, killing anyone at all didn't seem like an option to me.

I wasn't alone. Private First Class Lucas felt the same way I did. He was the medic in the squad and, as a conscientious objector or CO, didn't carry a weapon either. The squad respected him because he really knew his stuff. He opposed the war, but did all he could to help the wounded and dying soldiers. Determined not to let the trailer parks of Philadelphia dictate his future, he had volunteered. He loved rock and roll, and thought that if the U.S. Army was good enough for Elvis Presley, then Vietnam was good enough for him. When his time was up, he hoped to take advantage of the G.I. bill and attend medical school.

"Maybe I'll write a book about my experience here in the bush," said Lucas. "I'll make sure I mention you."

"You do that," I said. "Just make sure you spell my name right."

I knew that Lucas was a Christian without ever asking him. He had volunteered to serve his country. According to the words of Christ, in order to follow Him, one must be willing to take up his own cross. Volunteering for Vietnam was a big decision for anyone. Drafted soldiers were forced to fight, but the ones that volunteered had to be mentally prepared and willing to die for their country. Lucas's actions were not an act. He wasn't a hypocrite. He took up the cross and, in order to save lives, put his own life on the line every day.

If that isn't God's work, then something's wrong, I thought as we loaded up for the helicopter flight to Landing Zone Lima.

The helicopter carried us just beyond the outer edge of the camp's southern perimeter. Most of the squad set up a hasty defensive position around the Huey while Private Jinx, the squad's M60 machine gunner and Corporal Saez from the Bronx, his ammo bearer, continued toward the wood line. They ran as far as they could to set up the initial secure perimeter, just outside the landing zone, but in the woods.

As they approached the edge of the landing zone, Saez observed enemy movement just beyond the tree line and stopped suddenly. Jinx stopped as well, but hit the dirt so fast that it looked like he had been shot. He swung the M60 machine gun out in front of him and, instead of engaging the enemy, hid behind it, frozen in place. He was playing possum.

Saez, on the other hand, thinking more about his team than himself, went above and beyond the call of duty. He ran straight into the enemy that lay in wait for First squad. Corporal Saez, full of uncommon valor, charged toward them engaging their fire.

A barrage of small arms fire bombarded him, but, before he went down, he managed to take three of them with him. The helicopter hovered over the drop zone as the onboard machine gunner returned fire into the woods, just over the heads of Sergeant Matthias and Johnson as they ran to recover Saez's body, firing their weapons into the dense bush as they ran.

They passed Jinx, who had practically dug a hole to bury his face in. Matthias grabbed the machine gun from him and opened fire on the enemy. The remainder of the squad, still in defensive positions, further spread themselves out at the spot where the helicopter first touched down and waited to help load Saez's body when the chopper landed again.

"Straight to base camp," Matthias ordered the pilot as the team loaded Saez's body onto the floor of the helicopter, saying a quick goodbye to their fallen friend. The landing zone still had to be secured, though it would be much easier now that the helicopter gunner had cleared about one hundred fifty feet of brush just beyond the clearing.

I thought that this was what I was here for, but it happened so fast I could barely tell who was shot and if they were dead or alive. I only had time to say a silent prayer for Corporal Saez.

"I have a feeling we'll meet again my friend. Yes, I'll see you again," I said to myself before I followed the rest of the team as they set up security for the departing helicopter.

"You know the deal, men," said Matthias, once they got deeper into the woods. "We don't get to mourn and we don't get to come out of the field until mission's complete, 'though I be the lone survivor'. Hooya!"

"Hooya!" shouted the men in unison.

"Stupid medal of honor-hunter," said Jinx under his breath, referring to Saez.

Hooya, I thought, remembering how Lump and I loved shouting that word when we went through Ranger and Airborne school. It made us feel pumped up and ready to drive on. Saying it now, I didn't feel pumped up or eager to move on anywhere. I noticed that, outwardly, it seemed to work for the rest of the squad. Then I realized that, if they had to get over it, then so did I.

We moved the patrol away from the assembly area. Eventually we would march back to base camp, escorting the villagers.

The first couple of hours after the firefight remained uneventful. First Squad split into two teams and went separate ways to inspect the claymore mine positions. Negotiating the flat, bushy terrain around the perimeter was pretty easy. The daily task of inspecting the placement of the mines rotated among the companies. A serious duty, it could easily become as trivial as a security guard making rounds of an abandoned warehouse.

The two teams reunited in a wooded area near the original landing zone, regrouping before continuing with the second part of our mission.

Episode Five

While on patrol, we planned to march through three small villages; the residents would attach themselves to our squad as we passed through each village.

The men of First Squad were used to humping through rice patties, swamps, and jungles. Ironically, though surrounded by the violence of war and the threat of dying, there were moments while walking on daylight patrols that seemed like just a carefree walk through the park. Some days, the only thing missing on a patrol was the big band sound of Dean Martin or Nat King Cole.

We were not expecting enemy contact before linking up with the first village, but we did wind up in another rather large firefight that lasted close to twenty minutes. Enemy fire came pouring down as fast and furious as rain hitting a car windshield in a summer storm.

"Take cover," shouted Sergeant Matthias, realizing that we were pinned down.

At first, the members of First Squad held their ground while returning fire, but soon we were slowly forced back. Sergeant Matthias positioned his team to cover each other's retreat to our original perimeter position. If we reached it, we would have to find an alternate route to continue with the mission.

"Listen up," shouted the sergeant, as he distinguished the sound of friendly M14 and M16 gunfire coming from the flanks.

A friendly platoon in the area returned fire in support of First Squad, turning the tables on the enemy, and causing them to retreat instead.

Two of the men from the friendly platoon approached First Squad and immediately engaged in conversation with Sergeant Matthias. Thanks to Second Platoon, who just happened to be in the area, First Squad made it out with no casualties. Second Platoon's appearance from nowhere became a miracle for us. They just happened to be over two thousand meters off the course of their own patrol mission.

"Thank God they happened to be in the wrong place at the right time," said Private Thompson, the M203 gunner from the great state of Missouri. He was just like they say, a true son of the "show me" state. There were no bones about it with him; if one of his five senses couldn't verify a thing, then it simply didn't exist. He believed in God, Jesus, and salvation, but that was as far as it went for him.

"Yeah, or our butts would be in a sling right about now," said Private Matthews, from Las Vegas, the other M203 carrier.

First Squad put about one thousand meters between them and the area of the last firefight. We moved through the jungle with a sense of urgency. So far we had run into two enemy positions and one member of the squad had lost his life trying to protect everyone else.

I thought about Corporal Saez's actions. He could have just hit the dirt and dug his head into the ground to avoid the enemy gunfire, but instead he charged right for it to protect his brothers.

I understood why First Squad had been chosen for this mission and, since we were taking a break, I decided to share the story about Gideon's three hundred.

"Listen up men!" I said, drawing the squad's attention. "That was my first real live firefight. It was nothing like that in school."

I looked at each of the men as they paused, then laughed it off, poking fun of me for being a college boy and a 'zero'—a nickname used for commissioned officers.

"Colonel Harris really believes in you men, he told me so himself. He also told me that First Squad was the best squad and that he handpicked each of you for it."

"Yeah, he got you with that 'these are my Michaels' line didn't he?" said Thompson, "but don't feel bad it works on the best of the newbies,' he added as the whole squad, including me, laughed.

I was setting up to tell them Gideon's story.

"There is a story in the Holy Bible that I think specifically relates to each of you and I would like to share it with you." I began explaining how God chose Gideon's men to carry out a special mission, a military confrontation where God would prove to be the victor against impossible odds.

"You men will be able to relate to the process of determining which men are found deserving enough to carry out God's crucial task."

As much as the men seemed interested in the story, they still had to maintain a secure position. They set up a circular perimeter with each man posted at a clock position at or near a tree for cover and high bush for concealment. It was a tight circle, so tight, in fact, that I could reach out and touch the boot of every man spread out around me. In the center of the circle, I literally knelt at the foot of each soldier. They kept their weapons pointed outward and ready to fire, but turned part of their attention toward me.

As the squad took their break, I taught from the book of Judges. I explained that in the book of Judges, Gideon, the second judge of

Episode Five

Israel—after the death of Joshua—led the battle for freedom from oppression against the Midianites. The army of Israel, under Gideon, numbered 32,000. They were greatly outnumbered, but, with God's help, well-positioned for victory.

"However, God had a change of plan," I said, switching to kneel on my left knee. "He wanted Gideon to trim the number of soldiers down to impossible odds."

"That's crazy, man," said Private James, from Detroit.

"Yeah, crazy, sir," said the other private James next to him, glaring at him for the slip of tongue.

"Why would God want to reduce the size of the army?" asked Peterson, before he turned away to scan the outside of the perimeter.

"It was God's way of proving to them that all victories came from Him," I answered. "God wanted Gideon to reduce his fighting force to the three hundred men who would battle an army that was so large it was considered numberless and actually compared to the sands of the sea."

"Who were they fighting anyway?" asked Private Johnson, from Atlanta.

I opened the Holy Bible and read from Judges, Chapter 7, "And the Lord said unto Gideon, 'The people that are with thee are too many for me to give the Midianites into their hands, lest Israel vaunt themselves against me, saying, mine own hand hath saved me.'"

"Sounds like God didn't want the men in Israel's army to get the big head," said Private Bart from Miami.

"Just call him Batman," said Johnson as he shrugged his shoulders and rolled his eyes at me. "They been calling him that since he was a little pinhead boy, got something to do with him wanting to be a superhero, or something stupid like that. If you say Bartman real fast, it comes out like Batman. He was some kind of whiz kid growing up, and some fool convinced him that his brain had superpowers.

"I can relate to that. Kinda happened that way with me too—some whacked out priest, though," I said, laughing and thinking back to my childhood.

"Yeah, but that was probably okay for you," said Johnson, "but Bart thought his brain was gonna beat off the bad guys. Naw! Don't think so. We really just call him Batman 'cause he really just super stupid."

"Yeah, no real superpowers, but plenty of real stupid powers," said Matthews.

"Am I right, though, sir—Israel, ix-nay on the ig-head-bay, right?" Bart asked.

"Exactly right," I answered. "In order to save man from destroying himself with foolish pride, God reserved the glory for Himself. This would prove to other nations not that Israel was strong, but that Israel's God was triumphant."

"See, what I tell you? I'm Batman," said Bart, defiantly tipping his steel helmet up with his middle finger so everyone could see it.

"How did God choose His warriors?" Johnson asked, using the heel of his boot to scratch his leg.

"God's first task was to cleanse the army of its weakest soldiers, those who would prove to be worthless to him in battle."

"Oh, you mean they got rid of folk like Jinx," said James as he looked over at Jinx, and then threw a handful of dirt at him. "Hell, we been trying to get rid of him since day one."

I heard the dirt hit the back of Jinx's steel helmet. They all laughed in agreement. Jinx, of course, who wouldn't have cared anyway, was sound asleep at his position, and didn't hear a single word of their taunts. In fact, Doc Lucas, lying in the position next to him had to reach over and kick his boots to stop him from snoring.

"Go ahead, Preacher, sir, don't worry about Jinx. Nothing you say's gonna help that fool," said the other James. "But, hey, we be hearing you though."

"Yeah, so what happened next?" Bart asked, ready to guess what would happen before anyone else could.

"God carries out His first cleansing by allowing the weak to return home," I said, wondering if they would pick up on my special word.

"Hold up," said Private Matthews, "did you say cleansing—as in bathed or something?"

"I sure did. God is thinning out the masses in order to sanctify His elect."

I threw out words that would ultimately suggest that there was more to the story than just a battle that took place thousands of years ago.

I read another scripture from Judges, Chapter 7, "Now therefore, go to proclaim in the ears of the people, saying, whosoever is fearful and afraid, let him return and depart early from mount Gilead. And there returned of the people twenty and two thousand; and there remained ten thousand."

Jimmy Jinx rolled over just in time to hear that verse. "Now... now I can say amen to that one. Damn, I can be scared if it will get me the hell outta here."

"Shut up, Jinx, you just a no account traitor," said Johnson from across the perimeter. "You ain't acting scared, you just scared. Go on back to playing dead again."

Episode Five

"Yeah, man, shut up. Go ahead, sir, finish your story," said Matthews. "Why does God need to send them back home? I mean, He must have a reason, right?

"God can't use anyone who is afraid of the enemy," I said, nodding. "He finds the fearful unworthy to serve in battle and orders them to return home. Never fear death, or God may decide that He can't use you," I said, a slight emphasis on the word death, as a hint for the future. No one took the bait, so I continued.

"How many were let go?" asked Peterson.

"I don't know how many, but however many, it wasn't enough. God insisted on a second cleansing, in the form of a test." I knew that the men of First Squad would relate to this part more than any others I had ever shared this story with.

"A test?" asked one of the James boys.

"Yes," I said as James turned over to adjust the mic on his radio. "There was a test that, as far as we know, only God and Gideon knew about. After the first cleansing, God tells Gideon that there were still too many soldiers. God wanted the numbers to appear impossible, making a victory unattainable by man alone. What happens next proves to be the most important part of the story."

I told them that, although God knows His elect, they still must prove themselves. God's elect prove themselves the same way they did it that day thousands of years ago. His elect will always be the ones who stand, always watching and waiting until the very end.

"Sounds like you're saying that God's elect are always on alert, hint, hint," said Matthias, sounding like the squad leader that he was.

"That's it exactly, sergeant."

"You got another verse for us, sir?" asked Matthews, who seemed more eager then the rest.

"Yes I do," I said reading from Judges, Chapter 7 again. "And the Lord said unto Gideon, 'The people are yet too many; bring them down unto the water, and I will try'—remember, that means test—'them for thee there: and it shall be, that of whom I say unto thee, This shall go with thee, the same shall go with thee; and of whomsoever I say unto thee, This shall not go with thee, the same shall not go.'"

"Sounds like God is making the decisions to me," said Bart.

"Yes, Batman," I said laughing and switched knees again. "He is going to make the decisions, but it's based on who passes or fails His test. He designs a test for the remaining soldiers to determine who is right for the task."

I wanted to tell them more, like God can only use those who have been tried and tested. When it comes to battle with His enemy, He will only use soldiers that He can count on. But this wasn't Sunday school and I didn't have time to teach the spiritual side of the story. However, if I could have, I would have said that God continues to separate the true warriors from the mediocre and, spiritually speaking, that meant those who have been tested by fire and then overcome it, are proven to be His elect.

"If it's something we can relate to, then it must be some type of tactical thing, huh?" asked Bart, thinking that he had figured out the test already.

"That's it," I said, hearing the others boo him for always thinking that he was smarter then everyone else.

"Hey, what can I say? Who am I? Why, I'm Batman, that's who I am," bragged Bart.

With the Bible still open to Judges, Chapter 7, I read Verse 5. "So he brought down the people unto the water: and the Lord said unto Gideon, Every one that lappeth of the water with his tongue, as a dog lappeth, him shalt thou set by himself; likewise every one that boweth down upon his knees to drink."

I told them that God's way of weeding out the masses, in this example, involves military tactics. He often segregates the strong in knowledge from those weak in understanding using similar strategies. In this lesson, God uses the tactical way of drinking water during a combat situation to determine those fit for His battle. In Vietnam, we called it 'tactical mess'. To prevent a gaggle formation at mealtimes, each company allowed one platoon at a time to drink or eat, while the rest remained tactical and alert at all times.

"In Gideon's case," I added, looking at each man within the perimeter, "his men have been fighting for days and have run out of water. They are practically dying of thirst."

"It's the dying of thirst that makes them so ripe for God's test, right?" asked Peterson before anyone else could.

"Correct," I said, nodding my head toward Peterson. "God gives each soldier a chance to prove his worthiness to fight for Him. It's also a way to prove their preparedness.

"It's kind of like the way you are set up right now," I said, pointing around to each man's position in the circle. "You all could have just plopped down and started eating your rations, but you didn't, right?"

"That's right," said Sergeant Matthias. "They know better than that; we stay ready to fight."

Episode Five

Hearing the squad leader answer the question, I felt like I was accomplishing something. I knew that if he understood the comparison, he would make sure that all of his men understood it.

"Go ahead, Staff Sergeant, finish my thought. I think you know where I'm going with this story about drinking water in a tactical environment."

"Well, I'm no biblical scholar," Matthias began, "but I been in a battle or two. A soldier who runs and then falls down on all fours and drinks water like a dog is totally defenseless. A soldier who allows the needs of his body to take over has no discipline and is no good in battle. They'll usually be the first to turn and run.

"Yeah, like Jinx," said James.

"Hey, that's enough," warned the squad leader as he continued. "The mind has to remain focused on security at all times, watchful and alert even when at ease. On the other hand, a soldier who drops down to only one knee, and scoops water into his hand can remain alert and armed, ready to move out, attack the enemy, or defend against the enemy at any moment. Hooya."

"Hooya," we all replied.

"That's it exactly, sergeant," I said before reading the final verse. "And the number of them that lapped, putting their hand to their mouth, were three hundred men: but all the rest of the people bowed down upon their knees to drink water… And the Lord said unto Gideon, by the three hundred men that lapped will I save you, and deliver the Midianites into thine hand: and let all the other people go every man unto his place."

"So how does the story end anyway?"

I couldn't tell who asked that question because everyone in the squad, minus Jinx, was nodding in agreement. I summed it up for them, switching knees again.

"God split the three hundred men into three groups. Each group had a hundred men; they approached the enemy from three sides. God used three groups of His elect to conquer hundreds of thousands of enemy troops by using a form of misdirection."

"You mean like a magician uses misdirection?" asked Matthews.

"Yes, almost exactly the same. Each one of the three hundred men carried a lantern and a trumpet. The opposing force knew that, usually, there was a lantern and trumpet for every ten thousand men. Believing that they were outnumbered and soon to be slaughtered, they ran for their lives, trampling themselves to death. God had worked His miracle and received the glory from the battle."

After listening to the story of Gideon, we finished eating. Right before we moved out, Peterson gave the signal for everyone to freeze. He heard movement out in front of his six o'clock position. Luckily for us, we were still set up for a defensive battle. Matthias and James exited the perimeter at the twelve o'clock, walked out about ten meters and then circled around through the six. While approaching they could hear the movement in the vegetation and got down. Noticing the speed of movement ahead of them, Matthias ordered everyone to hold fire until there was a sure target.

Whatever was approaching them turned and made a beeline straight for the perimeter, where Peterson would be forced to engage.

"Hold your fire, hold your fire!" said Peterson quickly as he lay there face to face with a wild boar. The boar squealed, then snorted at the barrel of his M16 rifle.

"It's a demon," said Peterson.

"Yeah, a demon pig," said Johnson, making everyone laugh.

Regrouping, we stayed on course for another three hours or so. Private James, at point, stopped, took a knee and signaled back for Matthias to join him at the front. The village we were looking for was just over the next ridge; he estimated that, if we continued with this pace, we would be there within the half hour.

"Roger that," said the squad leader, patting James on his steel helmet. "Let's get there, then."

"Roger that, Sarge," James replied as he led the patrol forward again.

First Squad successfully negotiated the ridgeline separating us from the village, but right before we entered the village Sergeant Matthias shouted at the top of his voice.

"Incoming! Incoming, everybody down, hit the dirt."

Peterson, right next to me when we heard the command, practically body-slammed me to the ground.

"Mortar attack, sir," Peterson said. "Now's a good time to start praying. There's no telling where those shells might land. We're just sitting ducks right now."

"Praying, now!" I said, placing my hands over my steel helmet.

While lying on the ground, Matthias looked around to get an idea of our surroundings. Even from ground level he could tell that it had been hit multiple times. Based on the amount of damage, he guessed the spot was sort of a test area that the Viet Cong would bomb as a 'who knows we might just get lucky' target area.

Episode Five

They would just bomb this particular place outside the village to keep the villagers trapped and keep outsiders away. If anyone got caught in the fire zone at the wrong time, they'd have the devil to pay.

After the mortar rounds ceased, Private Thompson, this time not believing his own eyes, sounded off frantically. "Man down, got a man down over here, Doc," shouted Thompson who had fallen a few feet from Private Bart.

"Ah, man, Batman's down, Sarge. It's Batman," said Thompson, checking to see if Bart was alive, and then checking himself to make sure he wasn't hit as well.

"Damn shrapnel made mincemeat outta you," said Jinx from the other side of Bart. He rolled over the other way to his machine gun. "I gotta get outta here; I can't take this place no more," mumbled Jinx, as if pleading to God.

"I hope you don't think God gonna listen to you, Jinx. That shoulda been you, lying here dead," said Thompson as he kneeled over Bart's body.

Lucas confirmed that Bart was dead and asked to stay with him until the medevac came, but Matthias ordered him to head to the village with the rest of First Squad. Private Matthews and Jinx would wait with Bart's body until the helicopter showed up and would join the team afterward.

The remaining squad, minus two men, entered into the village without any resistance. We kept busy gathering the villagers and preparing them for the march back to the base camp. With close to one hundred villagers, First Squad would have quite a task of keeping control of the civilian population when we got on the move. We would have to keep an accurate head count, keep them moving, and, if necessary, protect them from enemy forces.

Some of those random mortar attacks had hit inside the village as well. Several hooches throughout the village showed signs of near misses and fires that had been extinguished.

Jinx and Matthews rejoined the squad in the village about a half an hour later. Private James ran over to the squad leader and interrupted him. He had a message from the base; our mission was changing.

"Roger that, bravo whisky delta," said Sergeant Matthias, "Whiskey seven, out." He handed the mic back to James. "Listen up, team leaders, I need to see you, lickety-split," he said. "Let's go—pronto."

"What's goin' on, Sarge?" asked Peterson and Johnson. Johnson had taken over for Bart.

"There must be a God. It looks like someone in HQ is using their head for something more then hanging their 'catch me-screw me' sunglasses on. We got a change of plans, men," said Matthias. "We gotta link up to make."

"Oh yeah, Sarge?" said Johnson.

"Oh, yeah, we gotta drop off the villagers to Third Platoon and they'll take them off our hands. Where's my pointman?" asked Matthias, looking around the village. "James!" He waved the pointman over to join the meeting. "Get over here."

"What's up, Sarge?" James trotted over to join them, dropping to one knee like the rest of them.

"I need you to plot out a course about 1500 meters south to south west," instructed Matthias, pointing to his map.

"Sure thing, Sarge," said James, pulling out his protractor and grease pencil.

Matthias realized that this trip would take them away from the next village, but it was better than trying to shepherd residents from three different villages at the same time. After making the exchange, the squad would be free to move onto the next village more quickly.

They lined up all the villagers on the trail, in as close to a file formation as possible. There were at least one hundred villagers with farm animals prepared to move out. Thompson and Johnson had orders to burn the hooches still standing in the village and catch up with the formation afterward.

We instructed the villagers to sit down, but stay in the formation. As they sat on the trail, the team leaders counted heads to make sure the headcount matched the count taken when we first arrived. After checking at least three times, we lined up and began to move out. It would be difficult, but we would try to remain as tactical as possible.

Towards the end of the formation we overheard a woman arguing with a man and shouting at the top of her voice in Vietnamese and broken English. "You leave now!"

Everyone in the squad knew who the man was—Jinx. He was trying to see to it that a certain young, attractive Vietnamese girl, no more than thirteen years old, was more than comfortable. "Take you hand and you go, now!" shouted the woman again as Jinx fell into formation.

Sergeant Matthias continually paced up and down the side of the slow-moving formation, which now stretched well over fifty yards. Once

Episode Five

he passed them, he would look over the whole group, then wait for them to pass by him. He literally made eye contact with every person in the formation. It was standard procedure for him to continue this action until the mission was completed. The formation moved constantly; the rest of the platoon remained alert to every security risk. It was quite a gaggle, but very much under control.

Three hours later we joined up with Third Platoon at the rendezvous point to make the exchange. The villagers remained in a makeshift resting area that encircled the trail. There was a small pond located just forward and to the left of the villagers. I walked toward the designated link up area, but straying slightly off to the side of the trail.

"Stop, sir, stop!" shouted Peterson from the rear.

As noisy as combat can be, and as peaceful as it can get out in the fields, it's easy to hear the sound of metal clicking together. In that moment of bizarre silence, Matthias heard a subtle clicking sound and knew exactly what it was.

"Freeze!" he shouted. "I mean nobody freakin' move!"

It was too late. There was a loud crackling sound, then a penetrating boom as the familiar sounds of battle erupted. The booby trap hurled the body tumbling through the air, landing in the thick vegetation at the edge of the pond.

Fortunately for First Squad, there was no follow up attack.

Everyone froze and remained motionless as Matthias, also standing completely still, quickly gave his team a visual once-over. On point, James had stopped instantly, already looking back toward Matthias as he shouted the command to freeze. Jinx had plopped himself and his gear on the side of the trail to light a cigarette. James, the RTO, stood right next to Matthias. Lucas was all the way in the rear, checking on the condition of the villagers. Including himself, Matthias could only visually account for six of the now ten-man team, but he knew that Thompson and Johnson were standing guard over the villagers.

Thompson refused to believe that another member of First Squad was a possible K.I.A, ran toward the pond to confirm it.

The only squad member that Matthias had not accounted for was Matthews.

"Matthews, sound off," ordered Matthias.

"Over here, Sarge," he shouted, hidden behind the tree, where he had been relieving himself before the commotion began.

Matthias knew that he had seen a body hurled through the air. As much as he hated to admit it, he hoped it was one of the villagers and not who he thought it was.

Everything seemed to be moving in slow motion now. He didn't want to call out the last name. He pressed his fist up to his chin, then opened his palm to cover his mouth. He exhaled forcefully into his palm, trying to catch his breath. His hand stayed over his mouth, as if preventing him from calling out the last name.

The whole ordeal took less then three minutes, but time had slowed down, moving intermittently, like a fingertip run over the jagged edge of a knife.

For Mathias, it was one of those moments in time that he wished would just go away, but, instead, seemed to stubbornly stand still.

"Chaplain Christopher, sound off, sir," said Matthias, hoping, but not expecting, to hear an answer.

Peterson, forgetting—or not caring at all—that they might be in a live minefield, ran over to where he last saw me walking, with Matthias ordering him to stop the whole time. Peterson ignored him, running toward the pond and tripping over a boot, which sent him spiraling to the ground. On the ground, he laid eyes on a second boot, spilling over with fresh blood and splintered bone fragments. He knew whose boots they were. Peterson managed to get himself up on one knee and looked toward the pond. A lifeless, mangled body lay half floating in the pond, half on the marsh and unresponsive.

"No… God… no, this can't be right. I… I…It's Chaplain Christopher, Sarge, it's the preacher. Call for the medevac," cried Peterson, stuttering.

"Gimme that radio, James," said the squad leader, switching to the emergency evacuation frequency. "This is whiskey seven, over. Prepare to copy. Grid number hotel gulf dash 3-7-5-4-7-2. S.O.S! I repeat, S.O.S, emergency evacuation-- over."

The radio was silent. The whole squad waited impatiently for an answer, but heard only the hissing of static.

"Man, nothing but dead, air," said Peterson, anxiously yelling at them to check the frequency again.

Private James took over on the radio, calling the transmission in again. He would continue to do so until help arrived.

Doc dropped what he was doing, gathered his gear, and ran as fast as he could to where my body had landed, using Peterson as a guide.

"Hurry!" shouted Peterson as he moved out of the way for Lucas. "He's still alive, Doc, look, he's… he's still breathing, right? You gotta hang in there, sir."

Hysterical, Peterson felt powerless. After vowing to protect me in the field, he hadn't been there when I needed him the most.

Episode Five

"It's my fault," cried Peterson, pacing frantically about near the body, close to hyperventilating.

"Damn! It is the preacher," said Doc, as if he didn't or couldn't believe it at first.

He could tell right away that I was still alive. He needed to stop the bleeding and prevent me from going into shock.

"Peterson!" yelled Lucas. "Peterson, I need you to stop freaking out right now. Get down here and help me."

"Okay, okay. Sorry! You're right, Doc, damn, sorry, man. What you need me to do?"

"Keep talking to him, so I can dress his wounds before the chopper gets here. Take his helmet and elevate his feet for me," instructed Lucas.

"Yeah, okay, yeah," said Peterson, looking around for my helmet. "No helmet, Doc."

Peterson removed his own. "I'll just use mine to elevate his… damn—damn. Oh damn, Doc, his feet been blowed up, ugh," groaned Peterson, remembering the scattered boots he saw. He turned his head to the side and threw up.

"You're going to be okay, Holy Man," said Doc Lucas. "Just hang on. Look at me, sir. That's it. Just keep looking at me. Try to keep breathing, sir."

Lucas pulled out everything from the inside of his medical kit bag.

"You gotta keep breathing for me, you hear? You can't die today. Not on your birthday. That's right, Lieutenant, we all know about it. Colonel's planning a big surprise shindig for you for when we get back, so you hang on, Lieutenant. Lieutenant!" He spoke louder, trying to get my attention and hold it. "Good, good, hang with me, sir. We got you a medevac on the way. Yep, you're gonna be up and away any minute now. I'm gonna take good care of you. Don't you worry about a thing, birthday boy.

After looking at my fragmented veins, Lucas gave up on the intravenous saline. As he dropped the bags of saline back into his kit bag, my body went into uncontrollable seizures. Doc held me securely, but I kept convulsing. My body had so much shrapnel protruding from it that Doc had to literally wrap it from head to toe. He tried to stop the bleeding by fastening tourniquets around my legs and forearms. He caught a glimpse of protruding intestines in my abdominal wound, but my sunken head wound was probably the worst. Doc was tempted to remove an oddly shaped piece of shrapnel that seemed to be causing the bleeding, but decided to leave it in.

"We need that medevac, Sarge, ASAP!" demanded Lucas.

Matthias nodded. "It's en route, Doc," he called, then said softly, "We already lost two men." He wondered why they had to lose the preacher too. Jinx stood behind him, listening.

"I told you the holy man was bad luck. See? You done lost three men already 'cause of him, you just got yo self a holy day from hell. How's that gonna look on yo' freakin' record? Lifer!" mocked Jinx, blowing cigarette smoke in Matthias's face.

Matthias stared at Jinx, barely restraining himself from killing him for saying what he did. For the moment, it was gratifying enough just to imagine him at the end of his M16 barrel with a large hole in his head.

As horrible as the situation was, Matthias had to maintain security and control of his squad. He knew that, normally, we would have been attacked by now. Most landmines were nothing more than early warning devices used to initiate an ambush or key in indirect mortar fire. Luckily for us, Third Platoon was ready to back us up if we were attacked.

Peterson called Matthews over. Teamed up they put together a temporary litter from his all-purpose poncho.

"On the count of three. Ready? One, two, three." They lifted my body onto the litter, remembering to elevate what was left of my legs, while Doc Lucas held my head in place. After that they took their shovels and, using them as sickles, cleared away a large amount of tall vegetation so the medevac could lift my body from the jungle floor with the helicopter's jungle penetrator.

Thirty minutes had gone by before they heard anything that resembled helicopter propellers.

"It's approaching." Private James popped a flare of white smoke to mark the area for the pilot.

Peterson, Thompson, and Matthews counted to three, then carefully loaded me onto the stretcher and held it in place until the onboard medic signaled to raise it up. Doc Lucas, after searching the vicinity between the pond and the trail, followed with whatever dismembered body parts of mine that he could recover.

On the stretcher, fighting to stay alive, I felt myself being lifted up from the jungle floor. A deep burning sensation ran through my whole body. At this point, I wondered if I was actually conscious. My stomach was on fire, but then it began to warm me, like the warmth of a campfire. After a bit, I could tell that the very strange sensation wasn't from my injuries. The heat felt more like it came from outside my body; something around me was causing it. Maybe it was the hot sun beaming over the rotary blades of the helicopter. Whatever it was, it felt comforting.

Episode Five

"Is this what dying feels like?" I said. "Well, it's not so bad then."

The squad's attention turned skyward toward the chopper, the stretcher, and the whopping sound of the rotary blades. The rotating blades blocked the sun, like the shutter on a camera lens. As they continued to stare upward, it seemed more like they were looking into a kaleidoscope. The glare from the intermittent sunlight impaired their vision slightly.

As they looked heavenward, they heard a thunderous sound, like the implosion of a skyscraper, its voice directed toward the jungle floor. The energy created by the earthshaking voice caused their small patch of land to tremble. It seemed like the earth moved momentarily, but without any noticeable damage.

I felt as if an elastic band had taken hold of my body, attempting to thrust me back onto the jungle floor. Against the resistance, the stretcher spun out of control.

And then, slowly, everything began fading away. Maybe it was all the spinning. Afterward, surrendering to the pull—and possibly by divine intervention—my body knelt in the pond where I had just met my potential demise. All of First Squad, Third Platoon, and the villagers that we were escorting stood astonishingly by as they watched me, apparently resurrected and unharmed. The reflection staring back at me from the pond looked vaguely familiar, but was it me? I wondered. No longer in my military duty uniform, I wore a brown robe and tunic, like someone from the time of Christ.

It was December 31. I had just turned twenty-one years old, and I was dying. Apparently, I was also about to have the dream of a lifetime.

Episode Six

December 31 and 30 AD

I peered through the crowds of people collecting around the pond where my dying body had lain. I didn't recognize any of the villagers standing closest to me. From where I stood I visually parted the crowd to look for familiar faces.

I saw each of the remaining members of my squad staring back at me, as if they expected to see something great—Peterson, Matthews, Matthias, Lucas, Jinx, Thompson, the James boys, and Johnson. I felt a sense of loss when Bart and Saez came to mind, knowing that they would not be present. Disbelief filled my mind.

Am I dead? Who? Where...what...is going on? Why are they staring at me?

Grasping at anything to get control of my mind, I went over the last thing I remembered.

If I'm supposed to be dead, who is this in front of me, and why am I kneeling in water? I...I must surely be dead. Is this the afterlife?

I couldn't figure out my unsettling situation. To top it off, I kept hearing the name of Jesus mumbled in the background.

"Jesus?" I said. "Where?" I looked with wonderment into what now seemed like an audience. "Why are they calling Jesus' name?"

Obviously hallucinating, I had traveled back in time to the year 30 AD. For some reason, I stood in a pond up to my waist.

I tried to inhale deeply, but couldn't. I tried to touch my face, but couldn't lift my arms. I felt paralyzed, trapped in what felt like my own body, but robbed of all motor skills. In fact, I thought how a marionette doll must feel, if it could feel. My body suddenly bent over at the waist without me even thinking about it.

Episode Six

Taking advantage of the moment, I attempted to see my reflection in the pond. I could see everything from my waist up clear. At first I wasn't sure, but now my vision had cleared. I recognized my face, arms, and hands.

I had no clue about the person standing next to me—actually, over me—as I knelt in the water. That had me even more puzzled. I noticed that my squad members had repositioned themselves closer, standing in the pond with me. However impossible or unlikely it was, I finally figured out what was going on when, without warning, the person standing over me sent me falling backward into the pond. From the sudden flash it made me think of the story of Christ's baptism, which occurred shortly before His ministry began.

"That just felt like a baptism," I said, remembering what if felt like from my youth, and how disappointed I had been.

But this time, spiritually, everything about me felt brand new. Curious, my eyes followed the flight of a bird, shooting toward the heavens. It soared toward the brilliant sun, then miraculously transformed into one of the helicopter rotary blades right before my eyes, or so I thought.

As the bird vanished I could have sworn I heard a voice saying, "Thou art my son, in whom I am well pleased."

Feeling as if that same elastic band had suddenly released its tension, catapulting me back to reality, I came to as I was hoisted aboard the medical helicopter transport.

My God, that was some dream. I think I was just baptized by John the Baptist. Wow!

Slightly disappointed, I wondered why I never saw Jesus. I remembered my recent conversation with the colonel about the baptism of Christ. It seemed odd to have such a vivid dream, so similar to the story, and so soon after.

Dream or no dream, in my present state I wasn't sure if I was alive or dead. As far as I knew, this was still part of the dream.

"We'll have you fixed up in no time, sir. Got a couple of scrapes, that's all," said the onboard medic, doing his best to reassure me that the situation was not as serious as it was.

The medic immediately set up an IV, somehow finding an intact vein. I felt a cool rush as the solution entered my blood system.

You're not a very good liar, I thought, but at least now I know that I'm still alive.

Back at base camp O.R., the surgeons worked diligently for hours on my mutilated body. They gave me a chance to survive if I recovered from my head wound and didn't develop any life threatening infections. At least, that was the prognosis they relayed to Colonel Harris, who knelt in the chapel tent, praying for my recovery.

My body was near death, my brain unconscious, but my soul seemed restless. I felt that warm sensation in my stomach again; certain that death was attempting to pay me a second visit.

Oh, no, I can't die yet! I thought about all of the work I wanted to accomplish in Vietnam, but wouldn't be able to. There is much too much work for me to complete here. Did I transfer here for nothing?

In my dream state, I replayed many of the conversation I had earlier with Peterson, especially the one about Christ's choosing of the twelve apostles. The story enchanted Peterson. He had confessed to me that he did not think the selection of the twelve was by accident; he wanted to know the significance of Christ just picking regular, everyday Joes to be in His squad, as he referred to it. Christ could have recruited any of the priests or teachers from the local synagogue, but He didn't.

"It's like they were soldiers, just like us," Peterson had said as we packed for the mission.

"Yeah, they were just regular guys," I reassured him.

It's true. There was nothing special about them before they met Jesus. They were just sinners like the rest of us. In fact, that's one reason He picked them. Regular men, with absolutely nothing to boast about, were to be the first ones set apart by God.

There was more to the story, but I decided to tell him later. I would explain that those chosen by Jesus were not random. Each of the first disciples were preordained, chosen before the foundation of this world age. The opportunity to follow Christ was their reward for their loyalty during the fall of Satan, prior to this present world age.

Thinking back on it now, I should have told him. I should have told him everything.

After a few hours in surgery, they transported my body to the infirmary for recovery. Colonel Harris made sure that the good news made it back to First Squad, still in the field, and it helped boost their moral.

I didn't know it, but while my body lay critically injured and my brain comatose, I would relive quite a few of my last conversations, interactions, and altercations before the attack. In fact, I would be a spectator as parts of my life, including my time in Vietnam, unfolded before me. It was God's way of saying well done. There was also another life I would be witness to and it was all part of God's plan.

Episode Six

The feeling in my stomach sped through warm, hot, and very hot sensations. I felt on fire again. I tried to think cool thoughts, hoping my body temperature would drop and my stomach would settle. I felt like my insides might erupt at any moment.

This must be it, I said. I'm a goner for sure now, I just know it. The fire burned in my stomach; it must have just killed me for sure. Then came that pulling again.

I felt like I was being dragged to hell. I fought as hard as I knew how, but, just like before, the room dissolved, fading into nothing. Nothing I did could stop it.

To my surprise, I went to the beach. Am I in paradise? I smiled inside. I can feel the sand between my toes. I can smell the salt from the sea, and I can see men… fishing? Hey, I can see men fishing! I felt as if I had a new chance at life.

I belched loudly. Excuse me. I certainly had not expected to make a sound. I did it again, only this time it made my stomach rumble even louder.

Okay, now that was kind of painful, I thought, wishing I could hold my stomach. I couldn't move my arms.

A group of men working along the harbor shore caught my attention. They were preparing their boat, but stopped working as I approached them.

I couldn't understand why I was perspiring so heavily. My stomach was boiling and my mouth was full of saliva.

Where am I, and why do I feel so sick? My body didn't look different to me, but as I looked down, I didn't see my boots or work fatigues. I wore that same robe again, and I had felt the sand because I had on sandals. I had no way to see my reflection. Involuntarily, my hands reached for my face. I felt my profile.

A couple of day's growth, I observed before my hands were forced back to my sides as if by someone else. As strange as it all seemed, I felt entirely like myself. When it came to moving my body, it felt like someone else was pulling the strings, but, other than that…. As my hands rubbed my face again, I peered through my fingers. Corporal Peterson approached me, with Lucas and Johnson behind him.

Okay, all my men seem to recognize me. I'm convinced that I am still me. Dear Lord, what happened? Did everyone from First Squad die in that blast? I noticed that their clothing had changed as well.

Whatever bubbled in my stomach now rose up to my mouth. It felt so painful that I wanted to curl up in a ball, clutching my stomach in my hands. My guts were about to erupt.

Whatever the problem is with my stomach, it's about to come up.

I wanted to bend over and vomit, but still couldn't control anything. I wanted to tell the men to stand back, but I couldn't. Saliva welled up in my mouth; I had to release it. And I did. Everything in my mouth spewed forth like a volcano spilling over.

Instead of enough saliva to fill the kitchen sink, a strong voice issued from my mouth. I heard the voice commanding, "Follow me, and I will make you fishers of men."

Who said that? I noticed all the moisture built up inside my mouth and throat had gone. In fact, now my mouth felt as dry as the desert, leaving my body feeling somewhat comforted but extremely thirsty.

Not only Peterson and the rest of the squad followed me, but everyone who heard the words 'follow me'. Hundreds followed me through the town, the places of worship, and even to the office of the tax collector. I saw someone resembling Private Matthews, looking very official and standing behind a table. He seemed to be in charge of a small group of men busying themselves with records and data. I recalled seeing him earlier, at the shore, but without his staff accompanying him.

I felt my mouth filling with saliva again. It felt so full that I dreaded spewing on everyone around me. I wasn't sure what would happen next, but hoped it wouldn't be embarrassing. I wanted to tell Matthews to come along, but my mouth wouldn't open, and I wasn't at all sure what would come out if it did. Then, I heard it: "Follow me."

Who keeps saying that? I felt frustrated by not being able to look for myself. My mouth feels completely dry again. My stomach has settled itself, too.

I tried to speak, but still could not utter a word. Deciding that the voice must come from someone standing behind me, I tried to look behind me, but couldn't.

Confused, I rethought my dream theory when Matthews left his desk to follow the crowd.

If I'm dead, and if everyone in the squad is dead, too, are we all in heaven?

Just then I saw Jinx, standing in the background like he was up to no good. Well, maybe we're not in heaven after all. Forgive me, Lord. I'm just joking.

We walked until we ended up at what was clearly Peterson's home. Parts of this dream started to seem very familiar.

My stomach felt strange again. In fact, my stomach even growled, but this time I recognized the discomfort. I don't have to wonder about that one, I am so hungry.

Episode Six

The aroma filling the Peterson house emphasized my hunger.

I don't remember the last time I ate. I was invited to stay for dinner that afternoon and accepted eagerly.

During the meal, I could not relax. I sensed danger filling the room, like there was an enemy among us.

I don't see any Viet Cong, I thought, thinking back to Vietnam. All the other men are acting as if nothing is wrong, so it must be my imagination. After all, they're trained to notice things like that.

I eagerly devoured the warm bread, gulping down the baked perch smothered in hot sauce and onions. My hunger soon satisfied, I noticed someone mumbling something in Doc's ear. I couldn't hear it, but, strangely, knew what had been said.

I was correct. There was an enemy in the room, but it wasn't the V.C. This man carried himself importantly. Though his robes were cut like ours, the cloth seemed finer and was dyed. He must have been a priest or someone official. He wasn't alone. A small number of similar, royally clad connivers were also in the room. They had followed us from the harbor and invited themselves to the table. One of them was bold enough to speak. He had been very inquisitive, observing everything, and now wanted to speak his mind.

It sure is getting hot in here, I thought, wishing I could fan the heat away.

I heard the priest speak again, then heard the name of Jesus whispered a few times.

The priest, still speaking softly, but hoping to provoke an answer, asked Doc, "Why does your master eat with tax collectors and sinners?"

I knew he was gonna say that, but wondered how I knew. I also wondered who the priest meant. Who in the room had the nerve to claim they were some type of master—master of what?

I was just curious. As out of place as I was, I didn't really have any stake in the matter. I thought about how empty my stomach felt, when hot sauce was invented, and what I might like to eat next. Nevertheless, the words of the priest weighed on my thoughts. Anger soon replaced my hunger pains. The soft growling in my stomach churned with a ferocious vehemence.

I tried to sit back and relax, while contemplating the words spoken by the head priest. Once again, I felt too sick to settle down. This time, I noticed that, before my mouth filled with saliva, my tongue felt as if it swelled, pressing against the roof of my mouth. Swallowing became impossible.

My tongue rolled as my mouth watered, just as it had earlier, before the mysterious voice became audible. Again, I experienced every sensation that comes right before vomiting. Burning up, I wanted to wipe my brow, but could not lift my arms.

I feel like I'm going to vomit again.

I tried to leave, but remained in my seat at the table.

I can't move and I got to get outta here. I panicked. I need to get to a bathroom.

I was beginning to realize what was happening. My fear that I might have traveled back in time only added to my discomfort. Once again I heard the name of Jesus spoken and wondered where He was and why I couldn't see Him.

He's got to be here somewhere.

My legs remained folded under me, both arms immobile. I looked straight into the eyes of the priest as I heard that same commanding voice speak again.

Ugh! I shouted at the same time that the voice cried out.

"It is not the healthy who need a doctor, but the sick. But go and learn what that means. I desire mercy, not sacrifice. For I have not come to call the righteous, but the sinners to repentance."

Those were the words of Jesus. I heard the voice of Jesus speaking, but still had no idea where He was.

This is too much for me. I wondered if the men of First Squad had conspired to play some type of trick on me.

This is some strange dream. I thought, feeling my stomach roil again.

I knew those words. In the past, I paraphrased them for my students. I taught that Jesus was saying, 'you righteous priests don't need me, but these humble sinners do.'

In their pomposity, the Pharisees would take this as a compliment, an acknowledgement of their spiritual supremacy over the commoners. Although He knew they were likely to take it that way, Jesus had another meaning in mind.

Spiritually speaking, everyone needs Christ. Any priest who thought himself truly righteous was nothing more than a theological sociopath. This type of priest lacked the wisdom to recognize spiritual irony, even when it was directed right at him.

Haven't they read that there are none righteous except God?

Episode Six

In Luke 16, Jesus says to them, "Ye are they which justify yourselves before men; but God knoweth your hearts: for that which is highly esteemed among men is abomination in the sight of God."

But these so-called holy men, soaking in their own self-esteem, think very highly of themselves, I thought, remembering a discussion with Colonel Harris a few days before the mission.

"They desire to be revered by others while investing in their own so-called wisdom."

"Roger that," agreed the colonel. "They sound more like scheming false prophets, seeking approval and needing admiration from common folk who don't know no better. I think God finds their self-administered admiration to be an abomination and, whenever God deems something to be an abomination, it becomes the lowest form of degradation, below which there is nothing worse."

"In reality, Jesus was saying that He wasn't there for the self-righteous, or so-called men of God. In this case, Jesus ate with those who needed spiritual healing. He ate with those who would not only accept the spiritual healing, but partook with sinners who were aware of their spiritual need."

I told the colonel that these self-righteous priests were no more spiritually healthy than other sinners, and that Jesus knew that they were more than sinners. They were His enemy.

"I know the type," said the colonel doing his best to keep up with the conversation while working at his desk. "Around here, we call 'em 'Hollywoods.' To them, proving worthiness to God means pretending to sacrifice while parading a charade of suffering in public.

"That's true," I said, watching the colonel fastidiously signing form after form. "Their definition of self-sacrifice was absurd, and they sold it to willingly uninformed congregants, who bought or brought in sacrifices in hopes of receiving favor from the false priests. For-profit seeking priests, selling salvation to the highest of bidders. The more one had to offer, the closer to God one could become."

As I became more entangled in this unusual scenario, I realized what was taking place. I wasn't sure if I was dead or just detained somewhere between life and death. I wasn't sure if this happened to everyone when they died, or if I was specifically chosen for this near death dream experience.

I felt the burning sensation cooling as a freezing chill came over me. As my surroundings ebbed away, I felt sure that I would see them again before this life or death experience was over.

Feeling like someone suddenly yanked me away by the back of my shirt collar, I found myself back in Vietnam. Odd—I had thought my body was recovering, and now I stood over the base camp surgeons as they worked on my head wound.

"Blood pressure, nurse, what's his blood pressure?" asked the surgeon positioned on the right side of the table.

"Blood pressure is 89 over 48," said the nurse.

Don't let me die, Doc. I'm too young to die. I haven't done enough yet, I thought. There's the whole U.S. Army that needs to be saved, so it's almost impossible for me to run out of work to do. Doctor, as long as you don't give up, I won't give up, and that's a promise.

I felt an immediate drowsiness, and wasn't surprised when, once again, my spirit drifted away as if tugged from behind.

"Incoming! Incoming, six o'clock—take cover, sir," Corporal Peterson yelled to me, at the top of his voice. "Mortar rounds coming from behind us at the six o'clock position."

While Peterson yelled, I, dazed, tried to figure out how we were back on patrol and not in the surgery room, and why some of the transitions seemed illogical. I had just witnessed my surgery, but knew that my body was already recovering in the infirmary. As unreal as I knew it had to be, these dreams began to seem very real.

How did I get back here again? I thought. I'm not really here; this is just a dream. I… I don't want to see this again. I braced myself emotionally for what I was going to see. "Out of the frying pan and into the fire."

"What's that, sir?" Peterson yelled.

"Nothing, just talking to myself," I said, "I think," mumbling under my breath.

This has to be déjà-vu, I told myself. Everything is happening all over again. Does this mean I'll be killed in action twice? I didn't feel anything the first time, so maybe it won't hurt the second time around either.

The squad was under fire from the Viet Cong mortars. I remembered that this attack happened earlier during the patrol, on our way to link up with the first village. We could only freeze in place until it was over. In addition to the mortar rounds, the enemy also used psychological audible warfare tactics.

An enemy soldier, doing a bad job of speaking English over a loud speaker attempted to antagonize the patrol team. The idea was to get First Squad to expose their position, preferably by shooting at an imaginary enemy presence. The area was set up as if there was an enemy patrol near, but it was just an illusion. The Viet Cong, well aware that this area saw heavy traffic from U.S. soldiers, knew better than to use the area themselves. They would bomb it regularly, hoping to get lucky.

Meanwhile, they used loudspeakers mounted to trees in an attempt to fool U.S. soldiers into thinking that they were nearby, when, in fact, they were securely hidden hundreds of meters away. And, if soldiers found themselves in the area during the enemy fire missions, they would hear taunts of inflammatory propaganda that included everything from 'you're fighting a losing battle' to 'your country has abandoned you.'

Recalling my officer training military tactics class, I remembered that the success of this enemy strategy depended on stress levels of the patrol team caught in the kill zone. In our case, First Squad, somewhat stressed out, ended up under indirect fire from the enemy mortars because of the location of the village.

"We got you now, Americans, you can't run that way, we got you now," the enemy voices crackled over the speakers.

"Don't worry about them, sir," said Peterson. "They can't really see us. It's just one of the mind games they play."

I didn't buy that because I was hearing what sounded like a personal attack directed at me. "Your holy man can't help you, G.I. you gon' die, you gon' die, die, die," taunted the enemy voice.

"Are they talking about me?" I said, stunned. "How did they know I was with this patrol if they can't see us? I don't remember it happening this way before," I said, recalling the actual attack earlier.

Peterson looked at me and shrugged his shoulders, as if answering me.

The voice over the loudspeaker sounded as if it was specifically haunting me. The voice morphed into the type of sound that spooks children in the night, like a scratching sound from the inside a closed closet door.

Those haunting words became blasphemous as well, insulting the name of Jesus. I could only take so much of this; my blood boiled at the offense. Focusing on the voice screeching from the loudspeakers seemed to twist my anger, sending me into an almost hypnotic spell.

"How dare you curse the name of the Holy Spirit," I said.

I heard the squad's M60 machine gunner firing in bursts of three at what he thought were moving enemy troops, but there was no one there. Jinx, who had not been ordered to fire at all, had panicked.

"He cursed the name of Jesus that time. Let me get my hands on him," I said. "I could drive that demon out of him by using the same name he's cursing."

I still heard the voice over the loudspeaker as I felt my spirit slipping away again. When I regained my sight, I took in my surroundings, noticed that my garments were soaked with sweat and that my stomach was cramping from the heat.

I could tell that I had returned to the other time and place. This time, I was ready to admit that I thought I was in Jerusalem, around 31 AD. It looked a lot like the place I visited the last time I felt sick. The same roads, the same clothing, and it looked like the same city.

This time I recognized every remaining member from First Squad. Peterson stood in front of me, still shrugging his shoulders. As difficult as it seemed, I had to admit that I was dreaming about time traveling to the days of Christ. I still wondered why I had not actually seen Him yet.

I figured out on my own that everyone had not died, so, this time around, I entertained the thought of how possible or impossible for everyone having the same dream at the same time. Thoughts of The Twilight Zone kept going through my mind.

As we walked I noticed what looked like a church just up ahead. I was happy about that—how great would it be to witness a sermon given by Christ? After all, why visit 31 AD and not see Jesus? What a waste of time travel that would be.

That would make this the greatest dream ever, I thought.

Arriving at what seemed like a church, I heard a man speaking all sorts of wickedness inside. He threatened me personally as the squad and I entered the building. I could tell right away that this strange, ungodly man had an unclean spirit within him. He pointed and yelled at me. He insinuated that I was trying to kill him.

I'm just trying to get out of your way, I thought, since no one could actually hear me. My eyes shifted around the church; I kept hoping to spot Jesus this time.

"Let us alone," screamed the unclean spirit in anguish, looking straight into my eyes. "What do you want with us, Jesus of Nazareth? Have you come to destroy us? I know who you are, the Holy One of God."

Episode Six

Up to now, I had been suspicious, wondering why I heard Jesus' words, but had not actually seen Him yet. This time, I couldn't believe my ears. I could not deny it this time, either; someone had looked straight into my eyes and called me Jesus.

I knew my faith was strong. I had always followed Christ and hoped others would find me, at the least, Christ like, but being referred to as Christ had to be blasphemous.

Well, the man is mad, after all, I thought, trying to dismiss what just happened.

Like most people, I believed that the Holy Spirit was in me, but in no way could I be mistaken for Jesus Christ. I tried to walk away from the man, but my feet seemed rooted to the floor. Obviously, I wasn't going anywhere else until I confronted this madman.

With my stomach practically convulsing, and my tongue rolling along the roof of my mouth again, I looked at the squad for help. They seemed unable to do anything; they waited for my next move. My eyes shifted back and I peered directly into the eyes of the demon.

Ugh! The others still could not hear me, but I clearly heard that same voice of authority.

"Hold your peace and come out of him," said the voice. My body experienced sudden, profound relief, but my mind fell into a state of shock.

With a loud shriek, the demon came out, almost tearing the man's body in two. A stream of black soot bled from the man's pores, but his eyes were sane again.

I stood silent for a moment, marveling at what just happened. The demon had looked right into my eyes and called me Jesus.

Why are they calling me Jesus? I wondered. I need a mirror.

I prayed for an answer. I didn't understand what was happening. I was reminded of verses from the book of Mark. In the synagogue, an unclean spirit had confronted Jesus and the disciples.

In the past, I had always found it ironic, considering Christ's teaching style and how He initially tried to stay a little under the radar around the clergy. Yet the demons knew that Jesus was the Christ and that His ministry was one of salvation, while the clergy in the city of Jerusalem saw Him as a troublemaker.

I remembered having a similar conversation with Lump the day the priest tried to swat me with my Bible. I had been so upset about the priest attempting to strike me for teaching God's word that, when Lump and I were alone, I speculated that a devil had possessed the priest.

"He was wrong for what he did," laughed Lump. "He musta' thought he was your daddy or something."

"I think he must have been possessed by the devil," I yelled, laughing and throwing the baseball back to Lump.

"Demons in the church. What will Satan think of next?" shouted Lump.

"That's how it was in Jerusalem when Jesus was there," I said, catching the baseball in my glove.

This particular incident of the demon acknowledging Jesus as the Messiah is an example for all followers of Christ. It happened when Christ was visiting the synagogue and, although this specific visit happened during his first advent, it will happen again in the future.

"You gotta wonder why the demons were so comfortable hanging out in the church back then. If they were comfortable when Jesus was around, think about how easy they got it now," I reflected.

I always used to ask why the demons were so comfortable in the house of God. I wanted to know why they had not been cast out prior to the arrival of Christ. Where were the watchmen, why weren't they watching for the enemy?

"I tell you what," said Lump, catching the ball, "There is something wrong when the world's Savior arrives, and the only person able to recognize Him happens to be the church member who's filled with the evil spirit."

"Shoot, man, that's what it's gonna be like in the future, too," I said.

"In the future there will be seven types of churches, but, upon Christ's return, only two of the churches will be pleasing to Him. When the true Christ returns, He discovers that the other five churches have fallen away from the true Messiah, and are found not only following, but also worshipping, the false Christ—not just a demon, but the Son of Perdition himself."

I had a lot to think about now. Demons were calling me Jesus. I was certainly not a savior. I asked God to forgive me for my blasphemous thoughts. I knew that God wouldn't judge me for my dreams—after all, how could a person control what they dreamt about? However, this seemed like more than a dream and I hoped it wouldn't be held against me should I meet God that day.

―――――――――――――――――――――――

Episode Six

The sound of the battlefield interrupted my thoughts, pulling me back to Vietnam. I realized that I must not have been gone long at all. Jinx was still unloading the M60 machine gun at nothing, pretending it was the helpless body of a Viet Cong soldier.

The stuttering sounds of the gunfire reminded me of the demon being torn from the body of the man in the synagogue.

"Talk about my mama, huh! Yeah, well bump you and your loudspeaker," shouted Jinx, as he ripped the tree apart, bringing it and the loudspeaker crashing to the jungle floor.

"Ah! Damn, my leg," Jinx screamed in pain, "Doc! Yo, Doc."

Doc, Lucas, and I ran to his aid, but it was just a leg cramp.

"Stay away from me holy man," reminded Jinx, kicking at the air, "I done already told you once. You bad luck, man. Why you wanna' be out here in the bush, anyway? Why don't you go to church or something? Ain't that where most sinners be at? I mean, man—you ain't got no souls nowhere else you can save? You just waistin' your time here, holy man, cause you see, everybody over here goin' ta hell, don't matter, dead or alive."

"Man, you sound so stupid," said Matthews. "'Dead or alive, we all going to hell'." He turned away, adding under his breath, "You a idiot."

As I walked away, Jinx whispered to Doc. I could hear him begging Doc for a shot of morphine.

"You not dying, Jinx, you just got a leg cramp, soldier!" snapped Lucas

Jinx was an incurable heroine addict. I knew that Jesus could heal him, but Jinx would never give the power of Christ a chance.

"Come on, Doc," he said, "Fix me up."

"Doc, we got a man down over here!" shouted Thompson.

"Yo! Doc, where you going, man? You gotta fix me up," he whimpered.

"Hold up, Jinx. Just hold on. Who is it?" asked Doc.

"Shoot, man, it's Batman. Is he dead, Doc?" asked Johnson.

Lucas could tell that he was dead. He didn't have to examine Bart's body, but he did anyway. "Yeah—he's gone, man."

"Squad leader, we need a medevac," said Doc.

"Yeah! I need a medevac, too, Sarge," yelled Jinx.

"Shut the hell up, Jinx. Preacher," continued Sergeant Matthias, "His wife just had a little girl. It's all he been talking about lately. He ain't had no chance to see her in person, only seen her picture."

I remembered the picture Bart had shown earlier of him and his family.

"He was a short-timer, too," added Matthias, "Just like Saez. Just a few more weeks and he woulda' been back in the world with his family. This place woulda' been nothin' but a bunch a bad dreams. It ain't fair. I tried to get him and Saez sick-called out of this mission, but they turned it down and now both of 'em is dead. Preacher, will you do whatever you can for him? Poor soul, he just wanted to go home in one piece. He really was a good dude, sir. Gonna miss you, Batman."

My eyes watered. I had heard and seen so much death and dying that, for a moment, I wished I really were Jesus Christ. I had seen more dying in one day than anyone should ever see.

"This child of God should not have died this way, Lord. None of your children should die this way," I said. I fell to my knees and wept. "If I were Christ, I could bring him back."

My tears grew heavier, mixing with the trail of Bart's blood draining away beneath me.

Remaining trapped in this memory while continuing to hold Bart's lifeless hand I remembered one of the last conversations we had at the base camp before leaving for the mission. Me, Bart, and a small group of soldiers discussed the forty days that Christ spent fasting while preparing for His ministry. After we talked about the part where Satan tempts Christ, they wanted to know where Satan was now. Some said he was in hell, while others said he was on earth. I assured them that Satan was not on earth, though his spiritual influence dominated the minds of the unrighteous.

I explained why Satan was only here on earth in spirit at this time, using verses from the book of Matthew.

"The fourth chapter begins with Jesus being taken away to be tempted," I began. "By the way, it's no accident that Jesus' first real biblical lesson is about overcoming Satan."

I always figured that the New Testament recorded lessons according to importance; how to defeat Satan should top the list. The verse went, "Then was Jesus led up of the Spirit into the wilderness to be tempted of the devil."

"This is an example for us," I said. "After God prepares us and is sure that we are well-learned in His complete plan, He will allow us to be tested. The wilderness represents the place where death exists, and our task is to overcome death, or Satan. In fact, we should think of every temptation as practice for that day when we are called to stand against him."

"And when he had fasted forty days and forty nights, he was afterward hungered." I read that much, then stopped.

Episode Six

"Forty days of fasting, man, now that's a long time," said Peterson, "Jinx couldn't make one day."

"Yep, Christ's flesh, at this point, is at its weakest and is tested by Satan. I read on. "And when the tempter came to him, he said, If thou be the Son of God, command that these stones be made bread."

"You know," I warned, "Satan has a way of tempting us when we are at our weakest. He knew that Jesus was the Son of God, but that's how Satan tempts us. He wants us to prove who we are and then be gratified by it. He wants us to be proud, and then take credit, making the blessings we receive from God void."

"Satan wanted Jesus to step outside of God's will and act all bad, like He didn't need His Father's help?" asked Johnson.

"Exactly," I said, "he wanted Jesus to commit the same sin he was guilty of."

"And that was pride, right?" said Saez.

"Yes," I answered, "pride was the most costly sin, the one that led to Satan's fall."

I read some more. "But he answered and said, It is written, Man shall not live by bread alone, but by every word that proceedeth out of the mouth of God."

"Christ continues to defeat Satan by using the wisdom of God's word," I said. "The next part of Christ's test follows when Satan proves how well-versed he is in scripture. He tries to tempt Jesus by twisting the words of God."

I read: "Then the devil taketh him up into the holy city, and setteth him on a pinnacle of the temple And saith unto him, If thou be the Son of God, cast thyself down: for it is written, He shall give His angels charge concerning thee: and in their hands they shall bear thee up, lest at any time thou dash thy foot against a stone."

"Satan tested Christ with the words from Psalm 91," I said. "The real test was Christ's knowledge of God's word. Satan added words when tempting Christ."

"How did he add to God's word?" Johnson asked.

"God's word does not mention the words 'lest at any time'. By adding these words, Satan suggests that it's okay to ask God to prove Himself," I said.

"Like to test Him?" asked Saez. He seemed to be thinking about something personal.

"Yes," I answered, and then continued to read. "Jesus said unto him, it is written again, Thou shalt not tempt the Lord thy God."

"For the final test, Satan takes Jesus up to a higher place of worship and tries to tempt Christ with glory and power. Claiming them as his own, he points out the kingdoms of the world and says he has the authority to give Jesus the world—all He has to do to is bow down and worship him. Christ has no desire for the kingdoms of the world, or anything Satan can offer. Besides, they're already His. However, Satan makes the mistake of revealing his true intentions. He wants to be worshipped."

"Seems like the devil just got busted," said Peterson, "and I been listening to you speak enough to know what's comin'. The fact that it's written in the scripture must have something to do with the future."

"Right again, Corporal. This will also be his desire when he returns to earth posing as the true Christ."

"So, we know he's coming back," said Johnson, "but if he ain't in Vietnam, where the devil is he now?" Johnson joked. "Get it—where the devil is he?"

"Yeah, we get it, funny man," said Peterson.

"The next verse reveals the location of Satan," I said, "and where he will remain until released onto earth. Verse 10 reads, "Then saith Jesus unto him, get thee hence, Satan: for it is written, Thou shalt worship the Lord thy God, and him only shalt thou serve."

"Here, Jesus gives Satan a command, and he must follow it. He tells Satan to get behind Him. Speaking plainly, if we believe that Christ resides in heaven then we should also believe that Satan is behind Him, locked away until he is released."

"Is that it?" asked Bart, "just that one verse? 'Cause I can tell you now, you gonna have a tough time trying to prove that one to Private 'show me that' Thompson from Missouri."

"There are a few places that talk about Satan's whereabouts," I said. "It's written in Jude, Verse 6, that the fallen angels are chained and held in a place of darkness waiting for judgment day. It's written in the book of Revelation, Chapter 12 that there will finally be peace in heaven when Satan is cast to earth to tempt man into worshipping him. It's written in the book of Thessalonians that, prior to the second coming of Christ, the archangel Michael will release Satan onto earth from heaven."

I assured the soldiers that, although Satan is locked away, the war between the two seed lines is real and continues to this day.

Bart understood the lesson. He believed that good and evil existed, but I wasn't sure if he believed there was a heaven, and that some day

Episode Six

God would create hell, or that Christ was the path to salvation. I wanted to ask Bart if he had accepted Christ as savior, but decided to wait until our next conversation. I made a costly mistake that day. I forgot about the preachers golden rule: there is such a thing as being one day too late with God.

Episode Seven

December 31 and 30 AD

I welcomed the fiery sensation this time. The inside of my body felt like a piece of paper held under a magnifying glass in the scorching sun. My flesh associated the symptoms with each hallucination, like muscle memory. Watching as Bart's body lifted high overhead, I was overcome with grief, welcoming the stomach cramps and the swelling of my throat.

"Pull me, yank me, drag me, I don't care… just take me away," I shouted louder, knowing that no one could hear me. "Any place is better than here."

Witnessing death in war takes a toll on a person. It transcends the carnal to the spiritual, and cannot rightly be comprehended by the natural side of man. I witnessed the deaths of two people I had come to call friends. Now I realized why so many soldiers had such a long, cold, blank stare. In that stare you could see every time that witnessing death or taking life claimed a part of their souls.

It wasn't just any casualty; it was the violent death of friends and the inability to mourn that made the difference. I had to witness the deaths of Private Bart and Corporal Saez before I understood clearly what I couldn't figure out before.

Initially, I thought the men were looking beyond death. Now I thought that the combat veterans actually pondered what waited for them on the other side. As long as they remained actively engaged in combat, they had no peace of mind because death, and what waited beyond death, constantly chased after them. They could not rest because that other dimension haunted them, and beckoned their souls. Many hoped to find nothing on the other side, that death was the end. But others, like Jinx, felt certain that the pit of hell waited for them.

Involvement in either way left soldiers feeling an internal void as if part of their own existence was torn away. When death becomes a way of life, it makes men search exhaustively for something that no longer exists—peace of mind.

Doc Lucas, who felt he could never take a life, had the look worse than many who had killed. Doc saw it differently. As the team medic, he saw death coming for each man, but was unable to prevent it.

A lot of soldiers saw medics and preachers the same way; they were only there to locate, arrange, and rearrange fragmented body parts. Some reject them because, seeing a medic or a preacher at the wrong time usually meant that death was closing in.

Before I was wounded he confided in me, "Preacher," said Doc unsteadily after carefully wrapping Bart's body for travel. "I carry the howling of the dying in my medical bag. Every time I open it, I hear their wailing souls attacking me, crying, 'Save me, Doc! Don't let me die!' And it haunts me."

Doc had the look worse than all of them. Many times he was their last hope, their last chance, the last comforting face they would ever see. Since he never took a life, death didn't chase him the same way. He wasn't running from death; he fought it. Doc was running from the souls of the dead and dying. In his guilt-ridden mind, the dimension that haunted him was full of dead soldiers he hadn't saved.

I had a poignant understanding of Doc's emotional state as he focused on Private Bart, who didn't have to worry about killing anymore. He didn't have to worry about dying or protecting his buddies anymore. I prayed that the next face Harold Bart saw would be the comforting face of Jesus.

I took a moment to think about how this mortar attack was different. Originally, Doc and I left the site with the squad, heading toward the village while Jinx and Matthews stayed behind to wait for the helicopter. This time all four of us waited. I wondered if anything else would change along the way and hoped I would have that option.

"Father in heaven," I said, "we ask that you please receive the soul of our fallen brother, in Jesus' name, Amen."

"Amen," said Matthews, standing over me.

Matthews's words were the last ones I heard as the fire raging in my stomach finally took over, transporting me back to Jerusalem.

Finally, I thought, where's a good death-induced hallucination when you need one? Looking at my new surroundings, I felt content for the moment.

I had returned to this peaceful place on the road again, safe and sound outside of the city. This time I noticed a crossroads, where I met up with First Squad. The people, the environment, and the circumstances surrounding each hallucination were more acutely familiar to me each time. I wasn't sure if that was good or not, but, for the time being, it sure beat watching my buddies dying in Vietnam.

As much as I could tell, I wore the same clothes as in the other hallucinations; so did the rest of the squad. I had not seen my face since the baptism and was curious to see what I looked like now. All of the disciples—or squad members—looked slightly older, but had not changed much. I did feel as if my beard had become a little heavier. Everyone still called me Jesus and, honestly, I was beginning to like that part of the dream.

Hearing those words in my own thoughts, I suddenly remembered the Immortal Keepers. I tried to recall the stories that Father Shelly told me long ago, but couldn't.

"Darn, I should have paid closer attention," I said. "My fault for writing him off as a crazy person."

All of my life, I tried to live as Jesus did. All my life, I praised God and prayed in Jesus' name. It seemed rewarding, that, at the hour of my own death, I was not only called home by the Father, but dreaming of what it was like to be Jesus Christ.

I surmised that the first apostles must have been much like the men in first squad. Whenever my dreams sent me back in time, the disciples usually briefed me on our situation. It was like the operation order before each mission. I appreciated this; it helped clear up the confusion of where I was and what was occurring.

I just seemed to arrive on a thought. I noticed that I usually went to Jerusalem after an emotional event took place in Vietnam. Then it seemed like I had to figure out the biblical significance of my journey to move on from Jerusalem.

This is a gift worth dying for.

I had not yet recovered from the current journey and was still kneeling on the ground when, from a distance, I saw a woman approaching me. She looks, familiar. Who is she? I've seen her face before. Of course, no one heard me. My body stood up and I could see better.

Episode Seven

She dressed as if she were mourning the death of a friend or a family member. I didn't know this woman personally, but I had seen her face before. A scarf covered most of her long, black hair. Even though she had pulled part of the scarf across to protect her face, I recognized something familiar. I had seen an image of her and was just as pretty in person as in her picture.

Is this Bart's wife? I wondered, as it finally dawned on me that Matthews was asking a question.

"Will you make Lazarus well, Lord?"

Who? Harold? I thought, Bart's death still fresh on my mind.

Oh, Lord, is this the story of Lazarus? Am I... I mean... is Jesus going to raise the dead? I thought, trying to forget about Vietnam.

I waited impatiently to hear the answer come from within me this time, even though I knew how painful it was whenever the voice spoke. This time, the pain and all of the other symptoms came, but my anticipation of the next words spoken completely strangled the usual accompanying seizure.

The question about Lazarus rang in my ears. Then I heard the voice respond.

"This sickness is not unto death, but for the glory of God, that the Son of God might be glorified thereby."

Whoa! I remembered the story of Lazarus and how God, through Christ, raised him from the dead.

The disciples asked Jesus about returning to the city. "Master, the Jews of late sought to stone thee; and goest thou thither again?"

"Jesus answered, "Are there not twelve hours in the day? If any man walk in the day, he stumbleth not, because he seeth the light of this world. But if a man walk in the night, he stumbleth, because there is no light in him.' "

When I was younger, I thought that Jesus had the strangest way of answering questions. But as I matured, I recognized the lessons to be learned from Jesus' technique. His answer about returning to Jerusalem appeared to have nothing to do with the question asked. I concluded that, if Jesus' answer didn't seem to fit the question He was asked, then it was directing us to the future. Then I would apply an end time theory, and focus on God's complete plan to figure it out. In this exact, though seemingly evasive answer, Jesus shed light on how certain darkened teachings regarding the days leading up to His return would develop into stumbling blocks for Christians.

"Are there not twelve hours in the day?"

I remembered having that conversation with Vanessa. One day, when I was studying and she was doing homework, I asked her why Christians found it hard to understand Jesus' teachings. I never really had that problem. I loved hearing Vanessa talk about Christ.

"Sometimes Jesus' answers don't seem to go along with the question, so when Jesus answers a question this way," said Vanessa, "they should do just like you're doing right now."

"What am I doing?" the younger me asked.

"You're sensing there's something funny about His answer and trying to figure out what it means, right?"

"Yes, that's what I'm doing," I affirmed, nodding at the same time.

Vanessa laughed at my response. "Just like you, students of God's word should recognize that there is something hidden that needs to be revealed, right? And if I were to give you a hint do you think you could figure it out?"

"Um, maybe," I said, trying to outthink her by rushing to the eleventh chapter of John.

"Okay, but you don't have to read it to find the clue. So put the book down and figure this one out in your head."

"Okay, it's all in my head," I said, putting the Bible in my lap.

"It's not all in your head, silly," she said laughing, "but I want you to use your head. Okay, here is the clue."

I sat there, alert and listening.

"If I told you that the key to applying the death and resurrection of Lazarus to the second coming of Christ is found in the time frame that he died, what would that mean?"

My mouth dropped open, but I was still alert and listening.

"Did you understand the question?" asked Vanessa, laughing as she watched me this time shaking my head no, but saying yes.

"Um, a little bit, I think," I said, unsure of the question and the answer. "Okay, ask me again."

"If I said that Jesus came after death had taken His friend…"

"Oh, oh—I got it now," I interrupted.

"So then how would you apply that to Jesus' second coming?" asked Vanessa, feeling excited for me.

"Um, I think…" I was still unsure of the answer.

"Okay, basically we know that Lazarus is physically dead, right?" asked Vanessa as she looked over the top of her notebook. I nodded.

Episode Seven

"But if we look at it in the future, it symbolizes a spiritual death. Does that help? Can you figure it out from there?"

"Okay, I know this one," I began, anticipating how excited she would be when I got it right. "In the future, prior to the second coming of Jesus, those who follow the false Christ will be spiritually dead. Jesus shows us in this example that He comes after the world has been taken by death. Is that why He waited until Lazarus was dead already?"

"Exactly," said Vanessa, "He wants the people in the future to know that He comes after death. It's a warning for them not to be taken by Satan. And Satan is death, right?"

"Right," I agreed, laughing as she tickled me with her foot.

———————————————————

With the remaining squad, I went straight to the tomb, where it seemed like the whole city had gathered. Hundreds, if not thousands, of people jammed their way into the gravesite.

As we approached the tomb of Lazarus, it felt like I was watching a movie, but before the cameras rolled. Every character seemed to be in place and now all the players needed was for the director to command 'quiet on the set… action'.

I knew this story very well, and could even recite the dialogue. The spiritual significance of this miracle meant more then the actual act, but, to those watching and waiting to see a miracle, that part meant little. I realized that, no matter how much Jesus explained to the disciples, they would not understand until after the Holy Spirit empowered them.

I grew more excited to see this miracle for myself. Honestly, it seemed that I didn't care much about its spiritual significance either.

Lazarus's sister earnestly approached Jesus and greeted Him with the news. "If you had only been here our brother would be alive."

"Your brother will rise again," said the voice of Jesus.

I no longer had to guess who was speaking or where the voice of Jesus came from.

"She answered, I know, Lord, as will all rise at the hour of resurrection."

Whenever I would come to this verse, I would make it a point to teach a vital lesson. Jesus told her not to worry because God will raise him from the dead for all to see on that very day. Martha, however, thought Jesus referred to the future and the end time resurrection.

"I am the resurrection," said the voice of Jesus. "I am the

resurrection, and the life: he that believeth in me, though he were dead, yet shall he live: And whosoever liveth and believeth in me shall never die. Believest thou this?"

"She saith unto him, Yea, Lord: I believe that thou art the Christ, the Son of God, which should come into the world."

Initially, I thought Martha was Harold's wife. I remembered seeing photos of Harold' wife and sister, noting how much they favored each other.

Mary, Martha's sister, fell at His feet, and said, "Lord, if you had come sooner our brother would not have died."

I felt the agony caused by her misunderstanding and wanted so desperately to explain to her what Jesus meant.

I could see Mary, Martha, and their family members, crying softly. However, the genuinely sympathetic whimpers from the family were drowned out by the overwhelming wails of the professional mourners surrounding the tomb.

It seemed like everyone was crying, except First Squad and me. I felt a spirit of compassion moving within me, but I couldn't cry. I wasn't allowed to for some reason. My mouth watered and my temperature instantly rose.

Anticipating the size of the miracle, I figured that this was really going to be painful. The idea of witnessing such a miracle left me feeling both excited and afraid; I figured the impact would probably send me traveling straight back to Vietnam.

Is this really going to happen? I thought, wishing that I could close my eyes.

My body turned toward Mary and, looking upon her, I heard the voice of Jesus ask, "Where have you laid him?"

In my heart, I wept in sorrow and fear. Mary's family and friends could not see my compassion or fear. They could only see Jesus' outward show of confidence and magnificent surety.

They felt His love, but still doubted why He had not come sooner, to prevent the death. Hearing their disbelief, Jesus groaned inwardly. I felt the groan, and hoped that wouldn't happen again. I also knew why Christ waited so long. The people needed a sign. Bringing someone back to life when they were so certainly dead, should be sign enough.

"Remove the stone," said the voice of Jesus.

I think I am ready to go back to Vietnam, now, I thought, as my fear grew.

"Martha, the sister of him that was dead, saith unto Him, Lord, by this time he stinketh: for he hath been dead four days."

Episode Seven

Wishing that I could manage my own body movements, I now lost all control of my speech. Words seemed to spit involuntarily from my mouth. Just like before, I felt as if I was actually vomiting these words from deep within me.

"Said I not unto thee, that, if thou wouldest believe, thou shouldest see the glory of God?"

The stone was removed. I found myself looking toward heaven.

I thought I understood God's glory. Having completed exhaustive research, I came to a very simple conclusion: God receives glory when He is proven to be God. When His prophecies, promises, and revelations are proven, then He is proven.

I wasn't sure at first, but it seemed like I felt the wind blowing into my face. I was sure when my eyes began to water, but I could not raise my hands to wipe them. I could hear birds singing, dogs barking, hundreds of people wailing and the wind rustling, as the crowd moved closer, and tighter, trying to see.

What a way to draw a crowd, I thought.

While I looked skyward, the voice of Jesus spoke again.

"It is not my will but the Father's. Father, I thank thee that thou hast heard me. And I knew that thou hearest me always: but because of the people which stand by I said it, that they may believe that thou hast sent me."

I felt my shoulders tense up, specifically my rear deltoids as both arms extended toward the tomb.

Ugh, ugh! My body instinctively resisted the action. It wasn't painful, but felt inexplicably heavy.

Why am I resisting this? I thought.

What felt like a ball of fire rose from my stomach. I thought I should cover my mouth. I didn't know what was going to come up from me this time.

My whole stomach is on the way up, I thought. Do your will, Holy Spirit. I am ready.

The inferno within me erupted; the thunderous voice bellowed.

"Lazarus, come forth," said the voice of Jesus, leaving me feeling like I had just collided with a linebacker.

From the inside of the tomb, a hand grabbed mine.

Oh! God! I thought, afraid to look at what approached.

Unable to physically close my eyes, I settled for blanking out my mind. The fear I felt reminded me of staying up all night with Lump, watching Boris Karloff horror movies, then having nightmares until sunrise. Back then, I would lie frozen in bed, thinking that, if I didn't move a muscle, I would be safe from whatever waited in the darkness.

Now, I tried to imagine yanking my arm away from the tomb, but it was too late. Before me stood a man, wrapped as if he had been the star of one of those classic horror films.

Could this really be Lazarus? I thought.

"Loose him, and let him go," said the voice of Jesus.

I wondered if one of my squad members could possibly be wrapped in the bandages. After all, most of the squad was with me in Jerusalem—except the two who were killed in action.

As my insides calmed, thirst overcame me. My sweating stopped and my heart rate returned to normal. But there seemed to be an abundance of pressure in my forehead. I felt like I was dwindling away to nothing. It was as if I watched a picture become smaller as it shrank, then faded to black.

"I feel like I'm shrinking," I said as the black took over.

As the body of Lazarus faded from view, I could still see Bart's body being airlifted from the jungle. I had traveled back to Vietnam as if only moments in time passed. While watching the jungle penetrator swing, spinning Bart's body through the air, I thought about Saez and the question he asked me before the mission began. Most soldiers thought about it at all times, but were afraid to ask.

Saez asked me, "Where do people go when they die? And what happens to soldiers killed in battle?"

I wondered when someone would get around to asking me that question. I didn't bring it up because talking about death during a war was considered unlucky.

Not wanting to spend too much time on the topic of death, I answered. Jesus was our example and, since He returned to heaven after His resurrection, so will we all.

Saez and I talked about the parable of the rich man and Lazarus. I read, "And it came to pass, that the beggar died, and was carried by the angels into Abraham's bosom: the rich man also died and was buried."

"Both have died," I said, "and a comparison is made of their afterlives. Of course, upon their deaths, common sense tells us that both men were buried, but one man was with God, and one was in a place without God," I said, trying to give him the short answer.

Episode Seven

"The Holy Bible's comparison shows more favor towards the poor man, who had it tough in life, as opposed to the rich man, who apparently acquired his wealth illegally or possibly cared more for his earthly riches than his eternal life.

"And in hell he lift up his eyes, being in torment, and seeth Abraham afar off, and Lazarus in his bosom."

"So, Saez, what does that sound like to you?" I asked, looking behind me to where he stood.

"It sounds like the poor man is now living well, while the rich man is tormented," he said, reading the words over my shoulder.

"So it seems," I said, leaning back to let him read more. "The torment he feels is his lack of connection with God. He's cut off. The verse says that the rich man is in hell, but, since he can see Lazarus in the bosom of Abraham, we have to reason that he must actually be in heaven.

"How can hell be in heaven?" asked Saez.

"That's a good question," I said. "Originally, the word hell also meant grave, or simply put, the place of the dead. The definition of hell is the dimension where the dead exist—all of the dead, good or bad doesn't matter—and since the rich man can see Lazarus and Abraham, it's safe to conclude that they are all in this dimension together.

"In this case, his soul is also in heaven, but separated from the love of God. Jesus wants us to know that, in that dimension, being separated from God is what we today call hell. The shame that he feels is his torment."

"Like his own personal hell," said Saez.

"Exactly," I said turning the page.

"And he cried and said, Father Abraham, have mercy on me, and send Lazarus, that he may dip the tip of his finger in water, and cool my tongue; for I am tormented in this flame."

"Since this is a parable and being true to it, Jesus uses the example of a man dying of thirst to express what life will be like without the love of God."

"So hell isn't made up of fire?" said Saez.

"God is the fire, He's the consuming fire. Besides, there's really nothing to burn as we think of burning."

"Oh, that's right," said Saez, snapping his fingers. "In the new age there's no flesh to burn anyway."

"You know what? That's right," I said as I began to read again. "And beside all this, between us and you there is a great gulf fixed: so that they which would pass from hence to you cannot; neither can they pass to us, that would come from thence."

"But, if it's that big of a gulf, how can they see or hear each other? That must be like yelling back and forth over the Grand Canyon," said Saez, laughing.

"Yeah, can you imagine that?" I said, also laughing. "That's why it's a parable. You have to see stuff like that and then make sense out of it."

"Yeah, that makes sense too," agreed Saez. "So they can't really see each other, but Jesus wants us to know that they are in the same place, but separated."

"Right," I said, "There is a gulf separating, in this case, the souls of the spiritually dead from the souls that are spiritually alive with Christ. Jesus also wants us to understand that this is not the eternal hell simply because the soul of the rich man still exists."

"So, if it was the lake of fire, there would be nothing left of him at all, right?" Saez asked.

"Right again," I answered. "In this example, this cannot be the eternal hell because we will not see those sent there. In fact, if a person's soul is still intact then they are not truly dead and cannot be in eternal hell. Once there the soul becomes nonexistent. This will not occur until after judgment day, when souls in hell will be turned to ash from within and never exist again."

"Is that all there is, just that one parable?" asked Saez.

"There's more," I said, "the apostle Paul mentions that when we are not in our flesh body, we are with God. In 2 Corinthians, Chapter 5, he writes, " 'Therefore we are always confident, knowing that, whilst we are at home in the body, we are absent from the Lord.' We are confident, and willing rather, to be absent from the body, and to be present with the Lord."

"For we must all appear before the judgment seat of Christ; that everyone may receive the things done in his body, according to that he hath done, whether it be good or bad."

"If Paul is talking about death, then he's pointing out that in the end, God will judge everyone, but it doesn't happen until after the return of Christ," I said. "Any person who dies before that time, according to scripture, returns to heaven. There may be a separation in heaven, but no soul remains in the dirt, and certainly no one goes to hell until after they have been judged. So far only Satan, by name, and his angels are condemned to the final death."

Episode Seven

"Are you saying that if we die in combat, only the flesh dies and that we aren't really dead, our soul lives on and instantly returns back to God?" asked Saez, sounding somewhat relieved.

"Yes, that is exactly what I said, and I believe the Apostle Paul backs me up."

As I watched Bart's broken body taken onto the helicopter I thought about Saez and how he had died not long after that conversation.

I felt emotionally exhausted, overwhelmed, like a child moving away for the first time, crying in the back seat of the car as their childhood home faded away.

I seemed to be floating away now, but, as painful as it was to witness again, I was happy I had returned from the Lazarus dream in time to witness the recovery of Bart's body.

Like Bart's body lifted up by the helicopter, I felt myself lifted up, along for the ride. Hoping that I would finally wake up, I found myself back in the O.R. during my surgery.

"Why am I here again? Why do you keep showing me this instead of letting me wake up in the infirmary?"

"We need more units! Find me some more blood, nurse," ordered the surgeon.

"Yes, sir," replied the nurse.

Somewhere, my body attempted to recover from the surgery, but my dreams kept directing me back to the O.R., as if I needed to witness something that took place during surgery.

"Everywhere I go death seems to be waiting. I can't escape it. What did I do to deserve all this grief? Not only do I have to watch my friends die twice, now I have to witness my own death."

I was being forced to watch myself dying in front of my own eyes. That just didn't sound right.

Episode Eight

December 31 and 31 AD

I was afraid to know why I was drawn back to the surgery.

When I convinced myself that this was only a dream, everything seemed simple. Either way, I decided to revel in this experience for as long as it lasted. "It must be all over for me. Wow. But what a way to go! I'm not only spending a day in the life of Christ, but spending a day as Christ."

By now, some of Father Shelley's stories about the special souls chosen by Christ over two thousand years ago had come back to me. If they were true and I was one of them, then this would be the night of my initiation into the Immortal Keepers. I think he mentioned something about having dreams. I remember him saying there would be a couple of dreams and that one was about the ministry of Christ. He never mentioned that part of the initiation was actually portraying Christ—I would have remembered that.

"Gotta wonder why he left out that really important fact," I said.

I tried to remember the priest's words concerning the night of initiation. He said something about how, initially, the Keeper won't know if he is caught between worlds, and won't be sure if the dreams will ever end.

"Well, that's exactly how I'm feeling right now," I said to my memory of Father Shelly.

But, since I'm continually dreaming of Christ, I decided that, by remaining positive in this new realm, I would be able to enjoy the experience. I remembered that the priest mentioned a down side, too.

Episode Eight

Before the end, the initiate's euphoria would be replaced with shame, guilt, anger and fear.

"I'm not sure how or why that happens, but, if this is my course, I guess I'll find out."

If I understood correctly, my soul had experienced the dream nearly thirty times plus or minus a few depending on age of death each time. As a rule, the dream occurred and, the next day, the Immortal awoke with supernaturally acquired knowledge, various supernatural gifts, and a full understanding of his identity. They woke to a new life with enlightened understanding of God's complete plan, and a new commission: to seek out those chosen by God to understand the hidden messages heralding the second coming of Christ.

"I just gotta hang in there," I said, discovering myself drifting away from the OR. "This will all be over soon."

I still wondered what kept calling me back there.

After leaving the operating room again, I found myself standing on the steps of a chapel in Nah Trang. This was more of a memory than a dream. During my first few days in Vietnam, I found Christian fellowship at a small local chapel. One night, after the meeting, I noticed a fight further up the road.

Running toward the fight, I saw about six or seven G.I.s harassing a Vietnamese woman and man. When I tried calming everything down, I realized the woman was probably a prostitute and the man with her was her business associate.

"What's the problem here, men?" I asked, directing my attention toward the soldiers and trying to make sure that the shouting didn't escalate into violence.

"Yo, Preacher, with all due respect, sir, you should stay outta this-here. This ain't really none of God's business, if'n you knows what I mean, sir," said one of the soldiers.

"Wrong, soldier. It's all God's business, if'n it's no one else's," I said, shrugging. "How about letting them go so we can all go have a talk?"

"She ain't going nowhere, 'cause I'm gonna' cut her up," said one of the soldiers, hiding something behind his pant leg. The street lamp caught the reflection of a shiny nine-inch blade in his right hand.

"This tramp burnt me and just about my whole damn squad last weekend, and this one was in on it," said the armed soldier, pointing to her business partner.

I could see his lips moving, but could no longer hear any of the words. The light reflected from the exposed blade distracted me, practically blinding me.

———————————————————

I grew more at ease with the understanding that, however it was possible, I was sharing the life of Jesus. As painful as the transitions were, I knew what to expect now, making them more tolerable for me physically and spiritually.

"After raising Lazarus from the dead, everything else should be a snap," I said, noticing the ease of this transition.

As my travel back to Jerusalem happened instantly, my body barely experienced any side effects. It all happened in a flash. I saw the knife, then my vision cleared and I saw another knife, somehow in a woman's hand. She waved it around, doing her best to fend off her attackers.

Four to five men stood before me, trying to take hold of the woman. Although she had been accused of something, she was not the same woman, nor were these the same men, that I encountered in Nah Trang

The men, dressed as clergy, attempted to bind her, arresting her for committing the act of adultery. Given the chance, they planned to find her guilty and have her sentenced to death by stoning.

I immediately tried to defend her, but my efforts only wasted whatever inner energy I had. I remained helpless, only able to watch. I could see her naive vulnerability as I stared deeply into her dark, lovely eyes.

As my body turned around, my eyes followed. I could see the temple behind me. I also noticed the large crowd of people following me, and assumed that Jesus had just left the temple building. As my body turned back toward the lady with the knife, I noticed a gap forming in the middle of the crowd, which was taking on the form of a human arena. This left me, the woman, and her assailants clustered in the center. Apparently, my squad was not nearby. I had no idea what was really going on.

"What can it be this time?" I said, trying to remember this part of Christ's ministry. "You poor child," I said, my pain for the woman distracting me. I watched her struggling to defend herself, but being overpowered by the temple guardsmen.

Even on a bad day, no doubt this woman appeared both elegant and exquisite. But today she seemed like a once beautiful swan, smudged

Episode Eight

with remnants of a toxic spill. Through it all, a natural inner beauty emanated from her face, beginning with her eyes. I thought that such beauty could only be a gift from God.

The clergy seemed so determined to oppress her that I became suspicious. Something about the way everything was going down suggested that she had been set up to take a fall. Her unveiled visage showed that she possessed the wonderful power of love, but had been misused by men of self-proclaimed authority.

This just feels all wrong, I thought, and I know a set-up when I see one.

I compared the confrontation in Nah Trang with what I saw here. I remember the soldiers and the prostitute, now the priests and this painted woman. Could she be the adulterer? I thought, searching my memory for details of the Bible story.

"Teacher," said the clergy as they accused the woman, "This woman was caught in the act of adultery. The Law of Moses commands us to stone her. What do you say?"

I remembered how the scriptures said that they were trying to trap Jesus into contradicting the Law of Moses. They pretended to test His knowledge of the law, but, in reality, Christ's enemies wanted to build evidence against Him. It was all part of the conspiracy, and they would use it to arrange the murder of the Son of God. I felt offended. I was beginning to take these insults and deceptive attacks personally.

You fools are way out of your league, I said, feeling my body bending over, then resting upon my right knee. My hand wrote something in the dirt.

All right, this is going to be great. I always wondered what Jesus wrote in the dirt, and now I'm going to find out!

I wasn't the only one. Every priest, pastor, and evangelist wanted to know what those infamous words were. Everyone had an opinion, but now I was in a position to know. I would see what Jesus wrote that day.

I did see, but the words were written in a language that I couldn't decipher. Man, that is just so unfair, Lord, not fair at all, I thought, laughing.

It wouldn't help me now, but I really wanted to kick myself for not listening to my mother while I was in college. She kept suggesting that I study Hebrew and Arabic, which might have helped me understand some Aramaic. I could hear her now, "In your line of work, you'll never know when it will come in handy."

My tongue swelled; the feverish symptoms returned. My body stood straight up, but my eyes remained on what was written in the dirt. As

96

my stomach erupted, words rained from my lips in the authoritative voice of Jesus.

"If any of you is without sin, let him be the one to cast the first stone."

My body bent over again; I was fully confident that Jesus' words were enough to rebuke their wickedness. Remembering the story, I knew, without even having to look up, that they left. When Jesus finished writing in the dirt, He saw that only the woman remained. He stood again, asking her, "Woman, where are they? Has no one condemned you?"

"No one, Lord," she said.

"Then neither do I condemn you, go now and leave your life of sin."

As she walked away, I noticed that she picked up the knife from the ground. As I focused on the knife, my vision blurred as before. I watched Jerusalem fade once again.

Then I heard an engine revving and a Jeep pulling up. I was back in Nah Trang and the Military Police had arrived to break up the fight.

"Break it up here, men. Move out," they ordered. "You don't want to spend the rest of your R&R in the brig, do you?"

Noticing my presence, the MPs' tone softened. "Good evening, Father. How are you?"

"Doing just fine, Sergeant. Great night for fellowship, huh?"

"Yes, sir," said the MP, missing the humor in that statement. "Can we give you a lift anywhere?"

"No, I can manage, but thanks for your help. God bless you, men."

I remembered that incident clearly. I remembered the service that night. Even though it had been difficult to understand the Vietnamese preacher's broken English, I had enjoyed the service. Watching the MPs driving away, before I could take a breath or reflect on what happened, I was carried away in spirit.

As I felt myself being whisked away. I saw the Jeep's high beams, then felt the transition. I hoped this one would wake me up. Instead it whipped me around like a speeding car skidding out of control. I found myself back just before the mortar attack. It felt like I was on a

Episode Eight

continuous bypass looping around a city, seeing the same stops every time, but no exits.

"Hey, whoa, let's slow down a little," I said. "A dying man could get whiplash by stopping so fast, you know?"

"Chaplain Christopher, if I die in combat over here, will I be forgiven for what I have done? Will I go to heaven?" asked Private Bart, after seeing Saez killed in action.

"All sins can be forgiven, Private Bart," I said, thinking about the deaths of Bart and Saez and hoping I didn't have to witness them again.

"But what about us, sir? We're killing people over here. Some say that we are murderers, and that we won't be forgiven, ever. Can I still be saved? Can I still be born again? What about the unforgivable sin?"

We talked a long time that day about topics that were near to my heart and were concerns of Bart's.

"You're doing your job, Bart. All sins can be forgiven except…"

"Incoming! Incoming! Take cover! Get down, sir!" That mortar round seemed to land right in front of the squad. The percussion of the impact caused the inside of my head to pound like a drum.

"That was close," I said, shoving my head deep into the dirt, almost burying it.

"You looking like a holy ostrich," smirked Jinx as he crept past me. He snorted, then spat out the side of his mouth. "You can come up for air now, holy man, it's all over." He kicked a pile of dirt from around my head in an act of insubordination.

"I don't remember this part," I said, removing my hands from my head. I realized that I wasn't wearing my helmet.

"What happened to my helmet?" I asked.

Still keeping my head down, I reached out in front of me to feel if it had rolled off as I hit the ground, but it wasn't there. It was Jinx. He had kicked my helmet out of reach.

I raised my head to look. Peterson and the rest of the squad stood around me as if waiting for me to finish a sentence or answer a question. I stood up to compose myself, shaking off both the dirt and the feeling of embarrassment.

Either the hallucination had started without me noticing or perhaps the impact of the mortar rounds had shaken me so fiercely that I didn't feel the transition symptoms. As I stood in amazement, I saw that I had reappeared on the same path with the temple at the end of it.

"I'm on the right path," I said, noticing a man walking further ahead of the squad. "He's heading toward the city."

A group of elders and priests followed us along the road. They walked behind the disciples, but whispered about me under their breath.

I overheard them talking about Beelzebub. Beelzebub? I repeated to myself. I'd like to tell these false priests a thing or two.

I figured that the man walking toward the city must have been the blind deaf-mute, and Jesus had just cured him. The clergy accused Jesus of doing miracles arranged by Satan, and now they wanted to stone Him.

They called Jesus the prince of demons. Boy, were they on the wrong track, I fumed.

We continued walking toward the city, entered, then stopped near the center area inside the main gate. Many people had already gathered to hear the news.

My stomach jumped. My throat swelled. It felt like I was having an allergic reaction. Then the words came up as the voice of Jesus spoke out loud.

"He who is not with me is against me, and he who does not gather with me scatters. And so I tell you every sin and blasphemy will be forgiven men."

Forcing myself to think about the question I was asked on my last stop in Vietnam, I scanned the crowd for Private Bart, hoping to see him alive, but he wasn't here

"Anyone who speaks against the Holy Spirit will not be forgiven," continued the voice of Jesus. "Anyone who speaks against the Son of Man shall be forgiven, but anyone who speaks against the Holy Spirit will not be forgiven, either in this age or the age to come."

Jesus spoke the words recorded in Matthew, Chapter 12. I didn't understand why people had such a difficult time comprehending the meaning of the unforgivable sin. He specifically defined it, but the definition continued to elude even the brightest religious minds. Anyone could recite the verse, but so few had a specific example of what it meant to speak against the Holy Spirit.

When I was younger, Vanessa and I talked about the unforgivable sin all the time. I would hear her talk about it with her friends when they walked home from school. Most of them didn't agree with her, but I believed in my heart that she was probably right. It was so simple that I wondered why our church never explained what it meant.

"What is the unforgivable sin?" I remembered beginning to explain to Bart. I was glad that I had that conversation with him before he died.

"You don't have to worry about committing the unforgivable sin," I told him while walking through the jungles of Vietnam.

"Why not?" asked Bart, kicking the dirt as he trudged along, as if walking through a combat zone was old hat. "It does exist, right?"

"Yes. As simple as that question is, it's a very good one. In fact, pointing out that such a sin does exist proves how much He loves us."

"Jesus mentions it, but leaves it sort of unexplained," said Bart. "Seems like that can do more harm than good."

"Right again," I said. "It's dangerous because the definition is left up to priests, pastors, and reverends who haven't really taken the time to learn how it applies to the children of God, leaving many Christians in fear."

"Wait, did you just say beasts, pastors, and goblins?" laughed Bart. "Seriously though, that sort of sounds unfair. If they don't study it right, they can say whatever works best for them. So, why is it easy for you to understand it?"

"I've made it easy because I have learned that God forgives the sinner when the sinner asks for it."

"So what happens if a sinner can't ask for forgiveness?" asked Bart.

"It may not be that a person can't ask for it, it may be more like God won't be listening," I said, "Let's face it, some soldiers, especially over here in the Nam, find themselves unable to ask God for anything."

"That makes sense, but when would God not be listening?" Bart asked as we took a break with the rest of the squad.

"For me, that has to do with the future," I answered, sitting down on the ground and leaning against my backpack. "I believe that the unforgivable sin has more to do with the end times than everyday life."

"Are you saying that prior to the end times, sinners won't be able to ask God for forgiveness?" asked Bart, sitting on top of his steel helmet.

"No," I answered taking a drink of water. "During the end times, prior to the return of Christ, sinners can and will ask for forgiveness, but once the true Christ returns it's too late to ask."

"But Jesus said that the unforgivable sin is blaspheming the Holy Spirit—what is that?" asked Bart.

I put the cap on my canteen, saying, "Blaspheming the Holy Spirit is to deny, hinder, or speak instead of. However, this sin can only be committed during the end times, just prior to the birth of the new age. It can only be committed by God's elect when the false Christ takes the world into captivity. God's elect are captured physically, but the rest of the world is willingly held in spiritual captivity."

"Right, 'cause we already know that Satan wants to be worshipped as God," said Bart.

"Exactly. The elect refuse to worship the false Christ, waiting faithfully for the return of the true Christ. The elect are delivered up to the false Christ as a testimony to him, but instead they testify for God. According to the words of Jesus, should God's elect give in to temptation and fall down to worship Satan, refusing to allow the Holy Spirit to use them, thus hindering Him during the eleventh hour, they will not be forgiven in this age, or the new age to come."

As the patrol got ready to move on, Bart repeated, "Jesus says that to blaspheme the Holy Spirit during this hour of temptation will not be forgiven in this age or the next."

"Yes," I said, as Bart helped me to my feet. "In the future, the false Christ will persuade the whole world that he is the true Christ and should be worshiped. Anyone that falls for the wiles of Satan and worships him will ultimately lose their salvation. This is the hour of temptation spoken of in the book of Revelation. In order to remedy this, the whole world will be offered salvation at the same time prior to the Messiah ushering in the new age. The whole world is given a chance to repent before the day of the Lord."

"So what about now, what do we do to be saved? How can I make sure I go to heaven, especially after all of this? It seems impossible after so much killing."

I didn't want to make the same assumption that I made with Saez. In my mind I was asking, "Are you saved, Bart? Have you accepted Jesus as your savior? Do you believe that He died for your sins?" but it didn't seem appropriate to ask during an actual mission. It would have felt like I was scaring him, telling him this could be it for you and you better do it now before you die. Turns out that I should have asked. It was too late now.

My mind drifted to Jerusalem, where I heard the voice of Jesus speaking, teaching about salvation.

"Jesus answered and said unto him, Verily, verily, I say unto thee, except a man be born again, he cannot see the kingdom of God."

Episode Eight

With Bart's last question still on my mind—"What do we do to be saved?"—I noticed that Jesus was having that same conversation.

During my studies, I concluded that being born again was totally different than being saved. I knew that the two terms had become synonymous, but I vehemently disagreed with this trend. Unfortunately, it left people in the dark. In reality, the truth about being 'born again' holds the answer to the meaning of life itself. It explains where we come from and why we are on earth.

During another break in the field, I told Bart, "Jesus makes it very clear. He says that, in order to be saved, or to see the kingdom of God, you have to be born again. He leaves no doubt that the two terms are completely different. In fact, the first must take place or the second will never happen."

"What's the difference?" asked Bart, "I always thought they were the same thing."

I remembered how a few of the other men tightened their security positions to join Bart and I for the discussion. I felt so excited that day as I taught the born again vs. salvation message in the middle of a combat zone.

I explained that only souls that are 'born again' have the opportunity to be saved by the blood of Christ.

"Isn't that what Jesus said, too?" asked Matthews, keeping a look out for the squad leader.

"Yes," I said, "it's exactly what Jesus said.

Over the years, I had realized that people thought teaching the being born again topic was old news, when, in fact, it was one of the most exciting doctrines to dwell on.

"A lot of Christians don't even question the possibility that it could mean something more than what they have been told," I said, looking out over Matthews's shoulder as well. I certainly didn't want to upset the squad leader and possibly spoil my chances at patrolling with them again. Sergeant Matthias was a stickler for maintaining security at all times.

"Since we know what it means to be saved, what does born again really mean then?" asked Bart.

"It means born from 'above'."

I opened my Bible to the third chapter of John and read verse three. "Jesus confirms this when speaking with one of the priests saying, "and no man hath ascended up to heaven, but he that came down from heaven, even the Son of man which is in heaven."

"Does that mean that man has to come down from heaven in order to go up to heaven?" asked Matthews.

"Absolutely, so remember the other definition of the word 'again'," I said.

"Right, you said it means 'from above'," said Peterson, at the same time pointing toward Matthias, who was checking each security position to make sure the men were awake.

I explained that man's soul descends to earth and is born in the flesh. Each soul enters the world through the womb. However, when man's flesh expires, that same soul ascends to heaven through resurrection.

"Isn't everyone sent to earth, though?" Sergeant Matthias asked, startling us. He had disappeared into the bush, then snuck up on the group. "I mean, aren't all souls born?"

I looked forward to hearing this question every time I discussed this topic. Not all souls are sent to earth to be born of water, blood and spirit. Understanding that every soul that God creates does not descend to earth, and is not born flesh, is the key to the difference between the two terms.

"Actually, some souls are not sent to earth and born flesh," I said as Peterson quietly vanished back to his original position before Matthias scolded him. "Some souls in heaven have either been denied a flesh birth, refused it, or have not been required to descend to earth. The archangels of heaven are not required to descend, but Satan and his angels have either refused or been denied this grace of our Father's."

They had never heard it put that way. Their eyes opened wide, and I could tell that they actually understood. A few of the men in the squad came up to me afterward to tell me how much more sense that made. That was certainly a day filled with the Holy Spirit.

I held onto this memory as I heard the voice of Jesus speaking to Nicodemus, taking my focus away. I really enjoyed my short time with First Squad and didn't mind this part of the dream at all. It was like having two conversations about the same thing going on at the same time.

"God so loved the world," began the voice of Jesus," that He gave His one and only Son, that whoever believes in Him shall not perish but have eternal life. For God did not send the Son of Man into the world to condemn the world, but to save it through Him. Whoever believes in Him is not condemned, but whoever does not believe is condemned already because he has not believed in the name of God's one and only Son."

Episode Eight

As I listened to the voice of Jesus, I remembered telling the men that Christ made a promise that His Father will reward those who believe that He is the Son of God with eternal salvation. I remembered that, as the conversation ended, I explained that those who are never born again or 'born from above' don't ever get the chance at salvation. In fact, Satan and his angels have already been condemned to death. But there is also a promise to those who do not believe. When Jesus says that the unbeliever is condemned already, it sounds like he doesn't stand a chance, when, in fact, each person born of water, blood and spirit will have the chance to accept Christ, either in this world age, or the next one, prior to the Great White Throne Judgment.

As the voice of Jesus continued, I heard Him say, "And this is the condemnation, That light is come into the world, and men loved darkness rather than light, because their deeds were evil. For every one that doeth evil hateth the light, neither cometh to the light, lest his deeds should be reproved. But he that doeth truth cometh to the light that his deeds may be made manifest, that they are wrought in God."

As the voice of Jesus fell silent, I felt a little concerned about the sermon I had just witnessed. I didn't know how long I had been in Jerusalem this time, but I had noticed that each visit seemed longer. I really only expected to spend one day with this gift from God, but it continued. And if it continued further, I knew what waited for me at the end of these visits to the past.

Maybe I would be stuck in Jerusalem until the end. After all, I had told God that I would lay down my life if it meant that my friend Lump could live. According to the latest letter from Dino, Lump was conscious and recovering. Now I was unsure about my own life. Had I finally died and gone to heaven, or was I still dying?

Episode Nine
December 31 and 31 AD

Father Shelly really got me good. Here I am dreaming, caught between two places, dying, and wondering if I really am one of those fictitious immortals he told me stories about.

I found myself with First Squad again, finding the village just where the pointman said it would be.

I overheard a few of the men remark how hard the mortar attacks had hit them as well. I felt relieved to have moved on passed the mortar attack, back to the village preparing the residents for departure.

"Man, this village has been hit hard," said Doc. "From the remains, there must have been close to fifty huts set up here."

As usual, the Vietnamese children swarmed all over the G.I.s.

"Candy, candy," they shouted, holding out their open hands. They wanted the chocolate-covered cookies found in the soldiers' k-rations.

My heart went out to the children of war. Even though they appeared unshaken by its effects at the time, I prayed that the war would not scar them emotionally. Only time would tell the true story.

"If everyone could all see the world as children do," I said.

Children find a way to maintain their innocence and adapt to harsh realities of life. Children would still be children, no matter how bad it got. I knew that one day this would seem very real to them. Their lives would forever be shaped by the traumatic impact of this war, but, for now, a simple piece of chocolate candy helped them forget.

An initial survey of the village determined that there were no serious injuries, but a few of the elderly villagers appeared to be disgruntled. I noticed an elderly man approaching the squad with great urgency.

Episode Nine

"He's staring at me," I observed. "He must be the leader of the village."

The elderly villager walked right up to me, insisting that I come with him to what remained of his hut. One hundred villagers or more pushed and shoved to get closer to the G.I.s, but this man was only interested in me. Shamelessly, he pushed through the squad without being challenged. According to Matthews, the squad interpreter, his daughter had been hit by some of the shrapnel from the mortar attack.

"But I'm not the medic," I said, as the crowd pushed and pulled me toward the hut. "Okay, okay, I'm coming. You don't have to drag me." I tried yelling for Doc, but I was beginning to feel light-headed.

"His daughter is dying," said Matthews, standing behind me. Hands pulled me around and I noticed a woman of advanced years and unwavering resolve staring at me as if she had known me my whole life.

"No, that's not it," I said. "She's looking through me like I'm not even here. Her eyes are saying 'what took you so long to get here'."

My attention was drawn away from her for a moment or two as I felt my body being jerked and tugged with such intensity that it spun me around. The sensation made me feel dizzy. In my confusion, one of the children snatched the canteen attached to the side of my ALICE pack and ran off with it, desperate for a drink of water.

I recovered, looking down and trying to feel around to my back, but I could no longer control my movements. I attempted to call to Private James and ask him to track down my canteen, but I couldn't. The voice from within murmured just as I attempted to speak. I could no longer distinguish my own voice from the voice speaking from within. It appeared that the two, at times, were the same. It was difficult to establish for sure if I was speaking or just listening.

My body traveled as the vision of the villagers vanished in a cloud. I tried to speak, but only heard utterances. "Who... who...?"

I sounded like an owl with a hoot that wouldn't end. I tried to force words out of my mouth as the transition took place, but failed again. I wanted to ask who snatched my water canteen but my lips were unresponsive.

"Who...?" I began again, as my mouth seemed to fill with saliva.

"Who touched me?" said the voice of Jesus. "Who touched me?"

"That was more then a touch," I answered the voice of Jesus, trying to recover from the stressful transition. My canteen had been snatched with so much force that it spun me around. It was only my canteen, but it felt like something much more had been taken. It felt like the earth moved under me.

It felt like I had been drained of all of my energy, like the time a helicopter's rotary blade passed inches from my head. I jerked away instinctively, missing it, then felt exhausted after realizing I had almost been killed.

With my mind's eye, I looked around for the woman who had been staring at me just prior to the transition. I didn't expect to see her here, but her condition concerned me. I had noticed that she was also injured, bleeding from a minor head wound.

She must have been injured during the mortar attack, too, I thought.

Now I could only see a swarm of people surrounding me, pulling and tugging at my clothing. Like the other times, I no longer wore my utility uniform—no pistol belt, backpack, or Bible. I stood there, trapped in my own body, but inside someone else's passion.

"I guess I don't need any water, or my backpack, but I...well, come to think about it, I guess I don't really need my Bible either."

"Who touched me?" said the voice of Jesus. This time the words sprang from my lips like a command.

I was very familiar with these words used by Jesus during His ministry. He used this phrase while being mobbed by hundreds of people. Jesus' popularity had grown as reports of His miracles spread. The miracle feeding of thousands of hungry people circulated like wildfire. Wherever Jesus went, crowds of people pulled at each other and followed Him as if He were a famous king without a home for His nation.

Everyone expected a miracle if they got the chance to be near Him. Thousands of people followed Him, hoping something good would happen for them. Of all the people pulling on Him that day, only one person had touched Him with unyielding faith. One woman believed within her heart that Jesus could heal her with a mere touch. This woman didn't simply hope for a miracle, she believed it would happen with all her heart, because she believed that He was the Son of God.

It was the bleeding woman! I thought. "That's it! Now where did she go that fast?"

I remembered more about the story of how Jesus felt virtue leaving His body. He had felt power, love, and faith being drawn from Him. And, although He knew who it was, He still asked who had touched Him.

Episode Nine

"Lord," said Peterson, "don't you see all these people crushing you? Why do you ask who touched you?"

I was still getting used to this notion that everyone including my own squad members were convinced that I was Jesus. I refused to accept it and knowing what fate waited, hoped not to experience it.

I had felt something too, but couldn't explain it. That must have been when I felt the ground move. I felt drained just as Jesus had. My body felt the virtue being drawn away as well, and it manifested physically. Until then, my body never really felt what Jesus went through, but that time I did. I wondered if, should my time traveling continue, I would feel more of His physical reactions.

The woman with the issue of blood had spent all of her money on doctors and fake faith healers who failed to cure her. In fact, over the twelve years she had become worse. But as a result of her faith, the real miracle of her healing occurred before Jesus ever said anything to her.

I kept looking for her despite distractions from the disciples. Finally I heard Peterson ask, "Crushing you, Lord?"

"I felt the power leaving me," said the voice of Jesus.

I didn't know who the woman was, but I knew that she would reveal herself according to the scriptures. And just as I thought that, the woman made her way toward Him and fell at His feet.

"Daughter, your faith has healed you, go in peace," said the voice of Jesus.

I became anxious as the crowd murmured over His choice of words. This can't be good, I thought.

I recognized this event from the book of Matthew, and recalled chapter nine. Saez and I had talked about it.

We also talked about him returning home soon. Just like Bart, he was a short-timer, due to leave Vietnam for good in a few weeks. Both men had wives who delivered children while they were away and really looked forward to meeting their daughters for the first time.

Before we left for the mission, Saez told me about his daughter and how she had been diagnosed at birth with an internal bleeding problem. Staring at a photo of her, Saez prayed every chance he got that she would survive and that they would one day meet. The doctors did their best to save her and eventually she recovered. Saez's wife felt sure that his prayers and the prayers of others helped save their daughter.

"They were saying that my baby girl was bleeding to death on her insides," said Saez, as he packed for the mission. "You already packed, sir?"

"Yes, corporal, packed and ready," I replied, looking at the photo of Carlos Saez's daughter.

"Do you think faith in God really helps heal people, sir?" asked Saez as he kissed the picture and put it under his hat.

"Definitely." I told him the story of the woman that Christ healed. I also explained how faith could work against someone by pointing out how many people put their faith in the wrong thing.

"Putting our faith in the wrong thing can be dangerous and, in some cases, even deadly," I said.

"They used religion to take advantage of her, didn't they?" said Saez.

"Yes," I said as I watched Saez continue to pack. "They had convinced her that she needed to give all of her possessions to the church as a sign of faith. She gave willingly and, in return for her faith, she became destitute. She had given all of her money and belongings in exchange for a healing that never happened."

"So, she got nothing in return, right?" said Saez, filling his water canteen.

"Exactly," I said, "The so-called men of God told her that she still didn't have enough faith."

"In a way, though, it showed how faithful she was," commented Carlos, "even though it was in the wrong thing."

"Right," I said, "in her heart, there was no lack of faith. In fact, she spent most of her days telling everyone who would listen, and believing, that she would be healed."

"Then the true Healer showed up," said Carlos.

"Yep, then her story changed," I said. "When she knew Christ and believed that He was the Son of God, she knew that just by touching His clothing she would be healed. Jesus felt something different from her touch."

"What do you think was so different about the way she touched Him?" asked Carlos.

"I think the difference was that she didn't believe just because other people were convinced that Jesus was a healer. She, herself, believed that Jesus was the Son of God. Jesus sensed her overwhelming faith in who He was, not in what He could do for her. Her faith was genuine."

I wish I would have known then what I know now, that Carlos would never see his daughter. I would have prayed with him and, if possible, warn him about what waited for him at the landing zone.

Episode Nine

Maybe Carlos would still be alive. But Carlos had been a highly decorated, courageous soldier. If I had been able to warn him, he probably would have just thanked me, then done the same thing. I wished I could embrace him as best friends or brothers do, but I couldn't.

Still in Jerusalem I felt heavy sweat pouring from my forehead. For some reason, whenever Jesus healed or raised the dead, my body felt differently than when the visions were initiated. The feeling began in my stomach and intestines, bursting upward like a ball of fire. I mentally prepared myself to be whisked away.

I saw the lady thanking Jesus, kissing the hem of His robe.

I was pleased in having the chance to see the joy in her face, happy to be healed and even happier to meet Jesus personally. I knew that I wasn't actually Jesus, but I took joy in her response. I felt a little guilty, too, like I was taking credit for some great achievement when I had nothing to do with it. It felt like I was cheating.

After helping her up, I noticed two suspicious men had arrived during the healing and witnessed the event. I overheard the others whispering that these men were servants from the house of Jairus.

The two visitors informed Jesus that a child, a young girl, had died and insisted that He return with them. When we arrived at the home of Jairus, the two servants seemed to be very distressed while speaking to him. After all, Jairus was prominent in the synagogue. Since the Pharisees envied and feared Christ, Jairus's position in the synagogue would undoubtedly have been in jeopardy for attempting to secretly meet with Jesus.

I noticed people crying and wailing as if they really cared for the deceased girl. In truth, most of the mourners never knew her; they were paid to mourn.

"Stop wailing," said the voice of Jesus, making it clear that wailing was a waste of time, "she is not dead but asleep."

The mourners mocked Jesus, "Asleep! Asleep?" They all laughed at Him because they knew the girl was dead.

So much for mourning, could you be more obvious? I thought, scornfully. They just went from mourning for the dead to the front row of the Comedy Room in Times Square without taking a breath. That was disgraceful. I overheard the two servants speaking to Jairus. "Your daughter is dead. Why bother the teacher any longer?"

Ha, what they really meant was, your daughter is dead, so why risk your job and ours? I thought, upset that they doubted the word of Jesus. Ready and determined to show them the power of God, I had my heart set on making a few believers that day.

Hearing the mistaken servants, Jesus turned to Jairus and said reassuringly, "Don't be afraid, just believe, and she will be healed."

With this assurance, Jairus knelt faithfully at the feet of Jesus.

Okay, I take that back, I'm really not ready for this, I thought. This is going to be more difficult for me to watch than when Lazarus was raised from the dead.

I never actually saw Lazarus rise up from the dead; I couldn't see inside the tomb. I never really saw how or when Lazarus's soul returned to his body. This would be very different. The lifeless girl lay there in plain sight. I thought about how peaceful she looked, like Snow White after taking a bite of the poisonous apple, but scarier. Afraid of what I would witness, I tried shutting my eyes, but couldn't. I wished I could at least squint a little.

I'm just an observant bystander, I thought. God's gonna' help me through this.

I felt my body take in a deep breath as if to prepare for an underwater swim. I knew it was about to happen any moment now.

No, no, I can't watch, let me think about something else.

My thoughts suddenly went back to my time in Ranger school. Ugh! The swim test.

If it weren't for Lump, pushing me and, in the case of the swimming test, holding me down, I would never have graduated. Whenever I wanted to give up and surface for air, Lump held me under. Surfacing too soon would have meant disqualification from the course and Lump knew how badly I wanted to qualify.

I felt my body exhale greatly. Wow! Here we go, I thought, as if plunging under water.

My arms extended toward hers. I watched as her hand was placed in mine. The voice of Jesus said, "My child, get up." Her spirit returned to her; immediately she sat upright. It appeared ghastly, almost demonic, with nothing gradual about it. If it were not a holy work, it would have been a scene straight from a horror movie.

"Ahh!" I yelled trying to jump away, though I knew I couldn't budge.

The room was suddenly still, all sound, hushed. Not a word was spoken inside or outside of the house. Then, just as abruptly, social chaos erupted everywhere, within and without the house. People ran into the house so feverishly that they forced others out. Jesus and the disciples were also forced out, but were glad to leave what seemed to be developing into a riot. Before they departed, Jairus thanked Jesus. Jesus ordered the family to say nothing of this to anyone.

Episode Nine

No chance of that, I thought noticing the hundreds of people gathering.

I used to have a great time teaching these two examples in my private Bible study group. On this particular day, as recorded in the book of Matthew, Christ used two miracles to teach just how far the children of Israel had veered from God, and how far the world will stray from God in the future prior to the return of Christ. Like the bleeding woman, Israel bleeds, dying a slow death. With all her desire to praise and worship God, she has turned to and become dependent upon traditions of man. She put her trust in church traditions, in this case, false church traditions, which in return, have succeeded in deceiving and robbing her of the healing she desperately needs.

During my classes I would show how her dilemma offers an example and a warning to the children of God who will be here on earth in the future. She loved the Lord. She had no true knowledge of the first coming of the Savior, and false teachers easily deceived her in her desperation. Yet, upon hearing about the true Christ, she repented for following the ways of the false teachers. She then waited for the true Christ, and because she trusted and acted upon that trust, she received her healing. Those who are alive and waiting in the end times must not follow the false Christ, but diligently wait for the true Christ, for those who endure until the end will be saved.

In the second example, Jesus raises the dead girl physically and spiritually, proving that He has the power and authority over all flesh and spirit. However, her lifeless body represents the spirit of mankind in the future, once they fall down and worship the false Christ. They will be found spiritually dead when the true Christ arrives.

Carlos and I had talked about that on the day before he was killed in action.

"Are you saying that the people who are not saved when Jesus returns will still have a chance before it's all over?" asked Carlos as we walked to the mess tent for lunch.

"Yes," I said. "When Jesus returns, those who are not waiting for Him, because the false Christ deceives them, are termed the spiritually dead."

"You mean like the young girl in the story?" said Carlos, "As an example, though, right?"

"Exactly," I said, "this story is an example for the future. When Jesus returns, everyone alive on earth will be transformed into the dimension of God. This is accomplished so everyone can see Him."

"Everyone is transformed?" asked Carlos, holding the door open.

"Yes, thanks," I said. "All are transformed, but some are resurrected with Him, while others, though also transformed, remain spiritually dead."

"Still alive, though?" asked Carlos as we got in line for lunch.

"Yes, because no one is truly dead until after they have been judged in the end."

"The White Throne Judgment determines the final death or reward of eternal life, right?" asked Carlos.

"Roger that," I said. "During the millennium period, those who are spiritually dead will not be resurrected with Christ. They face a different resurrection. They will be resurrected or transformed unto a spiritual death, and separated from Christ. They will remain that way throughout the thousand years with no chance at eternal happiness until after the Day of the Lord comes to an end. But there is still a chance for the spiritually dead, and this second miracle shows that."

At the end of the second miracle, my squad and I remained in the past. We struggled to make it away from Jairus's house alive. Word of the miracles had spread quickly, and the crowd around the house had doubled. People wanted to see the girl with their own eyes. We escaped high into the hills, looking for some place to be alone. We needed to get away from all of the people. Following wherever my body led, I went with Peterson and a few others.

I heard the voice of Jesus, praying. I also prayed, thanking God for the opportunity to remain long enough to complete both miracles. This vision seemed to have lasted much longer than before.

"It feels like I have been here for days, so I guess I'll be staying the night this time," I said as the sun began to set. What seemed like days to me had actually only been a few moments.

I wasn't sure why I was staying longer—or if I wanted to—but it didn't matter how I felt, because it wasn't up to me. Prior to being medevaced I was looking forward to staying the night out with the squad. It would have been my first overnight stay in a real combat situation. Unlike the first few weeks in Nah Trang, I would ride out with the trucks to check up on the troops in the field, but I was able to leave all the death, war, and darkness behind me each night. I knew there would be a new day, a better day tomorrow. It wasn't like that for this squad.

God, what does all this mean? I prayed. Is this all a dream? Am I dead or alive? Am I still dying? God, will you answer me? Will I awaken or will I remain asleep? I know you can hear me, Lord.

Episode Nine

Ugh, I don't feel so good, I thought, feeling very light-headed.

"Master, are you all right?" asked Peterson.

I looked at my clothing. In the evening light, it appeared as if the sun shone through my body. A ghostly brightness glistened through me. Daylight seemed to encircle me.

"Your face has become like the sun, Lord," Peterson marveled.

My body turned around, and I noticed two men standing behind me. Are they angels? I wondered. Have they come to take me away? I must be dead, I rejoiced. God has answered my prayers.

The two mysterious men talked to me. The voice of Jesus spoke to them, but I had no idea what they were saying. I knew that my lips moved and I could hear mutterings, but I couldn't understand any of it.

This must be a Spirit thing, I thought. That's right! It's the Transfiguration. That's right—Jesus, Moses, Elijah and the voice of God. I'm not talking. Jesus is doing it all for me.

Jesus' transfiguration on the Mount of Olives has a lot to say about the second coming of Christ. The inner circle of the disciples, Peter, James, and John, witnessed this miracle at Christ's bequest. Their witness tells us how our bodies will appear at His return. In the end, everyone on earth will be transformed as He descends upon this very mount. Jesus told us that, in the next age, we would be as angels, and showed this small group of men an example of what the future holds.

The angels left the mountain, leaving Jesus standing by Himself. A large, glowing cloud took their place. "This must be the Spirit of God," I said.

The cloud enveloped Him. The squad members were afraid, and became even more afraid as a thundering, yet whispering voice within the cloud said, "THIS IS MY SON WHOM I LOVE. LISTEN TO HIM!"

"Tell this to no one," said the voice of Jesus as the sun finally set.

God had allowed mere mortal men to witness a dimension that only the dead see. As fearful as they were, the disciples grew curious now and asked to see God. I didn't know what to think. I was speechless.

Did I just see three ghosts, or angels? Were they aliens? I thought.

Again Johnson asked, "Lord, show us the Father and that will be enough for us."

"Enough for us, are you crazy? Just hearing His voice should be enough for anyone," I yelled silently.

Jesus stood against a tree and rested. I figured that the transfiguration and the conversing with the angels or aliens must have drained Him.

I'm exhausted too.

I felt my stomach turning over again. In my mind I tried to find some resistance. I thought it would help balance me. I mentally tried to dig my heels into the dirt and press my back against the tree where Jesus rested. I felt sure that the vision was coming to an end. As dizzy as I was, wanted to be prepared.

This tree should hold me up.

I felt like fainting, while visions of falling flat on my face kept flashing across my mind. I certainly didn't want to appear back in Vietnam in the middle of losing consciousness and falling.

My eyes rolled back in my head. The energy within me felt strong enough to push the tree over. My lips parted.

"Don't you know me?" the voice of Jesus cried out with disappointed authority. "Even after I have been among you such a long time? Anyone who has seen me has seen the Father. How can you say show us the Father?"

The voice of Jesus spoke as I continued in anguish.

Ah, let's go already, I can't take this.

"Don't you believe that I am in the Father, and that the Father is in me? The words I say to you are not just my own. Rather it is the Father living in me, who is doing his work. Believe me when I say that I am in the Father and the Father is in me; or at least believe on the evidence of the miracles themselves."

Those last few words echoed in my ears as I returned to Vietnam. I was with the squad, gathering the villagers for the journey back to camp.

I felt like I had been away from the village for the whole day, but confirmed that the journey to Jerusalem only lasted for a few moments. As far as I could tell, it was still December 31. In fact, the wayward children were still running off with my water canteen.

My return to the village was a short one. It ended abruptly and I found myself in a familiar but grisly place.

"Anywhere but here," I said, standing watch in the O.R. as the surgeons operated on me.

"Good" I said, "at least I'm not dead yet. They haven't given up on me. Hey, guys, how am I doing? I'm still hanging in here. Colonel Harris must be somewhere praying for me. His prayers must be helping to keep me alive. Whatever you're praying, sir, it's working, so please don't stop."

Episode Nine

With that said, I let my mind wander away from the operation. Strangely enough, I began to remember more parts to the Immortal Keeper story. If Father Shelly were right, and this was my initiation into this secret realm, then this wasn't the first time I'd had these dream visions of Jesus. Was I really supposed to believe his crazy stories? According to him, I wasn't alone. There were probably other immortals turning twenty-one tonight, each of them having the same dream and asking the same questions.

If I chose to believe, then I was in the Jesus dream phase of a three-part initiation. The two parts remained including a visit from an angel. However, my situation could not be normal. I had been wounded, potentially fatally wounded. From the looks of things, I might not recover. I might not make it to the third phase.

According to God's plan, each of the immortals, upon discovering their true destiny, would continue living out their lives as soul gatherers. Their job is to awaken the souls of God's elect and prepare them for the second coming of Christ. As God's Immortal Keepers they, whenever necessary, would be endowed with the full anointing of the Holy Spirit.

Everything should be made clear to me when I wake up the next morning. I just had to survive the night in order to rediscover my true purpose. If I am one of God's Immortal Keepers, then I have been doing this for over two millenniums.

But, for now, I had to watch as my mortal body was cut, sliced and diced by the doctors attempting to save me.

"I almost got it!" said the surgeon, trying to remove an object from my head wound.

"What is that?" asked the assisting nurse.

"It's just another piece of shrapnel," said the surgeon, but his voice sounded peculiar.

"Yeah, but—look at it! Man! It's almost perfect," said the assistant with excitement. "You said he was a chaplain, didn't you?"

"Yes, but he's not dead yet. I haven't pronounced him. Until I do, he's still a chaplain."

"Come on, now!" said the assistant. "What are his chances of living with something the size of this lodged in his brain? A head wound this size alone is sure to kill him. Let me hold this thing over by the light."

I didn't know what this object was, but knew it was interesting enough to distract the assistant, who was annoying me.

It was a legitimate question, though. How could anyone survive a head wound larger than a silver dollar? If the wound didn't kill me, the surgery should have.

"He could at least respect me while I'm dying. Man, with this guy helping, I'm going to die for sure," I said, feeling somewhat hostile. "Yep, buddy, I'm a goner, alright."

I could also feel this object drawing me closer and closer. I felt pulled, like by a leash, but resisted the pull like a stubborn bulldog.

"Whatever this thing is, I don't want to see it," I said, moving a little closer while mentally preparing myself for a personal viewing.

As I was pulled closer to the object, I also got a better look at my mangled body. Uncle Sam had invited me to Vietnam and, for the most part, had been a gracious host, but you couldn't tell by looking at my body.

"Oh, God!" I said, "It's worse than I thought; I am dead."

I decided to stop resisting. Besides, after seeing my own head wound, I wanted to see what caused it.

"Are you going to keep it, sir?" asked the assistant. "You could clean it up, shine it, and buy a nice chain for it. Hell, sir, you could have yourself a perfect..."

"Crucifix!" I interrupted. "Is that what's killing me? A piece of shrapnel in my head shaped like a crucifix? How ironic. Not only is it killing me, but it's drawing me closer to it."

"So how 'bout it, sir, what do you think?" asked the assistant. "I mean, if you stop to think about it, it's already kind of been blessed. I'm sure this guy won't mind too much."

"Look, you," said the surgeon angrily, "For some reason this chaplain, this man of God, is still alive. He should be dead already, but he isn't. Whatever force is keeping him alive is definitely beyond anything we're doing. As long as he's still breathing, let's just help keep him that way."

"Okay, you're the surgeon," said the assistant.

The sight of the crucifix being dislodged from my skull frightened me, but I didn't get a chance to dwell on it for long. I felt my spirit rushed from the O.R., like a cat shooed by a broom. I found myself standing in front of a mirror, admiring my uniform.

"Hey!" I said excited by my new surroundings. "This is my bedroom. Home, sweet home. It's true what they say—there's no place like home."

It was a miracle that I was still alive. Perhaps God was manipulating my fate. If I really was being initiated, maybe God wanted to make sure that I completed all three phases.

Episode Ten
December 31 and 31 AD

I was back in Detroit, and able to speak. My lips moved while I stood in front of my bedroom mirror talking to myself. I could swing my arms and do whatever else I wanted with my body, or so it seemed.

"Great! I can talk," I said, touching my mouth with my fingers and listening to the church bells ring out as if announcing my return home.

I could hear my mother singing from the kitchen and I could smell chicken frying. "Amazing grace, how sweet the sound and smell of fried chicken sizzling," I sang with her.

The aromas of Sunday dinner filled our home very early in the morning. I loved my mother's Sunday fried chicken, which she actually cooked on Saturday—so much so, I joked that it was definitely one of the traditions in the Holy Bible that God insisted man keep until, and maybe even after, the second coming of Christ.

I knew I wasn't there by chance. By now I realized that the dream took me to significant places.

"But why am I in my full dress uniform?" I said, still admiring my image in the mirror.

While at home, I only wore it three times—at graduation, on the day I departed overseas, and one other time that escaped me for the moment. As I tried to figure out the situation, I heard a voice that I longed for.

"Are you talking to me, Vince? Who you talking to?"

"Dino? Dino!" I ran over to him sitting on the edge of my bed. He sat there, playing with my newly issued U.S. Army helmet and backpack.

"We're going to have some fun today," I said.

"Wait a minute, that's not what I wanted to say," I thought. "I wanted to tell him how much I missed him and how much I love him. I wanted to pick him up and wrestle him onto my bed like I always do. What good is it to be able to talk if I can't say and do the things that I want to do?"

"Toss me my hat, Dino boy."

Dino put the helmet down and picked up my soft cap. Even though I knew I was dying back in Vietnam, it would have been heartbreaking not to see my little brother again. What would he do with the rest of his life?

I won't be here to help him grow up, I thought. What else is a big brother for? I still thanked God for allowing me to see Dino again. He's such a good boy, no trouble at all. I sure hope you stay that way, D. I pray there is no war waiting for you when you become an adult.

"Race you to the door," said Dino as he took off across the bedroom. "Ready, set, go!"

"Hey, you cheated," I shouted, amazed at how fast he could run.

Only five years old, Dino towered over other children his age. He looked just like our mother when he smiled, which was all of the time. Whenever he entered a room, the first thing anyone saw was his smile. He just had a happy face and, to our mother's credit, he had every reason to be happy.

I spent a few years with my dad before he was killed, but Dino only had a few months with his, which he doesn't remember. Dino's dad had been killed in a tragic auto accident when Dino was still a baby, but our mother did everything she could to provide him with a good and loving home. Dino was innocent; I hoped he would remain so for as long as possible. He was very obedient and well- mannered. Our mother had been careful to shield him from the pitfalls of city life.

Thinking back on my own childhood, I recalled how Vanessa helped raise me when I was Dino's age. I glanced across the hall to the room where she had slept, remembering how she would walk through my bedroom door each morning to wake me, and how long she would let me pretend to be fast asleep before sitting beside me. Her hair would brush across my face as she whispered in my ear, "Ah...I wish you were awake right now." My eyes would instantly pop wide open, staring into hers, and wonder if I were still fast asleep, dreaming about her. I hoped that Dino would have a person like Vanessa in his life to help him continue growing into a decent young man.

"Stop that running in the house," shouted my mother from the kitchen.

Episode Ten

I wanted to run down the stairs to the kitchen and say goodbye to her, but I could not. I did recall what had happened that day. My mother and I had talked in the kitchen for about an hour. She told me how proud I had made her by graduating from college, and said it was too bad that my father wasn't here. I cherished my mom and would have loved to relive that moment with her. I grabbed the banister and tried pulling myself to the staircase, but it felt more like I was falling away from it. For some strange reason I had returned just after our conversation. No matter how much I wanted to, I couldn't change anything.

I did finally make it to the staircase, but headed straight for the front door. I couldn't go anywhere near the kitchen, though I tried with all my might.

"Mom, could you tell Lump we left already? Maybe he'll catch up with us."

Again I was unable to say what weighed so heavy on my heart. I wanted to start by telling her how much I missed her fried chicken and how much her smile meant to me, how I would give anything to see it one more time. I wished that she would come around the corner and meet me at the front door, but remembered that it didn't happen that way. I wished I could get just one more kiss hello or goodbye. I wanted to tell her to please be happy and not worry over me. I hoped she wouldn't end up crying herself to sleep again. I didn't want Dino to have to go through what I went through at his age, after my father's death.

I wanted to tell her how much I loved her and how she made me happier than any graduation day. I wanted to tell her that something must have gone horribly wrong with God's plan and that whatever she was feeling about my true destiny didn't quite work out the way she thought it would. Apparently God didn't have anything extremely special for me to accomplish after all.

"Love you, Mom," I said aloud, glad to hear that I had remembered to say that before I left that day, a month ago. My eyes welled up while I stood frozen at the front door waiting for her to reply.

"Okay, Vincey, see you later. Be careful out there. I love you too, son," she said from the kitchen as Dino and I closed the door behind us.

In the Midwest, in towns like Detroit, each of the four seasons inspired a different approach to conquering the trials of daily life. Two of the seasons were manageable, inspiring and encouraging. Spring showed how pretty the city could be. Each spring, I would sit and read stories from the Holy Bible to my mother while she stayed busy tending to her flower garden in the backyard. I noticed how most of the yards and, in fact, the whole city dressed abundantly in colorful hues of greens, yellows, and reds throughout the urban neighborhoods.

Standing on my porch and looking toward the corner of my street, I remembered the hot summers. With the climate change came a different way of relaxing, dressing, and traveling. Temperatures would get so hot that those who could afford to travel would vacation far away in much cooler climates. Those left behind to soak up or hide from the scorching sun, made the best of it or experienced the worst of it. My family and others like us, who made the best of the summer, played our part in making the city one never-ending block party. The neighborhoods rang out with music and dancing.

I only had to walk to the corner of my street to see dancers, musicians, and vocalists performing to their hearts' content. Local amateur entertainers performed everywhere they could—hoping for a chance at stardom, but mostly having fun doing what they loved. My favorite dance group, The Hollywood Swingers—Tim, Anthony, Troy, Brian, and Lorenzo—were neighborhood heroes; they won the summer dance festival each year. They would kid around and call me the little disciple. They even invited me onto the stage a few times to bless the audience before closing out the competition. Jokingly they would say, "You're the reason we always win." For me, as long as I had my Bible to read during the boring acts, watching the street shows was the perfect way to spend a summer vacation.

Fall exposed the starkness of the city and just how barren it looked when stripped naked of all its dressings. It showed what the city looked liked after the summer party was over. The fallen red, green and yellow dressings that once helped the city look pleasingly attired now seemed to be just an abundance of organic litter. The musicians, singers, and dance groups were huddled in garages and basements to practice in hibernation, preparing for the next season, the most treacherous season of the year.

The winters in Detroit, Michigan, were reminiscent of the Ice Age. The punishing snowfalls would leave the urban inhabitants praying for Punxsutawney Phil to hurry and see his shadow. Yet, the day after a fresh snowfall, there was nothing more picturesque. Motor City natives enjoyed the winter season by sledding, building snowmen and hoping for a white Christmas.

Walking through the neighborhood, trudging through the snow with Dino that day helped me remember my whole life. I reminisced every moment possible. I felt like I was in a story entitled This Is Your Life an I thanked God for it.

Episode Ten

During my childhood, in the turbulent 1950s, the city of Detroit had thirty percent black residents and seventy percent white residents. The racial imbalances led to friction, which led to battles throughout the city. It was like an airplane dangling over the side of cliff that must, eventually, crash into the gorge below.

Between Livernois Avenue on the west and Woodward Avenue on the east, our part of the city was zoned off by mile number markers. Between 5 Mile Road and 8 Mile Road, the middle class and lower income black residents lived south of 6 Mile Road. Unavoidable verbal and physical confrontations took place between residents on both sides of 6 Mile Road.

Black families like mine, residing on the southern side of 6 Mile Road, and white residents from the northern side, would take their lives into their own hands when venturing onto the wrong side of the mile markers. Extreme heat, lack of work and summer vacations left some residents with idle hands, so altercations like these escalated during the summer.

My elementary school, located right at the six-mile marker, placed me at the hub of the racial border wars everyday. Some days I could cautiously, but casually, walk to school; attending classes was even worse. Most of my childhood friends went to the predominantly black public schools, but the Catholic school I attended was predominantly white.

Influenced by their parents' bigotry and instigated by conversations among their friends, the older white kids would beat up on the smaller black kids. The fights would take place on the playgrounds, in the hallway between classes, before school hours, and then after. Every day meant constantly looking over my shoulder, around corners, and down stairways to make sure the coast was clear. It was like never being able to wake up from a bad dream. Most days, if I didn't stay after school to help Father Shelly, I found myself running as fast as I could to get back to the safe side of 6 Mile Road.

"Running home from school again, huh?" my black friends teased. "You so used to running from the white man, you should go on and try out for the track team; at least then you could get a medal for running from 'em. Hell, you done already proved they can't catch you."

Winter in my neighborhood felt a little relief from the racial flare-ups. Only three white families resided in the predominantly black area where my family lived; one of them had quite an effect on the neighborhood in winter. As Dino and I walked on that snowy day, we passed by homes that I knew from my childhood, and I took time to remember them.

One family originated from Germany. We hardly ever saw any of the family members in public. Unsubstantiated rumors claimed the man of the house was on the run for suspected Nazi war crimes committed during WWII. People speculated that the basement of their house held a bomb shelter.

The second family, from Canada, pretended to only speak French so they never had to venture out to meet with their black neighbors. However, on Fridays, late at night, the neighbors would hear the man of the house cursing to himself in perfect English.

The third family, the Wilsons, came from Iowa. Depending on who spread the gossip, the running neighborhood joke held that they were sent to the south side of 6 Mile Road either by God or by Satan.

The Wilson family had relocated to Detroit after Mr. Wilson was promised a managerial position with one of the Big Three auto manufacturers. He could not have arrived at a worse time. His first month on the job, he and hundreds of others were laid off, forcing the family to move to the south side of 6 Mile Road.

Having to swap his upper-class aspirations for the lower middle-class left Old Man Wilson feeling bitter, angry, and hateful toward most of his black neighbors. They moved two houses over from us, but had no intentions of being friendly with any of their neighbors. Mrs. Wilson never showed herself in public, and it was rumored that she didn't really exist. During most of the year, the Wilsons never invited neighbors over for a visit and never accepted invitations for visits. They wouldn't even let neighbors pet their dog.

Despite the fact that they hated living here, it was the Wilsons who made a big impact on the neighborhood. If it weren't for the Wilson boys, the black kids in the neighborhood, like me, would never have learned to ice skate. The Wilsons introduced the sport of ice hockey to black kids who would never have had the opportunity otherwise.

Granted, they did not do it because they were kind or nurturing. The Wilsons were raised playing ice hockey; it was a long-standing tradition in their family. Most of the men in their family had gone to college because of the sport. Since they no longer lived in Iowa, the new generation of boys had to figure out a way to continue the Wilson family tradition.

As Dino and I passed their house, I remembered how, each winter, we would all watch them build a rink. They would shovel the top layers of snow, using it to build up banks for the rink, then lay down layers and layers of painter's plastic, covering their entire backyard. Then they would spray water over the whole area. Once the water froze, the transformation was complete.

Episode Ten

We would all stand around freezing, but amazed, watching the whole process in anticipation of opening day.

"Can we help?" we would ask, knowing they would refuse.

"No," the Wilsons would reply, while hurling shovels of snow at us.

In order to build even higher snowbanks, they would drive around and shovel their neighbors' snow for free.

Acting as innocent as angels, the Wilsons would ask kindly, "Can we shovel your snow for you?"

Of course, no one would turn down the offer. These were the neighbors who said that the Wilsons were a godsend. The boys would pile all the snow on the bed of their pickup truck and then take it home. With the additional snow in place, they would end up with snow banks around the homemade rink, as high as eight feet tall.

"The better to crush you with," the Wilson boys would threaten.

Once the rink was complete, my friends and I were invited to learn to play hockey. The Wilsons couldn't get the white kids to play because they all lived north of 6 Mile Road. The only kids available were the black kids living on the south end, and we were more than willing to play.

The Wilson's provided skates for each boy who wished to play. Their family had played hockey for so many years that they had barrels of used protective pads, helmets, sticks, and skates.

The Wilson boys, coached by their dad, became demonic bullies on the ice. They wore full pads and played the sport like they were trying out for the Detroit Red Wings. Under the tutelage of Old Man Wilson, they would hurl flying hockey pucks at us, take slap shots and, every chance they got, bodycheck defenseless children into the frozen snowbanks. The black kids, unable to ice skate, did all we could to stand up on the ice without falling while wearing oversized skates.

Mr. Wilson would strategically place the young black boys on the ice in defensive positions, ordering us not to move and not to fall down. He instructed his sons to run offensive options from the traditional Wilson family playbook. The young volunteers were nothing less than targets for the slaughter of the innocent on ice. As the goalie, I was the main target. Old Man Wilson made sure I was extremely well protected from the pucks flying at fifty miles an hour. Even with extra padding, I still had bruises at the end of each day.

For me, the best part of the game came at the end. Ol' Man Wilson also taught his sons the art of rink fighting. Every game ended with the Wilson boys duking it out, ice hockey style. None of us wanted to leave without catching their half-time and end-of-game brawls. For the battered and broken black boys, watching each Wilson boy pulverize the other was pure revenge garnished with retribution.

Even without the Wilsons-only fights, three or four boys would return home with serious bruises, sprains, and even broken bones. The parents of the injured boys were the one who said the Wilsons were nothing but 'Satan-sent hell-spawns.'

I came home more than once, snotty-nosed, scuffed and bruised, but excited about learning the slap shot. My mom became one of the mothers who said the Wilsons were surely cast from Satan's lot. Swinging the front door open triumphantly, Vanessa would make me feel as if I were returning home from battle, a victorious hero.

Whether sent by God or Satan, the Wilsons and ice hockey was one of the positive experiences that I, and other black kids in the neighborhood, looked forward to every winter season. Just thinking about those days sent chills down my spine.

Those were the days, I thought as Dino and I stopped for the traffic light at the end of the street. Meanwhile, Dino appeared to be mighty proud as he strutted up the street with a full-fledged U.S. Army Ranger.

"What you all puffed up about, Dino boy?"

"Nothing," said Dino.

"Well, if you want to be proud of your brother, be proud because I'm a man of God. Got that?"

"Yes, sir," said Dino, snapping to a salute.

"And stop yessiring me, Shorty."

"Roger. General, sir," said Dino, laughing.

"You be sure and behave yourself while I'm away, you hear? And study real hard in school." I tried to cram every bit of big brotherly advice I could into our walk. "And stay away from those bad kids down the street. You know the ones I mean."

I began to forget that I was dreaming, just reliving what had already happened. I felt comfortable walking and talking with Dino, like I was never going to leave.

"Do you remember what Jesus said to do if someone slaps your face?" I asked, hoping to prepare Dino for future confrontations with those bad kids down the street.

"Yes." Dino answered.

Episode Ten

"Well, what did He say you should do?"

"He said to turn the other cheek so they can slap you again, right?" answered Dino, turning his cheek and pretending to strike himself.

"Hmm, well that's close but…"

"Why does Jesus want the big kids to beat us up? I don't like it when they pick on me."

"Jesus doesn't want you to get beat up. Do you remember those moves that me and Lump showed you?"

"Yes," answered Dino as he tried to demonstrate an over-the-hip take down.

"Very good," I said, impressed with Dino's technique. "But Jesus only wants you to offer the other cheek if you are the one who is in the wrong. In a way, it's like apologizing for upsetting someone by mistake. It's like saying you're sorry for doing or saying something that made someone mad at you. Hopefully, they will accept your apology and not smack you again, though."

"Oh, okay," said Dino. "So, only if I make someone mad at me first, right?"

"Yep, so don't make anyone mad at you, okay?"

"Okay," answered Dino, nodding in assurance that he fully understood the lesson.

"And so that means no fighting in school. But, if you have to protect yourself, do what Lump and me showed you to do. Got it?"

"Roger," said Dino, demonstrating the over-the-hip take down one more time.

"Now, do you remember how to get to heaven?" I asked as we prepared to cross the street.

"I sure do. Jesus is the way, the truth, and the life and no one can get into heaven except through Him." Dino pointed heavenward on the last word.

"Very good, my faithful student. I'm glad to know that you have learned this lesson well."

"But, don't that mean you have to die first?" asked Dino. "Don't people go to Vietnam to meet Jesus? That's what I keep hearing the Sunday school teacher say. She says the ones who don't come back are gone to meet Jesus. Are you going to meet Jesus, too? Is that why you're going? Can't I just go with you?"

"Right…" I answered too fast. I had forgotten that part of the conversation and wasn't prepared for the second part of Dino's answer. It jolted me back to reality. This was only a dream. My mind wandered off while I listened to myself stutter through an answer.

Up to that point, we had just been big brother and little brother casually walking down the street. That was soon to change.

"Look over there," Dino interrupted, pointing further up the street, "That's a lot of people. What are they doing?"

As I turned my attention to the crowd, I could see that they were carrying placards and yelling.

"Um, they must be protesting outside of the recruiting office," I answered. "Maybe the police will show up soon. Come on, let's cross the street."

"Christo, where you at?" shouted Lump. "Let's go," he said, hollering up the staircase back at my house.

"Isaac, is that you? Boy, stop all that yelling. He and Dino went to the store up the street," said my mother.

"Is he wearing his uniform?" asked Lump.

"I don't know for sure, but yes, I believe so," said my mother. "Why?"

"Because I just heard they was protesting the war outside the Recruiting Office."

"You mean next to the store?"

"Yes, ma'am. I'll go see if they're okay."

Lump took off running up the street to catch up with Dino and me, arriving in the middle of a disturbing scene. Dino had been pushed to the ground and was crying as the protestors turned their attention on me in my army uniform.

"Baby killer. Baby killer," shouted the protestors. "No more war. Stop the war now."

They had confronted Dino and I as we crossed the street, hurling angry insults, physical taunts, and even a few snowballs. When someone pushed Dino to the ground, I lost control and physically retaliated. With catlike reflexes, I unbuttoned my military trench coat, scooped Dino up off the ground, and stood him against the wall behind me. I went into my defensive fighting stance.

My arms and legs began swinging and kicking at the protestors. I could feel flesh giving way to my thrusts as I made violent contact with the crowding protestors. All of the fighting skills I had learned went on autopilot, but I felt terrible inside. If it were just me, I could have talked my way out of it or escaped inside the recruitment office until the police showed. However, I wasn't alone. Dino was there with me, hurt and unable run.

"Please don't make me do this," I pleaded as my left fist projected forward, crushing the nose of one protestor.

Episode Ten

I remembered bits and pieces of this, but it was happening too fast to avoid. Still dreaming, I had become so comfortable walking with my brother that I had forgotten the ordeal with the protestors. I kept trying to remember what would happen next, even though I was helpless to prevent it from occurring again.

"Man, I lost my temper. God please forgive me. Oh, sorry for kicking you there. Ah, please don't make me do this all over again."

With my lean body, a simple forearm block left an attacker moaning from the contact, then trying to recover from the pain. With long legs and ferocious, quick kicks, I was soon holding the crowd off just by winding up for a kick. They soon figured out that they didn't want to run into one of my sidekicks. I was locked and loaded.

Other than practice, I could not remember the last time I really had to hit someone with my fist. My stomach churned as if I wanted to puke. I picked up Dino, preparing to run for the recruitment office across the street, when a police car came to a sudden stop in front of us.

"Better get in the car, Ranger," said one of the officers as he opened the back door.

As the police looked around at the injured people in the crowd, the protestors continued verbally harassing me, calling me all sorts of names, and spitting in my direction.

"You looked like a one-man butt kicking team out there, Ranger," joked the police officer. "They should be glad that we came along to protect them from you."

I placed Dino in the back seat of the patrol car. Then, as the police officers held the crowd at bay, I remembered something. I tried to stand there long enough to look through the crowd. I wanted to tell the police officers that what happened next was all just a misunderstanding, caused by fear. I wanted to ask them to please remain calm, but my tongue was glued to the roof of my mouth. I got in the back seat next to Dino and watched. As the car door slammed behind us I could hear Lump's voice calling from within the angry mob.

"Christo, yo, Christo," yelled Lump, out of breath.

The protestors were frightened by Lump. He had been clearing the mob from the rear, working his way to the front. He knew that Dino and I were being harassed and he was trying to protect us. He had lots of practice using his body as a human shield and was really good at it. All of his life people had prejudged him. He was so unusually large that people automatically feared him. I tried to open the car door, but couldn't.

"Lord, do I have to watch this all over again?" I prayed, wishing I were back in Vietnam or Jerusalem.

It was 1967 and riots had nearly burned Detroit to the ground. Caused by the anti-war movement, racial differences and prejudices, the urban areas had finally boiled over, leaving the whole city at war with itself. Everyone was misunderstood.

From their prospective, the police saw innocent white people being attacked from behind by a large black man who appeared to be on a drug-induced rampage. I clearly saw that it was an accident. Lump never meant to harm anyone. As he ran forward, he was so wide that people were falling down all around him. Then he accidentally slipped on a patch of ice, toppling onto three or four of the protestors. However, to the police officers, it looked as if a giant black man hurled innocent white protestors down to the sidewalk.

The police wrestled Lump to the ground. I helplessly watched as the police officers unremorsefully brutalized my best friend without ceasing.

I could see that Lump just wanted to get up and apologize, but the police wouldn't release him. He just wanted to get up and explain, but he wouldn't give up struggling against them. The police officers felt more threatened with Lump's every attempt to stand up and free himself. They beat and kicked him while his face lay crushed against the icy brick pavement. The norm, during this time, was to beat them first, and then there would be no need to ask any questions. And now my best friend was a statistic, a casualty of the racial war that had been brewing for over a decade.

"Stay down, Lump, please stay down," I said.

"Turn the other cheek, Isaac, turn the other cheek," cried Dino.

The angry crowd urged the officers on. "Kick him. Kill him. Shoot him. They shouted kill him, kill him, but I heard something else. It sounded like, crucify him, crucify him.

I felt light-headed again. My stomach started boiling. I knew that this dream was coming to an end. I said a silent goodbye to Lump, who lay on the ground, beaten, handcuffed, and nearly unconscious.

With tear-filled eyes I leaned over and tried to kiss my brother for what I knew would be my final goodbye.

Be good, I thought, I love you Dino.

My heart seemed to slow with each strike, then stop beating altogether as I turned back toward the gang of protestors in time to see the near-fatal blow to Lump's head. I made eye contact just as his eyes shut tightly from the impact. They beat him Detroit style, and no one would expect anything less from the city's finest.

Episode Ten

"No," I yelled, as I watched and heard the nightstick crack against the top of Lump's skull. I pressed both hands against the window and tried to push through it, but was barely able to touch it before I was whisked away.

As the vision of Lump faded, I heard someone say, "I love you, too." I was sure it was my brother. I needed to hear that, especially from Dino, because what I was about to go through would require me to remember what love felt like.

"Dear God," I prayed, "I think I know what's coming next and I'm not sure if I'm strong enough. This journey has been quite rewarding, but I'm not sure if seeing it through to the end is necessary. I mean, it's okay to try to live as Jesus, but no man should endure the actual suffering He went through."

"Is it necessary for me to die as Jesus did to know what it was like?" I asked.

I thought of Lump, and how he always came to my rescue. I wished I could return the favor, just once. I pictured him in the hospital bed, in a coma. I recalled my prayer at the hospital before leaving for Vietnam. I had prayed that I could take his place. I prayed that if it would save Lump's life, God could take my life instead.

I felt a herculean surge of strength. For a moment, all doubt, fear and anxiety were gone. I was prepared to die if it meant giving up my life for my best friend. The words of Jesus flooded my mind. "Greater love has no one than this, that someone lays down his life for his friends." Armed with the knowledge of the Word, I became empowered with renewed strength.

"Then let's do it," I spoke boldly, "I can do this. God, I know you'll be there with me."

I was ready to die for my friend, but the reality of the situation went beyond my understanding. This circumstance was greater than dying for my friend.

I'd give anything to see that old priest again. All those years ago, the whole time he had been trying to tell me something. And now I faced a dilemma that transcended dimensions, periods of time, world ages — and even heaven itself.

Was it possible that God had not even made up His own mind about my predicament? Would He interfere? If He did, would it be before or after I died?

According to the story, none of the Immortal Keepers had been dying or dying the day of their initiation. I would be the first. If I survived I would, without a doubt, have a testimony to give to the others. However, should I die before completing the initiation, but be returned to earth anyway, my story would remain a mystery until the day I died, again.

Episode Eleven

December 31 and 31 AD

The sight and sound of the violent strike to Isaac's head remained vivid in my mind. Seeing it a second time made me feel even guiltier. I felt like a guilty man watching an innocent man convicted of my crime. After witnessing two of my friends die in Vietnam, watching my best friend beaten almost to death, again, and then having to say goodbye to Dino without getting the chance to see my mother, made me wish that my heart would simply stop beating. One way or another, I wanted the torture of this nightmare to end once and for all.

I was in that familiar place, and it was becoming my favorite. I was back in the garden of Gethsemane. A kind of penetrating peace resonated throughout my psyche. Even if I weren't dreaming about this garden, I would undoubtedly like to. And all of the squad members lay asleep on the slope of the grassy knoll just below me.

"Why me, Lord?" I questioned. "Why have you chosen me to dream this dream? Why am I experiencing this vision? I don't ever remember dreaming anything like this before. You really don't expect me to believe in a secret realm, do you?

"Help me walk in faith, Lord," I prayed. "Give me strength to remain obedient to you."

I counted the disciples. I had accepted my fate. I no longer thought of the men as squad members, they were Disciples of Christ. In the dark, I could make out the tops of their heads as I took a quick count. I thought that perhaps I counted too fast because I only counted eleven of the men. I knew why that one person was missing.

"The betrayal."

I wasn't absolutely certain who would be the betrayer, although I had a pretty good idea. Whoever was missing from the group would be the traitor, the one who turns Jesus over to the authorities. But who would it be? I knew it was Judas, but up to now, I had not comprehended that a squad member would take on that role. The dreams were coming so fast. It didn't matter, because both Jesus and I knew what would happen. We would both find out soon enough.

I continued telling myself that there was no better reward than to be chosen to die for all of mankind, to be obedient unto death. While I prayed for strength, I heard Jesus praying as well.

"O, my Father," began Jesus, "if it be possible, let this cup pass from me: nevertheless not as I will, but as thou wilt."

I stopped my prayer, totally spellbound. The greatest events in the life of Christ were unfolding before me. "I can't believe that I'm actually right here, right now, to hear Jesus pray this prayer. Of all prayers, this is the one," I said as parts of my life flashed before my eyes.

This verse inspired me to remain spiritually prepared for battle at all times. I would argue the understanding of this verse every time it came up in discussion. The popular interpretation, taught in Christian churches of all denominations, portrayed our Lord and Savior as a weakling, praying for a way out.

This offended me to my core. How could Jesus tell others that, in order to follow Him, they would have to bear their own crosses, then, when it came to Him, pray for a way out?

Jesus essentially told His followers that following Him likely meant death. In those days, the cross represented death, the most humiliating and painful method of execution. Telling someone to "take up your own cross" was like telling them, "You will probably be put to death one day."

I remembered having this same conversation earlier with Corporal Saez.

"But why did Jesus say, 'Let this cup pass from me'?" he asked, after hearing the passion in my voice.

"When we read these words, and given His circumstance at the time, it's easy to think He was having a moment of weakness or a human moment. However, it warrants deeper investigation."

"Do you really mean investigation?" asked Saez, cleaning his weapons.

"Yes," I answered. "Simply reading this verse and deducing that it refers to His death is spiritual immaturity. This is too powerful a verse to simply take at face value. To understand a verse as potent as this, requires knowledge and understanding of the complete plan of God, and all of its hidden messages."

"We always hear you mention the complete plan of God, but most people don't know enough to do that," said Johnson, joining in the conversation while sharpening his throwing knives.

"This is true, but, whatever your level of understanding, remember—the bottom line is that Jesus will return." I felt the Spirit rising up in me.

"Why is it always about the future?" Saez asked gently.

"In the future, as heir, Jesus holds the 'cup'. Upon His victory over death, this cup passed from God the Father to God the Son. At His return, Jesus will complete the gathering and separating of God's children. This marks the first pouring of the cup of God's wrath with all its disgrace, guilt, and emotional pain. After the millennium, Jesus will be judge and, unfortunately, executioner at the final judgment, which marks the final pouring of the same cup."

"Are you saying that because Jesus becomes judge, He holds the cup?" Johnson asked.

"Absolutely," I answered, happy that he was catching on, whether he believed me or not. "He inherited it from His Father. However, it's Jesus' prayer—even His will—that none perish in the end. Jesus is not asking God to spare His life. He's asking if there is another way out for the children of God who remain ignorant unto death."

"So all traditional teachers say that Jesus was praying for Himself and that, just for a moment, He was afraid to die? Aren't they saying that, for a mere second or two, He didn't want to go through the agony leading up to His death?" asked Peterson, who had been just outside the tent listening, but too busy to join the conversation until now. He took a few of Johnson's blades and finished sharpening for him.

"Of course, not all teachers," I said. "But think about it for a moment, the amount of passion in Him during this time certainly assures us that, if this were true, it was more than a brief moment. The Holy Bible says that Jesus prayed so passionately that His sweat turned to drops of blood," I said, shaking my head.

"There is no way I'm going to believe that Jesus, Emanuel, prayed and cried with that much passion for His own life to be spared," I continued. "That would bring into question the faith He had in His own resurrection. And the problem with that is that Jesus didn't have to rely on faith. He knew for sure."

"Believing that Jesus was praying for everyone else certainly makes more sense," said Peterson, sitting on a footlocker and throwing Johnson's knives into the dirt floor of the tent.

"Sure, it makes more sense that He was praying for God's elect who will be here in the future and will have to suffer through their own hour of temptation," I said, pacing around the inside of the tent.

I took a moment to think of Vanessa. A lot of my passion came from long days and late nights studying with her. She helped me, at a young age, recognize the bottom line and the hidden messages contained within scripture. She explained that some church members were taught that Jesus' prayer means that it's okay to feel skeptical, or doubtful when facing the adversary. After listening to Vanessa, I doubted this traditional teaching with a passion.

At times I would listen to her debate—and even argue—the topic with friends saying, "How dare you, Jesus was the Son of God. He knew exactly what was going to happen. He knew exactly where He was going when He died. He was the protector of the faith. He never showed a sign of weakness and wasn't merely covering doubt with confidence."

I felt so strongly about it in turn that, at seven years old, I ended up in a very heated argument with one of the parish priests. The priest had briefly mentioned the weakness found in Christ and said that, since it was okay for Him, then it was certainly okay for the rest of us. Young and immature, I was furious. I made up my mind to give that priest a thorough verbal lashing at the end of Mass.

"What did you tell him, sir?" asked Peterson.

"Basically the same thing I'm telling you now but with a much squeakier voice."

"From the mouth of babes, huh?" said Johnson.

"And boy did it backfire on me," I said.

"What do you mean, sir?" asked Johnson.

"I ended up receiving a lesson in humility that I would never forget. My mother knew that she couldn't stop me once I began, but, in the end, it would be up to her to reveal the importance of teaching and sharing God's word gently with others."

I remembered that lesson and how it later defined my tolerance level. Now, although still very much convinced that certain topics like the cup, Jesus' final words from the cross, and the rapture doctrine, needed a lot more explanation, I finish each lesson with the proof of God's love. These days I finish with: God loves us so much that He has given us all these examples to learn from.

Episode Eleven

"From then on, I never embarrassed someone by insisting I was right, or disgraced anyone for their lack of knowledge or contrary opinion," I said.

However it did nothing to change what I believed to be true. My understanding wasn't based on the emotion. I could actually back it up with what I had discovered. I understood that Jesus was addressing the future. After all, God's words never change. They're the same now as they were then. We only need to know how to apply them to the future.

Mentally, I was drawn back to Jerusalem when I heard the voice of Jesus continue, "O my Father, if this cup may not pass away from me, except I drink it, thy will be done."

After hearing those words in the garden, I remained silent. I was in a very dark and lonely place. I wished Jesus had said more, but there was nothing else for Him to say.

The memory of my earlier conversation brought me out of it, as my mind raced back to Vietnam.

"Preacher, are you saying that Jesus was praying that the decision of the final judgment or pouring out the cup of God's wrath, would pass from Him?" asked Peterson as he thumbed through one of the Bible's in the tent.

"Yes, that's what I'm saying. Jesus did not want to inherit the cup or be responsible for sending the willfully disobedient children of God to death, but it was God's will. It was part of His complete plan and Jesus knew it. Jesus had no fear of death, no sense of doubt, and certainly no human weakness in fulfilling the promise spoken of in prophecy. Love for God's children rendered Him weak, not concern for His own life."

"But the scripture says that He wanted the cup removed, right there in black and white, and red," said Bart smartly.

"That's right," said Thompson, "That's exactly what it says and I don't see how it can say something else."

"True," I began, "In order for God's plan to be fulfilled, Jesus had to drink from the cup. Sure, His death and resurrection are a type of cup, but not the cup that He asks would pass away. The cup that Jesus was to drink from was not a cup of God's wrath, but rather a cup that assured His victory. Jesus was more than willing to drink from this cup. In fact, it was His will and the will of His Father; their will is one and the same."

I still did my best to convince followers of Christ that I was right even if I wasn't.

"Don't believe anyone who tells you that Jesus became weak until you have investigated it thoroughly," I said, looking for signs that they at least understood what I was saying.

I knew that only God could truly convince anyone that Jesus' acted based on obedience and love. I was simply a guiding instrument. However, if sharing this understanding with believers portrayed Jesus Christ as a true combatant and warrior, courageous to the end, and helped in the conviction, then I would continue challenging most, if not all, teachers of God's plan who taught differently.

"Think about this, men," I said, looking around the tent. "Would any of you think it was fair if Jesus asked you to risk your life to save others if He had not done it Himself? Why would He ask you to be brave when facing death if He wimped out when it was His turn to die?"

The men could directly relate to the hero analogy; they knew that being a hero has its price.

In all my years, I never read any verses about the disciples of Christ fearing death after the Day of Pentecost. Prior to that day, the opposite was certainly true. In fact, in the book of Mark, Jesus told the disciples that they would eventually drink from the same cup as Him. During their later ministries, the disciples calmly faced suffering and death for spreading the Gospel of Jesus Christ.

"Doesn't the Holy Bible mention that God finds the death of His saints as precious?" interjected a fresh voice.

"Attention," said Matthews, sounding off, as Colonel Harris entered the tent. He had been standing outside, absorbing the lesson.

"At ease, men," said Colonel Harris as he continued. "God even declares that the death of His Son pleased Him. How dare someone teach that Jesus Himself became weak and fearful when faced with His own demise. If God's elect are not afraid to die, how could we even dare suggest that the Son of God would be?"

I was pleased to hear the colonel interject the discernment that Jesus was the Son of God.

"He was Emmanuel. How could He have shown any sign of weakness when facing His adversary, death? I'll tell you this much I know, men," said the colonel as he stood by the tent entrance. "Suggesting that Jesus fears dying, even for a moment, is like saying He feared death. If that's true, then He fears Satan, who is death, and, of course, that would be a lie. Carry on."

As suddenly as Colonel Harris entered the tent, he exited, leaving a powerful understanding in his wake. The soldiers rose to attention again, then settled down at ease.

"This lesson teaches how much God loves us," I said. "He's given us the supreme example of how to face death and be victorious. He provided His Son for us to follow. God's elect will ultimately have to face

Episode Eleven

death as they seek to enlighten those who have been deceived by Satan. It's God's end time plan to overcome Satan."

As much as I wanted to relive those prized moments with the men, I realized that I was still in Jerusalem once again when I heard some commotion further down the garden. I knew what time it was.

Thinking about what came next, my mind flashed back home. "I love you, Dino," I said, thinking of my brother one more time.

I looked at the disciples resting, as all sizes and shapes of men approached me. The ones making their way to the front of the mob were polished; their robes glistened with each step they took. They looked so holy, dressed in their self-righteous attire. These men from the synagogue were there to apprehend Jesus. Led by a small band of temple guardsmen, the majority of the horde looked more like farmers or hoodlums than soldiers, and held rakes, forks, and hoes as weapons. There also seemed to be a small squad of Roman soldiers standing further back.

Imagining these pompous men of the cloth climbing such a steep embankment would have been hilarious had I not felt so emotionally deserted. Needing assistance from others in the crowd, they were certainly in no shape to keep up with Jesus. Physically disgraceful, they also lacked the honor and decency to render the trumped up charges against Christ. There should be honor in victory, but this felt like being taken captive by an enemy unfit for duty. I actually felt embarrassed for them.

I know you have to be put to death, but you shouldn't have to be humiliated by these so-called priests, I thought. Surely Satan has a much more worthy opponent.

Not paying much attention to the eleven disciples, I forgot that one of them was missing in action. A familiar face in the crowd made a beeline directly toward me. Advancing my way, the man flung his arms spread wide as if to embrace me. I stood motionless as Judas tenderly placed a kiss on Jesus' cheek.

Private Jinx, I thought scornfully as I recognized the condemner. You really are full of the devil, aren't you?

Jinx's addiction to drugs had won. I tried in vain to help Jinx. He didn't want any help, only his next fix. I tried to help him overcome his addiction by leading him to Christ, but Jinx wasn't hearing any of it. I knew he couldn't win that battle alone. He resisted participating in any of the Bible lessons, and he certainly wasn't curious about salvation or if heaven and hell actually existed. If someone from the squad had to betray Jesus, Jimmy Jinx made the perfect candidate.

Good for you, I thought, you finally came through on something. We knew we could depend on you.

That's what I wanted to say, but I couldn't. I wanted to tell Jinx to snap out of it. I wanted to tell him to fight Satan.

"Don't do this," I said, recalling the pitiful fate of Judas in the end.

"Judas," said the voice of Jesus, "are you betraying the Son of Man with a kiss?"

"I told you, I knew he was a traitor all along," said Johnson. It was true; Johnson had uttered those words about Jinx during the mission to the village.

"Yeah, you traitor," jeered the rest of the disciples.

In the blink of an eye and, for a moment continuing to loop in my mind, a reflection of my face suddenly gleamed past me, catching me by surprise.

Full of fury Peterson lunged toward Jinx, his bayonet unsheathed. It swung past my line of sight, reflecting the moonlight. Jinx quickly bobbed and weaved, dodging the attempted assault. Peterson, committed and unable to retreat, followed through with his strike. As his arm descended, the blade's edge slashed the ear of a civilian guard standing near.

Peterson had removed the ear of one of the men in the mob with his knife. The act caught them totally off guard. The mob of angry men, startled, fell back in fear.

Catching the wounded man as he fell into my arms, I wished I could do something to relieve his agony. He wasn't a soldier. As a result of his ignorance, he was at the wrong place, at the wrong time. He was an unsuspecting bondservant recruited by the devious church leaders, who filled his head with baseless anti-Jesus rhetoric. Most of the men in the mob had no idea of the enormity of the stake. They had no idea that they were being cruelly manipulated by Satan's cowardly offspring, disguised as men of the cloth.

I knew that I felt the same compassion as Jesus. In that moment, Jesus pitied the man, and cried out in anguish.

"Stop; enough of this," commanded the voice of Jesus. All action ceased; half the mob fell back even further.

My arms still cradled the injured man. I watched as Jesus turned His attention tenderly toward the victim. He administered to him as if he were an injured child, embracing him without prejudice. The helpless victim, in the folded arms of Christ, cried out to God for a healing, then momentarily lost consciousness. Jesus, now holding the man's full weight, laid him on the ground gently, so as not to cause him additional pain. He sat with the man, supporting him as one would an infant. Then, with my right arm around the man's back, I felt my left hand placed on the gaping wound as Jesus restored the servant's ear.

My body straightened up. Peterson was still furious at Jinx. I placed my hand on Peterson's shoulder, instructing him to put his sword away. Realizing that the innocent man had been healed, Peterson's countenance changed from combative to sympathetic.

Peterson was like a ferocious attack dog, standing on its hind legs, foaming and gnashing its razor teeth one minute, then instantly sitting and wagging its tail for its master's approval. He felt sorry for his behavior and seemed apologetic. However, as Peterson focused his stabbing eyes towards Jinx, anger filled his heart again. He grimaced, as if hoping he would get another chance at removing the evil within him before the night ended. He wiped his knife and bloody hands on the grass, but held the knife ready, just in case that prospect came sooner rather than later.

Then Jesus paused, taking a precious moment to remind him that, at any moment, He could have appealed to the Father for aid, but then how could the scriptures be fulfilled?

Every miracle that Jesus completed, regardless of the lesson, was to glorify God. Because of this dream, I knew how to apply the truth, literally and spiritually. It was all for God and, yes, there were plenty of lessons learned, but the lessons didn't matter to me now. The reality of these events had taken over. I could forget the spiritual side, the understanding and the knowledge gained from studying as reality unfolded.

Each event came easier to me now. The works, the words, and the prayers all seemed accomplished without effort. The words that erupted from my mouth before, now flowed like an effervescent stream. It was still painful. My mouth still filled with saliva, my stomach still rumbled, my temperature still rose, but I could handle it now. I welcomed the discomfort associated with the dream visions and accepted my role. Exhilaration overcame my denial and fear. Feeling a sense of accomplishment, I emptied myself and became filled with the body of Christ.

Turning toward the mob, the voice of Jesus said, "Am I leading a rebellion? Why have you come with swords and clubs? All the days I spent with you in the temples and courts, you never laid a hand on me, but this is your hour, when darkness reigns. But before you become boastful, know this, all who draw the sword will die by the sword. Do you think that I cannot call on my Father and He will not, at once, send me twelve legions of angels to defend me? But this day worry not, for the Scriptures and the writings of the prophets will be fulfilled."

Deep in thought, I barely noticed when they took Jesus captive, bound Him and led Him from the garden.

For the first time I felt alone in the dream. I looked around and, to my dismay, all of the disciples had either fled or remained behind in the garden. But I felt happy that they were free. In a way, I felt like Corporal Saez rushing into the ambush to help save his buddies. One by one, the remaining eleven apostles, had escaped. I knew why. This too is a lesson for God's elect in the future. As brave as God's elect will have to be in the end times, that strength will come from the Holy Spirit. The disciples didn't have this help. Although they put on a courageous front, they still feared of death.

They were truly set apart for God, I thought. They have become sanctified.

God's love for mankind became more real to me. I was awestruck by the depth of such love.

God is love, I'm sure of it now. I've known it my whole life, but now it means more. I have been made free.

They escorted Jesus to the house of Caiaphas, the High Priest. From within the stone walls surrounding the inner offices, I saw Peterson standing in the outer court. Every few minutes, he wiped his tearful eyes and running nose with his sleeve. He looked like a little boy, lost and uncertain of the future.

Knowing the role that Peterson would play in this unfolding drama, I looked on with empathy.

The high priest, formally clad in his precious jeweled breast plate, fine purple linen, and blue sash, convened with other members of the clergy to determine Jesus' fate. I stood before the eight-foot-long wooden table, trimmed with gold and surrounded by a jury of priests. Each one sat in a thronelike seat, waiting to cast judgment. The foul stench of residual incense from the day's earlier offering remained, polluting the air in the room.

The six priests stood ready to pronounce a death sentence upon the Son of God. Each one speaking in turn, and at times in unison, as they

Episode Eleven

fabricated baseless charges against Him. Throughout His three-and-a-half year ministry, they had conspired to murder Christ. Now, as the feast of Passover approached, they had altered their deviously concocted plans, which originally called for His arrest after the feast days ended.

God, however, had different plans for His Son. These crafty clerics had no possibility of triumphing. It was God's plan that His Son be made a Holy Sacrifice not after, but during the feast of Passover.

Episode Twelve
December 31 and 33 AD

If I had merely watched this dream, I probably could not have remembered it. But as it stood, I could recall, respond to, and even resolve issues while dreaming. I realized how fortunate I was to be able to talk to myself while dreaming, and how either fortunate or unfortunate that no one could hear me.

How can they tell these lies? I asked, furious about the spectacle at Caiaphas's house. Even though I'm dreaming and I wasn't actually there, or here, or wherever, I know the scriptures. The scriptures say that these men are liars.

It was Jesus' turn to speak, but I knew that God would instruct Him. His words would set one of the most important examples in the Holy Bible.

The hour of temptation continued for Jesus as He stood before His accusers. I remembered that Matthew wrote about how, just as a friend betrayed Jesus, God's elect will be betrayed by friends, family members, and loved ones, and similarly be put on trial as well.

This is what it will be like for all the people who are betrayed by their loved ones, I said. They'll have to stand before the fake Christ, the accuser, and testify just as Christ did.

I remembered another conversation that I had with First Squad. Private Matthews asked why the Bible says that it will be loved ones who turn family members over to death. That discussion turned into a very hot topic that night in Vietnam.

Episode Twelve

"You keep talking about the end times, like there will be a difference, what do you mean?" asked Peterson.

I began talking as most of the squad sat outside the mess tent.

"The popular theory states that during the end, after Christ has already come in secret to gather His elect, the world will turn against itself. Satan will then come to torment all those who remain. Christians and non-Christians will be held in captivity by the convictions of Satan, tormented day and night."

"I remember this one." Bart stood up to impress the others. "It's called the rapture, and it's when times will be so hard that there will be no natural love toward family members. It's got something to with…" he hesitated, "uh… because of Satan's tribulation period, a mother will put her son or daughter to death with no remorse at all, or a brother will put a brother or sister to death. The way I remember it, everyone who gets left behind ends up betraying each other to death. Am I right, sir?"

"Yes, it's a tribulation period," I said, sitting down next to Peterson. "This theory, of course, looks at the end days in a natural or carnal way, while taking the words literally. When investigated differently, it can be understood in a more supernatural or spiritual way."

"Does any of this have to do with Matthew 24?" asked Peterson, pulling out his whetstone.

"Definitely," I said, watching Peterson sharpening his bayonet, something all soldiers automatically did when they had nothing better to do.

"In Matthew 24, Jesus talks about His return to earth and the end of this world age. However, this so called treachery between family members and loved ones is not the end, it is only one of the steps that lead to the end. The betrayals of family members during the end days—and here's the twist—are inspired by love."

"What? Wait a minute, how do you get love out of betrayal?" asked Thompson, who almost fell off the tree stump he sat on.

"I kind of see," said Bart, sure of himself. "If it really is a betrayal, then you can't betray someone if there is no love involved. Right, sir?"

"You know what, Bart is right again, men. A lot of people think that Jesus didn't love Judas and visa versa, but Jesus Himself claimed that Judas betrayed Him."

"Right, with a kiss, right?" said Thompson.

"Exactly," I said. "In a distorted way, Judas betrayed Christ, primarily because he was greedy and secondarily because he loved Him."

"Yeah, Jesus did call Him a friend," said Saez.

"During the end times, when the followers of Christ are divided into those who become deceived and those who continue to wait, many families will include those who are deceived, who will report on the faithful. The Holy Bible says that family members will deliver their own loved ones up to death or will put them to death. We must ask the question, why would a mother put her son or daughter to death, or why turn them over to death? Why would a brother put his own brother or sister to death, or turn them over to death?"

"Yeah, remember what the colonel said the other day, that death is one of Satan's names," added Peterson, testing the sharpness of the bayonet's edge.

"The colonel was right," I said, "and that means that they don't actually put their family members to death. They turn them over to death or over to Satan. Deceived family members turn their loved ones over to him because, to them, the consequences otherwise seem eternally devastating. The deceived family members believe the first Christ that comes to earth is the true Christ, while the true faithful wait."

"Even if the imposter does come to earth first," suggested Thompson like a true skeptic, "and let's say he does deceive the world, that doesn't tell me why family members will betray each other."

"Thomp, you always thinking somebody's lying to you, man," said Johnson, playfully shoving Thompson backwards with both hands. "Instead of arguing all the time, why don't you let the lieutenant finish telling the story? You might just learn something, corn-fed farm-boy."

"Hey, proud of it too."

"That's okay; actually it's good to question. In fact, you should question everything and make sure you get good, sound answers," I said.

"How do you like that, crater face?" mocked Thompson, pushing Johnson in return.

Laughing, I continued, "The first or false Christ will promise to take everyone to heaven with him as the children of God expect him to do, and will convince the world that he doesn't want to leave anyone behind, including the ones who don't believe in him. He'll deceive the world by convincing everyone that it is better to be "taken" with him than "left behind" to suffer through the tribulation to come. Of course it's all lies—every word from his mouth. He tells so many lies the Holy Bible refers to them as a flood. The flood that pours from the mouth of the dragon is a flood of lies, mentioned in the books of Revelation and Daniel."

Episode Twelve

"Why doesn't God prevent His elect from being taken with the deceived?" asked Bart.

"Another good question," I said pretending to keep score. "The main thing to remember is that God's plan calls for His elect to be taken into captivity as well."

"Dang, here we go again! First you say it's a betrayal, now you saying it's God's plan?" said Thompson, still sounding very doubtful.

"Fool," interjected Matthews, who had been listening intently for the entire three days. "Didn't you just hear the lieutenant say that Judas betrayed Jesus, that they were friends and that it was part of God's plan? You need to start listening with both your ears and keep your eyes open."

"That's another really good question though, Thompson," I said, nodding my head. "The Holy Bible says that the word of God must first be published. It will be God's elect, during this hour of temptation that will publish, or broadcast the word of God to the whole world while also exposing the false Christ. The book of Matthew warns God's elect. It says that, during this hour, they should not worry about what to say. In fact, they should not even speak because the Holy Spirit will give them the words to say."

"So are you saying the only way they gonna get to teach the Gospel to the world is if they get caught by the enemy?" said Thompson, shaking his head in agreement. "Dang, that's a pretty damn good plan, though."

"That's the plan," I said, as Thompson realized he'd said a bad word, covered his mouth, and shrugged sheepishly.

Bart jumped in with a comment, "Oh, right, if Jesus was never captured and put to death, we woulda never had the opportunity to be saved."

"Right," I said, "Jesus' trial is a lesson; His actions set an example for God's elect when they are the ones innocently accused of treason or other false charges and placed on trial before the whole world. They won't publish or broadcast the Gospel and expose the son of Perdition, but the cloven tongue of the Holy Spirit that will speak through them, just as He did on the day of Pentecost thousands of years ago when everyone heard about the 'New Way' spoken by the Apostles, but in their own languages."

A Dream Before Dying

That was a fun day, I thought. Bringing my mind back to Jerusalem, I tried to look around the courtroom, but couldn't. I could feel my head turning slightly to the right and left and, as far as I could tell, my eyes were still open, but my vision blurred. I felt like I was going blind.

"No," I protested, "I need to see this. I need to see all of it."

I thought I was leaving Jerusalem and going back to Vietnam, but Jesus still stood before the mock tribunal, and I stood right there with Him. Now completely blind, unable to see anything, I listened all the harder.

"This man said he will destroy God's temple and rebuild it in three days," said one of the accusers.

I laughed. Jesus didn't say it that way, nor did he mean it to be interpreted that way.

"Man." I said, "These people were with Jesus all this time and they just refused to listen. They were so busy prejudging Him that whatever He said fell on deaf ears. They would not or could not open their hearts to the truth."

Jesus remained silent, even after they asked Him to explain what He meant about the falling of the temple. I wished I could see the faces of His accusers. Convinced that, back in Vietnam, my body was dead or dying, I wanted to remember all their faces so I could personally hunt them down after arriving in heaven.

I knew that these so-called religious leaders accusing Jesus were hypocrites. He called them play actors. I remembered.

According to Jesus, they were not religious men at all, but, in reality, the offspring of the devil. I remembered that, in the book of John, Jesus told them that they were of their father, the devil.

"Well then," said the priest, "under oath of the living God, tell us if you are the Christ, the Son of God!"

"Yes, it is as you say," said Jesus, "but I say to all of you, In the future you will see the Son of Man sitting at the right hand of the Mighty One and coming on the clouds of heaven."

After hearing this, I felt absolutely relieved. The words came from my lips, but I wasn't speaking. I was sure that this is what it would be like for God's elect in the future. I wanted to shout 'glory, hallelujah' and 'amen,' but stopped myself. I didn't want to miss anything. I may have shouted one little amen before the thought occurred to me, though.

"Hey. Stop that," I shouted, alarmed when I felt my clothes being torn from my body. I couldn't see who did it, but remembered that the High Priest had ordered Jesus' clothes stripped from Him.

147

Episode Twelve

"This man has spoken blasphemy!" shouted the High Priest. "Why do you need more proof? You have all heard this blasphemy, what do you think now?"

Without any objection, the tribunal agreed that Jesus should be put to death.

I thought about Corporal Saez and how he sacrificed his life for his friends. Through this dream I was beginning to understand what it meant to die for your friends. If I remained trapped in the dream until the end, death would truly be honorable.

However, dying at the hands of these heathens would be shameful, disgraceful, and even dishonorable. I thought that dying at the hands of these despicable conspirators, disguised as holy men, would be the real source of pain.

They hurled my body to the marble floor. I thought I felt the impact in my knees and wanted to cry out in pain, but didn't. Blind now, it took me completely by surprise, but I figured that it had to hurt Jesus even more and He never whimpered.

The temple guards blindfolded Jesus, spat on him, and beat Him without mercy, striking Him with their fists and kicking Him.

"Who's hitting you now? Do you know?" They taunted him cruelly.

As they mocked Jesus, I thought of Lump, beaten, the angry mob spitting on him for no reason at all. This gave me an inner strength. I felt that witnessing Lump's beating a second time in the dream, although painful, had been a revelation from God, a sort of preparation.

"Thanks, Lump, for always being there for me. I love you, and I'll remember you always."

They moved Jesus along the outer hallway and then outside, to a pavilion. Still shrouded in blindness, I sensed a crowd gathered about. I felt we stood above the crowd. What a time to be blind—I wanted to see the brilliant architecture. Such a pity that this beauty would forever be associated with this abased corruption.

I could hear the crowd. Many sounded sympathetic, calling for Jesus to be released from custody. It didn't take long for that to change.

In my confused thoughts, I knew what had to happen, but lost track of reality. I wanted revenge. In my anger, I wanted to strike out at the false accusers. I wanted Jesus to do something, to save us both. In my blindness, I had a change of heart. I felt feverish and lost, thoughts of violence fueled my emotions.

"No," I said, "I don't want to die. I don't want to die, Lord. Can you hear me?" I pleaded in my helplessness. "I don't want to go through this. Save me!"

I was beyond powerless. I could not even attempt to struggle to free myself.

"I'm still here, Lord. Did you forget about me?" I cried out in anguish, knowing that no one could hear me. I wondered if God was even listening.

With the snap of a finger, my anguish turned into anger. "I'll get you for this, Jinx. You're going to pay for what you did."

It was ridiculous to blame Jinx for what I suffered. In my subconscious, I knew that. But I didn't like being in darkness. I didn't like feeling confused.

"I need to take control," I said.

I thought of Peterson and what he must be going through. After all, he had to stomach denying Christ, not once, but three times. I knew Peterson was still there, even though I couldn't see him.

Earlier, while detained in my cell with my vision still intact, I watched as Pete warmed himself at a fire with a group of people. The fire roaring in the barrel was always lit at night for cold and weary travelers arriving after the main gates to the city closed. I watched Peterson struggling to stay warm.

"At least Pete's still hanging in there," I said. All the other disciples were somewhere hiding, hoping they wouldn't get caught.

Peterson and I kept looking at each other. Our non-verbal conversation reassured both of us. Unfortunately, his Galilean clothes made him stick out like a sore thumb. Feeling out of place, he acted jittery as well, continually checking his surroundings and apologizing to passersby for the slightest thing.

I remembered seeing a woman and three officials approach him. I couldn't see her face, but she seemed like any other woman. The longer she stood near Peterson, the more her body changed. She slumped over. I wondered if her face changed as well. I noticed something extremely odd, and wondered about my sanity. As she extended her arm from beneath her tunic to point directly at Peterson, her hand appeared absent any signs of flesh. Her skeletal index finger seemed abnormally long, lengthening as she pointed. It looked as if she aimed an evil wand at him.

"I'm truly losing my mind now," I said.

Peterson ran from the woman as she pointed and screamed indistinctly at him.

I couldn't hear over the din of the crowd, but knew that Peterson had denied being with me. I thought about how painful that must have been for him. Peterson, just like Peter, felt the exact shame and misery for his

Episode Twelve

role during the denial of Christ. I couldn't hear it, but I felt the cock crowing in my heart at each of Peterson's painful rejections.

At war with himself, Peterson battled within his own spirit. I remembered that Jesus had said once, "It is better for you not to know me and sin, than to know me and sin. For you will suffer yourself more."

Although I tended to use this verse as a reference to the future, I understood it differently now as I thought about Pete. In the past, I compared it to the guilt a person would feel after cheating on the love of their life. I used it as an example of what the deceived would feel when the true Christ returned.

Sitting in Jesus' holding cell, listening to the disturbance of the crowd outside, I heard the final rooster's crow merging with the sound of the approaching wind.

"You'll be alright, Pete, I said, "hang in there."

In reality, no matter how far Peter ran, he couldn't change his destiny. He would be at war with himself over the denial, probably until the day he died. That's how I felt about Peterson. I couldn't bear the thought of suffering and guilt that he must be going through. I wished I could forget about it, at the same time wishing I could say something to comfort him, but the scriptures had to be fulfilled. Jesus, selfless and shunning His own pain, must have felt the same way. I surmised that Jesus felt the same way about Peter as I did for Corporal Peterson.

My emotions churned again. Compelled to feel compassion for Peterson's inner struggle, I was no longer prepared to feel his pain. Physical selfishness arose within me once again. I felt more concerned about my own life now.

"I'm so sorry for you, Pete," I said sadly, "but you'll be okay. I'm the one who's dying!" I shouted as the church guards took me from my cell.

The crowd's attitude toward Jesus had turned negative now. He had been transported to the Roman pavilion to be prepared for questioning by the Roman governor. I sensed that He stood before the person referred to in the New Testament as Pilate. I couldn't see what he wore, but had always pictured him in white and off-white.

The elders, the priests, and the teachers had me bound and whisked away to confront Pilate. They thought they had a capital case; anyone claiming to be king committed treason to the throne of Caesar. If found guilty, I would receive the death penalty.

"Are you the King of the Jews?" the governor asked as if he didn't really care.

I waited for a response but Jesus remained silent.

I no longer wanted to think of examples and lessons, but I couldn't help thinking about the role of God's elect in the future. "They'll be delivered up too," I said, "They'll have to keep their silence too."

"Are you as they accuse you?" he asked again, impatiently, then, louder, "Are you the King of the Jews?"

"Ugh. Jesus, tell them who you are and maybe I can get out of here," I said in frustration. "Don't you people know who this man is? You fools, you dare to mock, dare to strike, dare to spit upon the Messiah, the Son of God. Hello? He's not the King of the Jews. He's the King of Israel. He's the Son of God, you sons of… idiots."

Furious, I was even more afraid. I hoped that, as soon as this part ended, my dream would end for good. I wanted to return to Vietnam, no matter what my fate. It had to be better than what would come if I stayed trapped in this dream. My voice and thoughts came to a sudden halt. A soft voice, out of breath, flowed from my bruised and swollen lips.

"Is that your own idea… or did others tell you of me?" panted Jesus, slowly.

"Am I a Jew?" Pilate asked abruptly. "There is only one King, Caesar. Are you a rebel? It was your own people who handed you over to me. What have you done?"

Those words made me angrier, but for a different reason now. As tolerant as I was outwardly, inwardly, signs of biblical ignorance from ones expected to know better infuriated me. Traditionally followers of Christ are taught that it was the Jews who were guilty of the death of Jesus. I had a problem with this because I never believed that it was actually the Jews who conspired to murder Christ. After all, His first followers were those of the tribe of Judah. However, in those days, everyone called a Jew was not necessarily a descendant of Judah. Some were called Jews simply because they lived in the land of Judah or because they lived in Jerusalem.

I remembered the last conversation I had with Colonel Harris, who insisted the Jews had killed Christ.

"Sorry, sir, but I have to disagree with you, if you don't mind," I said apologetically.

"Son, you don't ever have to apologize for what you believe. Hell, you just might know better then the old man. Go ahead, let me have it."

"Well, sir," I began, slowly at first. "If you truly believe in the words of the Holy Bible…"

Episode Twelve

"I do, and you know I do," interrupted the colonel. "So, come on. Quit your jawjacking and spit it out."

"Yes, sir. Well, according to the very first prophecy recorded in the Holy Bible, in the book of Genesis, if you believe that the Jews are descendant of Adam, it could not be the Jews who caused the suffering of Christ. The offspring of Satan would betray, conspire, and ultimately be responsible.

"I knew this was going to be good, lieutenant," said the colonel, "But the scripture still says that the Jews killed the Son of God. Right?"

"Yes, sir, but we need to explore what that means. I'm saying that, if the Jews killed Jesus, then the words of the Holy Bible have become contradictory."

"Impossible," snapped Colonel Harris as he thought about what I was saying.

"Yes, sir, according to the first prophecy the Jews cannot be culpable for the conspiracy and murder of the Son of God. The offspring of the Serpent, however, could impersonate, infiltrate, and disguise themselves as men of God, thus fulfilling the prophecy that describes the complete plan of God from beginning to end."

"You're saying that the priests and everyone involved in the conspiracy to kill Jesus were impostors of some kind?" asked the colonel, ready and willing to listen to this possibility.

"Yes, sir, that is certainly, if nothing else, a well thought out theory with the words of God to back it up. God's word says that the seed line of the Serpent would perpetrate the murder of His Son, the seed line of Adam and Eve. If this is true, then the true seed line of Judah is innocent. Besides, who, other than Satan, would want the Son of God dead?"

Thinking about what I taught during my short time in Vietnam helped me forget about where I was now. I reminded myself again that I didn't want to focus on lessons. I didn't want to compare notes or remember the significance of this, or the history of that. Right now, I didn't care who was guilty or innocent. I just wanted to leave this dream. I wanted a chance to fight for my life back in the infirmary where I was dying. However, Jesus was still speaking, and I was still dreaming.

"My kingdom is not of this world," said Jesus bluntly. "If it were, my servants would fight to prevent my arrest by the Jews. My kingdom is from another place."

"You are a King, then?" asked Pilate.

"You are right in saying that I am a king," Jesus continued. "In fact, for this reason I was born, and for this I came into the world, to testify to the truth. Everyone on the side of truth listens to me."

"What is truth?" Pilate asked, throwing both hands in the air.

Pilate left Jesus standing alone, beaten, to go speak to the council.

"What is the truth?" I said. "Why don't they know? The prophecy had been written thousands of years before the coming of the Messiah. The religious leaders knew and taught the prophecy. Now that Jesus is with them, they refuse to believe the truth. The truth sets men free, and Jesus Himself taught that He is the way, the truth and the life. One cannot be free without knowing Jesus Christ."

I could hear Pilate telling the priests that he could not find any fault with Him. The priests wanted more; they wanted a conviction at any cost. They insisted, claiming that Jesus caused too much trouble and that he planned to raise an army to overthrow the Roman occupation. Their false claims continued, accusing Jesus of spreading lies and false teachings all the way from Galilee. They said he stirred up the people everywhere He went with talks of rebellion, revolution, and of a new age for Jerusalem.

Of course, the prophecy needed to be fulfilled, but I knew the real problem that the priests had with Jesus. He performed every miracle that the church only claimed to perform. Thousands of people followed Jesus everywhere He went, leaving the church in a financial decline. No one attended daily services, or made offerings. After three years of this, Jesus' ministry began to affect the high standard of living that the priests had grown accustomed too. Jesus fed the hungry, healed the sick, and restored sight to the blind. It affected their cash flow.

"Sounds like the same old song and dance to me," I said. "In the wrong hands, power and money are two of the most corrupting forces on earth."

Since Jesus had spent so much time in Galilee and likely resided there, Pilate sent Him to Herod Antipas, the appointed governor of Galilee, who happened to be in Jerusalem for the Passover feast. Pilate wanted to shift the responsibility.

Pilate felt relieved to send Jesus anywhere, as long as he had nothing to do with His trial. Herod, on the other hand, had heard everything about Jesus, and had wanted to meet Him for some time. Intrigued by His reputation, Herod felt quite overwhelmed at first meeting Him.

From what I could remember, Herod wanted Jesus to perform a miracle for him.

Episode Twelve

"What did he think he was going to get," I said, "a private magic show? Don't you recognize the King of Kings? Jesus, say something."

My thoughts wandered while standing waiting for Herod's questions. I seemed to be sporting dual personalities. My sudden blindness combined with fury left me bitter, sarcastic, and cynical most of the time, but, at other times, I felt totally free and full of the Spirit. I didn't like the fact that this part of the dream seemed endless. The thought of dying on the cross panicked me. Physically helpless, I couldn't defend myself. I was emotionally fatigued and now, blind.

Thinking of the crucifixion reminded me of the cruciform shrapnel in my head. Did it draw me closer so I could observe my own death? Why did I need to observe my own body lying there, mangled and dying? Jesus was being drawn helplessly to His death because of His obedience to God. Was I going to die because I was somehow disobedient? Afraid of God possibly finding me arrogant, keeping me here longer, I no longer wanted to compare Jesus' death on the cross and my own death.

I remembered the words spoken by Jesus, when He warned the Apostles that they would eventually meet the same fate. That warning applied directly to me.

I had been asking too many questions. They only made me more insane with rage and resentment. I decided not to question anything anymore. I attempted to psych myself into believing that it would all end soon. Surely God wouldn't allow me to suffer the agony of the cross. I knew that I couldn't be a part of the crucifixion that saved the world. I was a sinner; I wasn't worthy. I convinced myself that God would have to pull me out of here before the actual sacrifice.

"I'll be out of here soon," I said, not very convincingly.

At his palace, Herod Antipas found no guilt in Jesus. Just as with Pilate, he wanted nothing to do with condemning Him. Still blind, my heightened hearing observed the weight of Herod's robes. I could hear the rustling whenever he lifted his arms, lowered them, or rose from his throne. I could tell whenever he walked forward and backward. From the sound of his voice, I could tell that Herod was extremely overweight and in poor physical condition. I could even tell that he had a full beard. Herod met with Jesus alone. He did not allow any of His accusers to attend the questioning. He would do his best to set Jesus free.

Herod attempted to get Jesus to speak, to defend Himself, but He remained silent. Jesus accepted His fate. He intended to be obedient unto His death.

"We have nothing to say to you, you weasel," I said, as if from both of us.

Earlier, Herod had met with the chief priests. They repeated their accusations to him. Also uninterested, he found their hatred for Jesus suspiciously contemptible, to say the least. Now they played politics, which they made clear with their never-ending whining accusations. They showed no shame, even while addressing Herod, who felt compelled to do something just to end their nagging.

"If they're playing politics with a man's life, then they're all from the devil," I said.

Herod thought that, maybe, a sentence of corporal punishment and embarrassment would suffice them. Quite uncomfortable and anxious to appease the priests, Herod ordered his soldiers to beat Jesus. Afterward, they mockingly dressed Him in an elegant robe, gave Him a fake scepter, then took a three-foot-long thorn vine, fashioned it into a crown, and ferociously adhered it to Jesus' head. This was his judgment, and he was satisfied. He ordered Jesus sent back to Pilate for release.

"You're a sellout," I yelled.

It wasn't enough. The chief priests, obsessed with their own idea of sentencing, wanted Jesus dead.

"Let's see," I reasoned, "who actually wants Jesus dead? It's not the disciples. Even Judas, who may have had his own conniving reasons for betrayal, didn't want Jesus dead. The only one who wants the Son of God put to death is the son of the devil, Satan himself."

The priests pushed Pilate to put Jesus to death for treason. He looked guilty now. After being beaten almost to death, He looked like a criminal. The priests showed nothing but confidence. They met with Herod and Pilate and, sensing victory, conspired to remain persistent. Rome held Jerusalem captive, making peaceful coexistence imperative. The priests knew that the last thing Herod or Pilate wanted was conflict with the religious leaders of Jerusalem.

I sensed their confidence, and imagined them to be quite puffed up. They were breaking down Pilate, who had grown weary of the petty back and forth battling. Yes, they would ultimately win, but not because of their efforts. Satan inspired their religious, political, and financial motives, but God predestined all. Prophecy would be fulfilled, but heaven help the unrepentant ones who boastfully joined the enemy in fulfilling the completion of God's plan.

I contemplated my own circumstances. Things could be worse. Instead of losing my sight, I could have experienced total amnesia. What if I had been trapped in a waking nightmare and not been able to identify anyone at all? What if I had lost my sight and my memory? When most people dream, they usually have no control and no idea what to expect. I knew how my dream would end and, while each episode seemed to last longer, I was not worried about awakening from it.

What if I was still dreaming when Christ was nailed to the cross? What if I felt the spikes pierce my flesh? After all, though I had no control, it still appeared to be my body. Maybe it wasn't my body anymore. I was blind now, so I really wasn't sure. Maybe everything else changed, too. Anything could be possible in a dream.

I rationalized, wondering if it all could be just a dream. Maybe I wasn't really dying. Maybe seeing myself in surgery was part of the dream. For a moment, those thoughts gave me some relief.

"Maybe I'm in my tent asleep and just having the craziest dream in the world!" I said. "If that's true, God, please let me wake up." However, this part of the dream seemed physically tangible; I believed that I was there to see it through to the end.

"I can't believe that I'm praying outside of God's will," I said. "He must have me here for a reason."

I knew that Jesus carried out God's plan for reasons of salvation, love, and inheritance, and because He was obedient. He did what His Father commanded Him. If I truly believed that God had called me to this fate, then I must be obedient as well. No more anger or whimpering self-pity. It was time I stood like a soldier. If I was going to die, then I had to die with honor and dignity. I had to practice what I preached, achieving victory through discipline and obedience.

Now I submitted myself to God's will. "I'm going to die," I said, proudly, "but I'm not alone. Jesus is with me."

The congregation of priests and elders assembled in front of Pilate again. Still reluctant despite their pleas, Pilate refused to find Christ guilty. Pilate, finding no fault with Him, like Herod, decided to have Him beaten, hoping to placate those who hated Him.

"Hey, what's going on?" I asked. "Ha. I can see again; thank you, Lord," I said as the guards uncovered the eyes of Jesus.

With my vision restored, the world looked much brighter. My ability to see made me feel like part of the plan. I no longer felt left out or forgotten. I wasn't angry anymore. In fact, it felt like a new day, with anything possible.

"How did the colonel put it? Oh, yeah—like a light turned on in a dark room."

I noticed blood trickling from my head. Not only did I see it, but I could also feel the blood roll down and across the tip of my nose.

"Uh-oh. That can't be good." I watched the guards tether my wrists to the two whipping posts in the judgment courtyard.

All of my senses seemed functioning. If so, I would feel everything the guards thought to abuse me with. I was ready to endure any punishment they meted out. The more they tormented me, the more I would bear. I prepared myself for the pain that would follow the spilled blood. My body was slumped over, almost lifeless. They stretched my arms and bound my hands between the two pillars. This scourging would be much more intense than flogging at Herod's Palace—a much more severe sentence.

I readied my mind for every strike of the razor sharp whip, meant to tear the skin from my body. At times, the whip crackled in my ears, but at other times it seemed to whiz by. My lungs exhaled completely with each crack of the whip, then inhaled desperately, sucking the air back in.

Totally exhausted, my neck stretched forward and downward, unable to hold up my head. My eyes shut tightly with each strike as my body recoiled. My head continued to bleed, blood streamed from my arms and legs as my heart beat faster and faster, then slower and slower. Straining against the pain, my body buckled uncontrollably, dropping to my knees and then reflexively attempting to stand up again.

To my amazement, I was feeling quite strong. I felt like a conqueror. If I could manage this pain, I could overcome even the worst of it.

"I'm doing it," I said, proudly, "I'm doing it."

In the proudest moment in my entire life, I felt a soldier defending much more than my country, offering my suffering to gaining salvation for all humanity. I felt sure that this surge of energy, this high tolerance for pain came from my new commitment to obedience. Somehow, it allowed me to block the sensation of torture.

Attempting to rationalize the situation, I didn't know why I worried so much before. I had anticipated much more pain. Had my body become used to the pain? Had my nervous system just stopped sending pain messages? And then I heard Jesus' voice cry out in agony.

Something was wrong. Jesus cried out again, louder than before.

I didn't understand, but guilt consumed me. I had thought the pain was being controlled. I thought that I was controlling it.

I heard the voice of Jesus cry out again and again in anguish. His suffering caused the onlookers to turn their heads away. The sound of His cries vibrated the very stones of the courtyard. Loose topsoil trembled between the cracks. The posts that held Him upright moved

Episode Twelve

lightly; the ground beneath Him groaned. Jesus cried out again, shaking the heavens. Jesus' nervous system was working fine, and He was clearly in pain.

Jesus cried out one final time before losing consciousness. This time it seemed as if the earth quaked. The two posts gave way; Jesus and I crashed to the ground. Feeling the passion in that cry, I cried out as well, though no one heard.

Jesus lay prone and comatose. Wide-awake, I wondered how I could help. I felt miserably embarrassed. I felt pain now, though not the physical pain that Jesus felt. I felt pity, empathy, and disgrace to the ultimate degree. It hurt so badly that I wanted to die.

I would rather accept death than the feelings of shame and guilt I experienced now. How could I have been so cocky?

"Jesus did willingly bear all my pain," I said. "If I could, I would bear all of His agony, and mine."

After all, I should feel the injuries inflicted on my body. But, instead, absorbing each penetrating stripe, Jesus endured the humiliation, and bore the piercing thorns. Jesus stood in for me. I felt an echo of Jesus' suffering. Each lash of the whip caused my body to jerk, though I only felt the jolt, never the actual pain. I felt Jesus collapse to the ground, but I didn't feel the pain as my face and knees smashed into the earth.

Disgusted with myself, I longed to feel the pain now. I focused on Jesus' pain, certain that would allow me to share in it. As my body lay facedown in a pool of blood, my face turned to the side, I stared out. I noticed my trickling blood forming a pattern. It bubbled with each breath exhaled from my mouth and nose. There was something peaceful about this moment. I expected to see intermittent curdling of the blood stream, but noticed how surprisingly rhythmic it was. My breathing caused a sort of rippling effect, like a stone skipping across a shallow meadow.

There was still no pain and I grew angry all over again.

"Wait a minute," I said. "No pain?" While lying there, I started to understand.

I thought about the Old Testament and the wars that God fought for Israel. I thought about how God had hardened Pharaoh's heart in the book of Exodus. Over and over, God showed that He was in charge. He would mount up impossible odds in favor of the enemy just so Israel, as well as her enemies, would know that the God of Israel had defeated them. For me, God made sure that I understood that Jesus was victorious. No man could have endured that horrendous beating and survived, except that He was the Son of God.

"Thank you, Jesus," I said softly. "Once again, you die for me. My God has shielded me from all pain."

I still felt ashamed, guilty and remorseful, overwhelmed by my weakened emotional state.

"Not feeling the pain just makes it worse," I said. "If only I could find a way to relieve Jesus' pain."

Listening to Jesus cry out, I knew that the pain was excruciating. For a moment, I doubted that Jesus could survive any further torture. Knowing nowhere else to turn, I sought God's intervention. I asked that the beatings cease, not for me, but for His Son. I knocked on the heartstrings of Heaven. According to God's promises, my prayer was answered. The beating ended.

They dragged Jesus back to His cell, a broken shell. If Pilate's plan worked, He would certainly be released from custody.

Episode Thirteen
December 31 and 33 AD

Sitting in my cell, struggling against despair, I didn't want to think.

I didn't want to analyze my recent, agonizing experiences, which was unlike me. I did not care how they applied to the future. Depression and guilt devoured my soul, and I longed for Vanessa.

Vanessa's enthusiasm always brought out the best in me. I regretted losing touch with her. If she could see me, she would be so proud of me. She would call me her little hero again, and I would feel better. She used to tell me how great the world would be when I became a man, when I turned twenty-one.

Of course, in my mind, I heard that we would be married as soon as I turned twenty-one. I laughed about it later, but I still loved her to this day. I had spent my first few weeks in Vietnam trying to find out where she was stationed. She must be somewhere in Vietnam, but I had no luck finding her. I figured she must have gotten married and changed her name. The thought of her married to someone else left me searching to fill a blank spot in my mind. After all, I had followed her to Vietnam.

Now, on my twenty-first birthday, I was finally a man. Ironically, she had probably married someone else, and I was probably going to die without ever seeing her again.

"I would happily give my life to see her, Lord," I said, then remembered that I had gladly offered my life to save Lump's. "Lord, I guess I'm in a self-sacrificial mood right about now."

After Pilate decided that beating Jesus was enough and that He should be released, the devious elders and priests proposed another option. The priests invoked the custom allowing one prisoner to be

160

released during the Passover feast. When Pilate realized that the other prisoner was a well-known thieving murderer, he thought the matter would be settled. He assumed that the people would choose Jesus to be released, rather than a viciously brutal murderer.

Standing upon the marble pavilion, astounded, I let thoughts of Samson and how he brought the pillars down on top of the Philistines entertain me.

"That would be perfect," I said.

Positioned close to the stone-carved railing, staring at the horizon, I observed the beautiful day. The rainy season had just ended; the smell of spring surrounded us. The fragrance of blossoms filled the air. From high atop the pavilion I could see beyond the gardens, across the top of the crowd, to Golgotha, my destiny.

Golgotha made me think about the James boys from Detroit. They wrote a fancy poem after one of the evening study classes. Vietnam had Motown, and it also had the holy lyrics of Trent James and Kent James, also known as Holy Smoke. They had rhymes for everything. After every completed mission, they came up with a new poem and recited it for everyone.

After hearing my sermon on the death of Christ, they wrote a poetic synopsis. They gave me the honor of trying to come up with a title. I named it 'Victory Over Death'.

The sight of that horrid hilltop hypnotized me. How ironic that I was now the protagonist in that poem. I wished that I could recall all of those fated words summing up the entire epic of Christ's life in one neat package.

I knew that the crowd would choose Barabbas over Jesus, but watching it unfold dumbfounded me. The crowd sat so far below the platform that I wondered how they could possibly tell the difference. Barabbas looked as bad as Jesus had and not because he had been badly beaten. I wondered how they could choose an evil murderer over the Son of God. Had God hardened their hearts as He had done so many times before?

Some Christian churches teach that, during Jesus' ministry, the Jews disliked Him and that each of them, simply and without provocation, turned their backs on Him. From the time that I had spent witnessing Jesus' ministry, I knew that wasn't true. I could list evidence proving the contrary. They most certainly were provoked, since the local synagogue threatened its members with excommunication for following, promoting, or secretly meeting with Jesus. The Pharisees had total influence over the citizens, and their decisions were final.

Episode Thirteen

The initial cheers for Jesus' release were replaced with shouts of 'Crucify Him' and 'Give us Barabbas.' As I looked out over the crowd, I saw the priests, at times with their backs toward the pavilion, in groups of three, leading the cries from the people. And there was something even stranger. Observing the crowd, I couldn't tell if my vision had blurred, but the clergy seemed not only suspicious, but also non-human. They seemed almost alien. One by one, the votes changed as unholy threesomes converged on Jesus' supporters. The priests forced believers to choose death over life, a murderer over one who brought life, a thief over one who offered hope, a liar over one who preached truth.

"This is how it will be in the future," I said. "It will be unholy church leadership persuading followers of Jesus to follow the false Christ."

The prophecy unfolded; I could say nothing to influence the vote. Those who called for Barabbas's release didn't really mean it. The so-called holy men, who had conspired to murder Jesus since the beginning of His ministry, extorted their votes. What once sounded like many voices, now shouted as one voice. I knew that Satan had influenced this one voice. He had successfully infiltrated the people of Judah, the city of Jerusalem, the government, and the head of the synagogue. As per the prophecy, Satan's seed would murder the seed of Adam, right before my eyes.

Pilate pled for the life of Jesus three separate times, but the crowd still demanded that He be crucified. God used Pilate as a tool. God, through Pilate, had exposed the identity of the true enemy. It wasn't the Jewish people, but the clerics; those false teachers promenading as anointed men of God. How easily a few evil people could stir up a peaceful crowd and incite a riotous act. This was truly a war between good and evil disguised as good.

I knew, and often taught, that this was done for the benefit of those who will be here in the end as the examples of the Holy Bible continue repeating. As in the past, the children of God ignorant of the truth through no real fault of their own, had no way of knowing that they were portraying roles in the completion of the prophecy. The priests however, knew of the prophecy but had no idea that Jesus, despite all of his teachings, was the fulfiller of the promise. Their job was to teach about a coming savior who would free them, save them, and heal them. Ironically, even though they taught this very message and were undoubtedly prepared to identify the Christ upon His arrival, they totally missed it. If that were not the case, if it were not ignorance, then these religious leaders were truly vile men driven by pure evil. Simple ignorance, or evil, in either case, it was the hand of God choreographing His plan and seeing it staged to its final act. I often taught that Christians should learn from these mistakes and demand that truth about His second coming be taught. Relying solely on popular or traditional teaching will be detrimental to the salvation of many souls.

"Let His blood be on our hands," shouted the priests from below the platform. These angry people were asking to take responsibility for the killing of God's Holy Lamb.

"Be careful what you ask God for," I said. "This is the beginning of the new age to come."

I felt vengeful toward the religious extortionists and pity for the people forced to change their vote. I knew that God would judge them according to how they really felt. Yes, they should have stood against them, overcoming their threats, but they didn't know any better.

"Please have mercy on them, Father. They don't realize," I prayed from my heart. "Please, God, please forgive them, give us all another chance."

I didn't feel any pity for the priests. After all, they were murdering conspirators who might never truly be forgiven until they literally meet God face to face.

As the guards led me away to my cell, I could hear Barabbas being released.

I thought about something Vanessa taught me years ago. I had already known it, but loved listening to her talk.

"Vincent," she began as we walked home from church one day. "You heard the priest talking about how the Jews chose the sinner over the saint. Well, there's more to it then that."

"I know," said the younger me, taking her by the hand. "He was talking about how they chose Barabbas over Jesus and how the wrong man was put to death."

"That's right, but I want to let you in on a little hidden message," she said as she squeezed my hand in hers.

"You mean like finding a hidden treasure?" I asked, switching sides to walk closer to the curb.

"My, aren't you the gentleman," she complimented me, acknowledging the gesture. "Thank you."

"You're welcome," I said, reaching to hold her other hand.

"Do you want to find the treasure with me?" Vanessa asked, letting her arm swing freely with mine.

"Yes, I sure do," I replied, smiling every step of the way.

Episode Thirteen

"Finding the hidden treasure has to do with the two names and what they mean. If you know what they mean, not only can you find the treasure, but you can claim it as your very own."

Vanessa told me that, when the names are explained, a hidden message reveals the truth. By combining the circumstance of the prisoner exchange with the names, God's complete plan is explained.

"Do you understand so far?" she asked as we waited for the traffic light to change.

"Yes," I said, looking both ways for traffic. "But what do the two names mean?"

"The name Barabbas, in the Greek language means 'son of Abba' or son of the father," answered Vanessa.

"Does 'abba' mean father?" I asked.

"Yes," said Vanessa, rewarding me by pinching my ear affectionately. "Barabbas was a convicted murderer and so is Satan. In fact, Satan is the father of the first murderer. But, on that day, the children of God had a choice to make. They had to choose between the son of the devil and the Son of God, and they did, but they chose the wrong son and the wrong father."

"They chose the son of the devil, huh?" I asked, hoping to get another pinch.

"Right again, young man. You sure are full of surprises. How did you get so smart?" This time she leaned over and kissed my cheek.

I stood on the corner waiting for the light to change again, but this time in a daze, then looked around, hoping that everyone in the neighborhood saw Vanessa kissing me so I could brag about it later.

She finished by comparing the choice they made back then to the choice they would have to make in the future.

"Did we find the treasure yet?" I asked, convinced that I had all the treasure I needed as long as she was with me.

"Almost," said Vanessa. "Discovering the hidden treasure lies in understanding the example, then passing it on to those who will be here during the end times."

"In the future?" I asked. "You mean it's gonna happen again, right?"

"That's right, baby genius," said Vanessa. "In the future, there will be a choice between following the false Christ or continuing to wait for the Son of God."

Remembering that day with Vanessa, especially the kiss, always put a smile on my face. The lesson wasn't as exciting, but I did remember. If abandoned, the children of God, through provocation, deceit, and ignorance, would choose Barabbas over Jesus all over again. Vanessa emphasized that example after example shows how God's word repeated, how it will repeat in the future, and how God intended it that way for our own sake.

I remembered telling this same story, minus the part about the kiss, to the men of First Squad.

"God proves that He loves you by saying and doing the same thing again and again, so we can learn from the mistakes and, hopefully, get it right in the end when it really counts."

However, I still didn't understand the bigger picture concerning my own soul. As far as I knew, I was just having a dream before dying. A nightmare to some, to me, it was literally my dying dream. As much as I would like to stick around and continue to teach God's word the way I was trained to, it wasn't up to me. My time was up. As far as I was concerned, whatever job God wanted me to accomplish in life was over.

If Father Shelly's tale had anything to do with me, my duty would just be starting. I would wake up the next day and everything I ever studied, read about, and researched about God would mean something complete.

After so much time in Jerusalem, I felt myself being whisked away again. I wasn't surprised to find that myself at the base infirmary. I had no idea how long this last dream vision had lasted, but at least the surgery was over. It appeared that I was still alive.

I had thought that I would end up dying twice, once in Jerusalem and once in Vietnam. Now I felt certain that I would survive both ordeals.

Even though my current spiritual state seemed a mystery, I was glad that I had left Jerusalem, 33 AD.

"If I'm going to die Lord, let it be here with soldiers that know me," I said.

It was late at night and the camp was quiet, except for the infirmary. The infirmary shone like New Year's in Vietnam.

"This is definitely a birthday party. Looks like I got my birthday party after all," I said, remembering what Doc Lucas had told me after the landmine attack.

Surprisingly, I felt alive, like I was just hanging around outside and listening to Motown rhapsodies, the whole company gathered, happy about the recent news of my successful surgery. I could hear Colonel

Episode Thirteen

Harris' voice from inside the tent. He seemed pleased with my recent turn for the better.

Listening in on the colonel's conversation, I wished I could tell them everything I had seen back in the first century and how the dream was both frightening and enlightening at the same time, and how I was glad it was over.

My desires changed when I overheard the conversation between the doctor and Colonel Harris. I was in a coma and they were not sure if I would survive this part.

I inspected my body, seeing more damage than before. I noticed that bandages covered both of my hands and feet, but after looking closer, I could see that both hands, up to my forearms, had been removed during surgery. My left foot up to the heel and my right foot to above the ankle were missing as well. There were enormous wounds to my head and abdomen.

"Ah." I mourned. "No matter what happens now, my days as a soldier are over."

I wasn't sure if I even wanted to live. How was I supposed to live the rest of my life with no hands? I thought about Dino, and Lump, and how they would feel after seeing me. I thought about all those who warned, "I told you so." I thought about those skeptics who could never get enough of talking about me behind my back.

I could imagine my anger toward all of them, but thinking about my mother and how much she would just love seeing me home, alive, calmed me down. I thought about how Vanessa commented more than once that soldiers returning home deserving a hero's welcome. She would be proud; she would say that I was one of those heroes now.

I realized that, although I was dreaming, this wasn't part of the dream. This was as real as real could get. Recovering meant I would have to live the rest of my life as an overly ambitious amputee.

I didn't realize it yet, but surviving the night meant something more than just returning home to preach about the second coming of Christ in some local church. It meant more then proving that, although I was an amputee, the Lord still had plenty of work for me to do. Suddenly that sounded a lot better than dying. I would be much more than a mere example of how to overcome the hardships of an unfortunate handicap.

If this were my initiation, then there must be a lot riding on what happened to me, whether I survived or not. I was becoming aware that a supernatural element existed in my life, and that others might be concerned with my mortality as well as my potential immortality.

According to Father Shelly, there were a lot more like me. They would be waiting to see what my death meant and how—if—it would change their courses, too. If I survived the night, it meant joining the ranks of the other twenty-four hundred Immortal Keepers. My victory over death wouldn't matter if I were missing a few body parts. I would join them in their critical task of gathering, teaching, and preparing God's elect for their end time battle with the false Christ.

I had no way of knowing, but all the twenty-four hundred favored my death. In a way that only made sense to them, they saw my death as a win-win for the whole realm, including me.

While my body remained in the recovery tent, my emotions went elsewhere. My physical body just lay there, attached to every modern medical miracle available in Vietnam, struggling to stay alive.

My mind went blank, dark, and thoughtless. I wanted to conjure up thoughts about the good times with my friends and family, but couldn't. I tried to think back to playing hockey with the Wilsons and how much I loved catching the puck in my glove, but I couldn't focus on that either. Wherever this part of the dream was supposed to take me, it failed miserably. I wasn't going anywhere.

I felt another presence in the infirmary. In the corner farthest from the front entrance, a thick white cloud hovered, moving slowly toward me. It passed over each bunk, but stopped when it reached my bunk. I watched as it moved up my bunk toward me, getting darker as it got closer. I wondered if the now pitch-black cloud was death coming to swallow me up.

I took my eyes off what seemed like a dark black hole approaching me and looked back at my body lying on the bed. I wondered if I would ever see myself again. If this cloud took my soul, would everyone, inside and outside of the infirmary realize it before I did? Would the monitors sound off and alert the whole camp that I was dead?

Is that how I find out that I'm dead? I thought, Or have I died, but not been officially declared dead yet?

I tried being brave. I tried to be positive. If death did take me, I was sure that, when I woke, God would be present to greet me.

As death approached, blind darkness engulfed me, rendering me unable to speak or hear anything. My emotions had been displaced by numbness, absent all ingredients necessary for sustaining hope. I could no longer find myself. For the first time since the attack, I was elsewhere and nowhere at the same time. In this place I couldn't even find Jesus.

Episode Fourteen

December 31 and 33 AD

"Ah… I wish you were awake right now," whispered my past as I tried to regain my mental balance, thinking I would see her. The black funnel cloud spit me so far, and so ferociously, from its guts that it felt like I had been swallowed and then regurgitated, leaving my head feeling like the inside of a shaken maraca.

Back in Jerusalem, I connected with my surroundings. No matter the tragedy, anywhere other than that emotional void was a good place to be. I knew that bliss awaited the resurrected soul; I refused to believe that what I experienced related to the path to eternal happiness.

"That was something else," I said, sure of myself. "Whatever that was, or wherever it took me, had nothing to do with God or heaven."

I felt sure that my brief out-of body experience had taken me to a private place where my comatose mind existed after surgery. I gave thanks that I wasn't experiencing a continual dream loop, because I never wanted to feel that emptiness again. Each time I returned to 33 AD, my dream moved forward, giving me a slim hope for a happy ending. Now, back in Jerusalem, I believed that this dream was about to end, and it would end once and for all.

The trial was finished; Pilate had washed his hands. He would keep the peace and, if keeping the peace meant sending an innocent man to death, then he would.

"You're a sellout, too," I said with contempt, thinking back to Herod.

Thoughts of the black funnel cloud haunted me, but, in a way, I wished it were still with me. It would offer an escape from the torture waiting for me.

A Dream Before Dying

I listened, thinking I heard what sounded like church bells ring nine times. I didn't think that they had church bells in the first century. Did I hear them or just imagine that I did? It reminded me of the bells at my old church in Detroit, and the way they rang each hour of the day to remind people of the time. The ringing bells always seemed to comfort me; no matter how bad things were, the bells let me know that it would be over soon. They made me feel like home truly was a sweet home.

Now the rings sounded more like haunting tolls, weak and distorted.

"Nine o'clock in the morning, it's the third hour," I said, counting the numbers the way I always did, beginning with six in the morning. "Whatever happens from this point forward will all be over by the ninth hour."

I found myself on my knees. My body had fallen to the ground while climbing up a sharply inclined path. Before falling, I remembered looking at the trail that lead to the base of Golgotha while I stood on the balcony with Barabbas. It seemed much longer and steeper now, as my body struggled to take each step, only to fall again.

"Lord, I wish I could help you this time," I said, knowing that it was Jesus who had to make that trek up the steep, cobbled path.

Although I knew that it was Jesus carrying the cross, the unforgiving weight cut deeply into my shoulder blades, neck and back. I acknowledged that it was Jesus' strength alone that could bear such a burden.

Both of my hands had been tied to a partially flattened log, wider then my arm length, making it impossible to balance. I stumbled and fell every other step. While trying to avoid falling onto my face and head, my body instinctively turned toward the right side of the humongous beam. Sometimes my knees would help break the fall. I had fallen on my head a few times already, then used my forehead and knees to stand up again. The parading guardsmen, never helping to prevent my falls, would only help stand me back onto my feet. Their menacing presence prevented the sympathetic from lending a helping hand.

Extremely top heavy, the weight of the beam and the pressure on my lower back kept me bent over so far that I couldn't see anyone in the crowd. If someone could have looked down from above, it would have looked like some sort of creature, crawling, similar to a worm inching its way up a hill.

The road to Golgotha twisted upward, filled with smooth stones, chiseled rock, and gravel. Although the hill was high enough to be visible within the city walls, curious bystanders still lined the road.

Episode Fourteen

As my body stood up again, I saw that the path narrowed as I approached the base of the hill. The crowd of people made it impossible to crawl any further. Unable to catch myself, I fell flat onto my face with the full force of my dead weight. My mind focused completely, but, with my body unable to move, I wasn't sure if I was unconscious or if the fall had actually killed me.

"I wish these people would get out of my way," I said, helpless and furious.

I couldn't believe that some people were actually teasing Jesus and asking why He couldn't get up. "I thought you were the Son of God!" they scoffed. "Why can't you get up?"

As I lay there, I could see others weeping for Him. I hoped to see someone I knew. I hoped someone would be there, as the squad had been there earlier. But I recognized no one.

"I guess it's up to me, now. I'm completely alone. Stop feeling sorry for yourself," I argued.

I still had absolutely no control over any of my body. After falling and taking that brief second's rest, nothing more than an attempt to inhale once, my body found its way back to its feet. The tears of the sympathetic strengthened me. I knew that Jesus was the one who had been encouraged. The weight of the cross on my back prevented me from standing erect enough to actually see their faces, but I heard their weeping. On my feet again, my body stopped for a moment.

"Is Jesus going to speak?" I asked thinking that it would be better to conserve His energy.

"Do not weep for me," said the voice of Jesus, "weep for yourselves and for your children. For the time will come when they will say, blessed are the barren women, the wombs that never bore and the breasts that never nursed! Then they will say to the mountain fall on us! And to the hills, cover us! For if men do these things when the tree is green what will happen when it is dry?"

I remembered reading those words in Vietnam the Sunday before the mission began. One of the female nurses from the infirmary had asked why it was a blessing to be barren. I let my mind dwell on our conversation; it comforted me, especially now.

"That's a great question," I said to the nurse, "and I'm glad you asked it, since you're one of the few here who can actually bear children." The men of First Squad snickered; I failed to see the humor.

Speaking to the nurse, I said, "Instead of Jesus feeling sorry for Himself, He felt compassion for us and continued to teach, warning us about the enemy. On the way to being put to death, Jesus could have asked for a number of things, from a small drink of water to the whole power of heaven. He could have had a human moment, or even a moment of weakness, as they say He had in the garden of Gethsemane. Instead, He chose to utter this warning, prophesying a reminder to the women surrounding Him."

"It sounds like Jesus is making about three claims in that statement," said Sergeant Belinda Davenport as she read over the verse again.

"You're probably right," I said, "But when He said it is just as important as what He said."

"When He said it?" the nurse asked.

"Yes," I said. "When He says it proves again that God loves us, and how much. As much as Christ was suffering, He still taught us something."

"When you say us, do you mean us, as in the future?"

"Exactly. And in fact, just about every lesson in the Holy Bible is directed toward those who will be here in the end. The women that He addressed may or may not have understood the message. They may have found a way to make sense of it later, but ultimately it has to do with His return to earth."

"But how would a regular person like me know that Jesus was referring to the future?" the nurse asked.

"That's just it," I said, "It's important to have a teacher who understands how to pull all of God's mysteries together so they make sense. Combining this verse with a verse from the book of Matthew, where Jesus says 'cursed are those who are with child,' a student of God's word can begin to see the bigger, more spiritually complete picture."

"So…" Belinda turned to Matthew, Chapter 24. "Jesus says in one verse that it's a blessing to be barren and in another verse He says it's a curse to be pregnant? But that can't be true; it's never a curse to be pregnant."

"Are you sure?" I asked, raising my eyebrows. "Can you think of any instance where being pregnant might not seem so much like a gift from God?"

"Um, rape," she said. "Maybe if you were raped, that might feel like a curse, maybe."

"That's good, yes. Now think spiritually, what if you were spiritually raped?"

Episode Fourteen

"I'm not sure what that would be like," she said, adjusting the soft cap on her head. "Is there such a thing?"

I explained that spiritual rape would occur among those who are deceived during the end times, prior to His second coming. These victims lose their spiritual virginity by worshiping the false Christ, and are found doing so when the true Christ returns. These two statements seemed to say separate things, but were exactly alike.

I summed it up by combining both statements.

"Jesus merely said blessed are the barren, and woe to those who are with child when He returns to earth for His bride."

"But it doesn't say when He comes back, here," said Belinda as she read the verse again.

"No, you're right," I said, pointing to the third verse, "It doesn't say it there. You have to read the chapter from the beginning to know what it is about. At the beginning, Jesus tells His disciples all the events that will precede His return to earth and this is part of it."

I asked her if she could see the spiritual implication and how it applies to the end times?

"Keeping the context of the chapter topic, can you understand how Christ uses the comparison of a woman being physically pregnant, to being spiritually pregnant by the Anti-Christ?"

"Yes, I understand it when you say it that way," said the sergeant. "But isn't He just referring to women, because men can't become pregnant?"

"That's just it," I said, smiling. That question proved that she was really listening. "It's for that reason that this statement encompasses all of God's children. Jesus is talking to His bride, the church—we—are that bride."

I noted that everyone is included in this example, regardless of sex, and that's what assures us that it points to a spiritual pregnancy and not a physical one. After speaking on this subject many times, during my own ministry, and listening to other opinions, I realized that some people had difficulty looking beyond the bodily aspect. Some people could only hear a description of how difficult a pregnancy would be during the so-called tribulation of Satan.

I explained that, without referring to the complete plan of God, the spiritual application of these words, as it applies to Jesus' second coming, would remain a mystery.

Belinda seemed to understand; she asked another good question. "But Jesus finished the verse saying that they would pray for the hills to cover them and the mountains to fall on them. What does that mean?"

"Jesus referred to the prophecy of Isaiah and the shame that each person will feel when they discover that they have been spiritually raped. The guilt will be overwhelming, so emotionally devastating that those found guilty of being spiritually defiled, of being with child, will pray for their own deaths."

"I think I get it," she said.

But I didn't think she was quite there yet.

"Think about this simply," I said. "What would happen if you were caught in an avalanche or an earthquake and a hill or mountain fell on top of you?"

"Um, I would probably die, right?" she answered.

"That's right," I said. "In essence, the Son of God is saying, the emotional pain people will experience when they are discovered with the false Christ will be so great that they would rather be dead.

"Sounds like I don't want to be caught dead with Satan," she said as everyone laughed.

I summed it up with saying that Jesus used an image, like pregnancy, as a tool so we can understand the implication of following the false Christ. The Apostle Paul used the same analogy when he told followers that he wanted to present them as virgins. He referred to them as spiritual virgins, spiritually undefiled by Satan. Jesus, suffering beyond anyone's imagination, still taught the word of God in the presence of His enemies, in the ears of the sympathetic, and in such a way that shows how much love God has for His children. For Jesus to compare the compassion of His second coming to a mother with child was awe-inspiring.

———————————

As my body approached the base of Golgotha I felt a mixture of sadness and anger at the same time. If the children of God could stand by idly ignorant and watch the execution of the Tree of Life, then what would prevent their souls from being stolen by the Tree of the Knowledge of Good and Evil in the end times? If they didn't know Jesus when He was here during His first advent, how will they know Him in the end, especially if they aren't taught to understand the hidden messages concerning His return to earth?

I felt my body start to fall head first, but again was unable to twist to my right. Too exhausted to try and break the fall, the front of my body would surely crash into the pavement again.

Episode Fourteen

Just as my eyes shut, my battered body was held frozen. The guards had instructed someone to intervene, ordering him to prevent me from falling, to catch me as I fell. They barked at him to release my body once I was on my way up the hill again. He disobeyed.

Lunging forward, the man positioned himself under me and prevented me from falling. This hero untied my arms and rested the beam, which once loomed so large, but now appeared small in his enormous hands, across his left shoulder. With the soldiers shouting for him to stop, this giant of a man tucked my beaten body under his right arm, carrying me toward the foot of the hill.

With my eyes shut, I felt a very heavy hand come down my back from behind as the weight of the cross lifted from my shoulders.

"Thank you, Lord," I said, "What just happened?" I tried to see what was going on.

I wanted to thank the person, but could not. My head and arms dangled below him. I felt like a rag doll might look when carried in the jaws of a ferocious pit bull. Yet there was nothing ferocious about this person helping to carry my body up the pathway. As I looked toward the ground, something felt familiar about this savior. I had forgotten that someone helped carry the cross that day, but now I remembered reading of the African that helped Jesus.

"This must be Simon," I said, still unable to look up.

I experienced déjà vu; there was something familiar about the way he came to my rescue. The huge man held my body parallel to the ground, walking effortlessly. Lump. Lump had carried me during a training exercise when we were in Ranger school. Buddy teams had to take turns extracting each other's wounded body, while carrying both soldiers' equipment. Lump carried me like I weighed nothing, but, when it was my turn, I could only drag Lump's body to safety.

I felt sure that Lump carried me now. I could only see the stranger from the knees down, but I felt sure the legs belonged to Lump. I was absolutely sure I had seen those feet before. Lump had a very identifiable mark on his right foot. As a child he had a sort of cyst that sat on top of the skin leaving a large mark when he was older, discoloring the skin forever. Lump's very memorable birthmark, ironically, resembled the continent of Africa.

"Somehow I knew you'd be here. Lump, is that you?" I asked.

"Here let me help you, my friend," said the stranger, adjusting my body under his right arm.

"Thank you, my friend," I said.

Although the stranger could not hear me speaking, we communicated beyond words. I felt at home again, safe and protected from danger. I was with my best friend and everything was as it should be.

I remembered our boyhood plan for our military service. "You be the chaplain, and then put in a request for me to be the chaplain's assistant," said Lump.

He put every ounce of power and strength into making it to the hill and protecting me. Every time the guards approached, he would swing the giant tree limb as if swatting at an annoying bug. The board sliced through the air overhead, as if it were a rotary blade. Looking toward the ground, I could see the shadow of the wooden plank swung around him. Looking at the silhouette, I also caught a glimpse of the defiant bystander helping me. If my squad members had been there with me, maybe Lump was part of the dream too.

The stranger carried me as far as he could before a dozen soldiers finally wrestled him to the ground. As the guards forced us both down, I began to think that feeling at home wasn't so great after all. It felt like the Detroit police were beating Lump all over again. We both lay on the ground, my head turned away, preventing me from getting a look at him. I could hear the soldiers struggling to restrain Lump as he tried to stand. When he did finally get to his feet, he fled down the ridge, disappearing into the crowd.

"Thank you my friend, I'm glad you got away this time," I said, praying silently for him.

I understood the lesson involving the African. I often taught that, one day, all nations of people would come to know the Son of God and, like Simon, may end up putting their very lives on the line to spread the Gospel of Jesus Christ.

Earlier, from the balcony, I noticed how the hill was shaped like a skull. Now, too close to see the shape of the hill, I could see that its shape came from mounds of earth soaked in decades of blood, then hardened. An eerie sensation haunted the base of the hill, which seemed to spiritually consume me, as if it fed on me.

This is certainly the hill of death, I thought.

The cursed hill grew no grass, showed no signs of plant life. As far as I could tell, there was no life to speak of at all. Even the insects knew enough to stay away. No annoying bugs crawled or flew. Nature had long abandoned this land. On this mountain of darkness built up by layers and layers of death, the seasons never seemed to change. No

Episode Fourteen

matter the season within the gates of Jerusalem, Golgotha existed in a perpetual season of death with sorrow, bereavement, and grief always blooming. This hill, with evil as its fertilizer, didn't need water or sunlight. It hungered for souls and every heaping serving fueled its hunger.

As the eerie feeling took over, my eyes filled with tears. My limp body, with no strength left to resist, poured its sorrow out like an overflowing pitcher. Every sorrowful moment of my life flashed before my eyes.

I lay on the ground in a fetal position as the guards, preoccupied with preparing for the crucifixion, kicked dirt on me. I thought about my dad dying in Vietnam and how my dog was run over by a car. I thought about how I embarrassed the priest in church that day and how wrong it was for me to do that. I thought about the time I was watching Dino and he chased a ball into the street, almost getting hit by a car. I regretted losing contact with Vanessa and wondered why I came all this way to Vietnam for what seemed like nothing now. I did the math in my head again, imagining her at thirty-one and me at twenty-one. I thought about how much I loved my mother; how I would miss her most of all. She wouldn't want her son to go through this. I wondered what it would be like for her when the U.S. Army soldiers showed up to her door this time. Would it be worse? Was she already prepared? What would she tell Dino?

As far as the Roman soldiers were concerned, I was a common criminal and they treated me that way. Just before they lifted me and placed me onto the monstrous crucifix lying prone next to my body, I was forced to compare it to the shrapnel removed from my skull, which would ultimately take my life.

It was huge, at least ten times larger than the post I carried to the foot of the hill. Lying on my back, I noticed that two beams made up this new frame, the vertical beam eighteen feet long, and the horizontal beam ten feet long. About nine inches thick, both pieces still had bark on the sides. The vertical piece had a very small platform located about ten feet from the bottom; about three feet from the top was a notch, to hold the horizontal piece. Both of its massive pieces formed the letter T. Standing alone, it resembled a ghastly beast, driven by pure evil. Death was its only purpose.

In my mind, I heard my own eulogy passing before me, but I still hoped for some chance to survive.

"This is where Jesus will die, and I'm still here," I said, believing that God would pull me out before the end.

As my head turned left and right, I watched the Roman guards tie my forearms and ankles securely to the ends of the beam.

Still lying on my back, looking skyward, my eyes rested upon the man who would ultimately inflict the most pain. Everyone knew him as the local blacksmith, but, today, his identity was hidden. Through the hooded mask, I could see his apologetic eyes showed signs of pity.

"He doesn't want to be here, either," I said.

Looking into the blacksmith's repentant eyes, I was sure I heard, "Hold perfectly still so I can make this as painless as possible."

I felt grateful.

From his cart, the blacksmith removed two metal collars used to hold objects in place. Each collar came in two parts and with dangling leather straps. The two halves, combined, would hold my wrist. The soldiers showed no mercy as they tugged and snatched the straps, wrapping them around my wrists and the beam. With both wrists secured, it was time for the blacksmith to do his part. The blacksmith seemed to be stalling.

"Is he praying?" I wondered. "Yes, he is praying. He's probably praying for a way out of here too."

Haunted by my own past again, I heard eleven church bells tolling in my head, bells that would ring in my doom. It was the fifth hour.

"The fifth hour," I said.

I remembered that, biblically, the number five meant God's grace. I believed in my heart that the five church bells were a sign that, by the grace of God, I would escape this dream holding me captive, hopefully before the first spike. As the final three bells tolled, the infuriated soldiers demanded the blacksmith to carry on with his duty.

I realized that, since arriving at the bottom of the hill, I had not felt the presence of Jesus. I wondered why. He had not attempted to speak and I felt none of the physical symptoms I associated with the words or deeds of Christ. Jesus seemed unconscious, though my head moved from time to time, allowing me to observe the action.

While the giant cross lay on the ground, two of the guards positioned themselves, holding the collar in place. The guards sat on the ground, one above and one below the horizontal beam, bracing their feet against it and pulling the straps as tightly as possible. I could see the guard positioned below and to my left. I watched him intently as each pulled equally from both ends, keeping the hole aligned so the spike could not miss. A third guardsman held my extended left hand securely to the beam.

The commander of the guards, the only one standing, shouted to the blacksmith to hurry.

Episode Fourteen

My heart must have beat faster than normal, as I watched the blacksmith turn from his cart, inspect their alignment, and place a ten-inch spike into the top of the collar hole. The spike held its place, fitting snuggly and making an easy target. The blacksmith produced a large flat-headed mallet with a six-foot–long wooden handle. Holding the mallet like a posthole digger, he prepared, not to swing the mallet, but to plunge it down on the spike from above.

The blacksmith, in the role of executioner, met my eyes once again, as if to make sure I was ready, then clasped his gloved hands near the top of the handle. Trying not to look at me again, he focused on the head of the spike protruding from the collar. He raised the mallet handle to eye level and held still long enough to inhale, then hold his breath. His upper back and shoulders swelled as he swiftly exhaled, plunging the mallet downward and driving the spike head flush with the top of the collar.

The blood from my wrist spewed upward through the hole in the collar, and sideways out of both ends. To me, it appeared to be a volcano erupting. I watched it splatter the guardsman holding my hand in place.

That was the first strike of a two-strike procedure. Three strikes meant something had gone terribly wrong. As horrendous as it was, I gave thanks that the blacksmith was extremely good at his job.

While the blacksmith drew another breath, the guardsmen released and removed the blood-drenched collar from my wrist. I could see the metal spike protruding above my wrist, just where the base of the hand and wrist connected. The blacksmith hurriedly delivered the second strike, completing that task. The two strikes were amazingly quick, so fast that they appeared to be one. The spike went through my wrist, the horizontal beam and nearly into the ground.

As the guardsmen released the ropes tied around my left forearm, my mouth immediately filled with saliva as Jesus cried out in pain.

"Father," I heard Jesus cry out at the end of the second strike.

I had felt neither strike, but, ironically, was in a lot of pain as well. "He saved me," I said. "I'm the one that should be suffering, not Jesus. He saved me, a wretch like me."

As Jesus absorbed the actual pain from the strike, I felt a spasm, like a jolt through my body. I also felt excruciating pain from the sound of Jesus' voice. Unlike any of the other discomforts I felt during the dreams, this felt more like an earthquake and explosion combined. Jesus' voice reached heaven and the effect, though mostly emotional, was inexpressibly painful.

My head rolled to the right as Jesus seemed to lose consciousness again. I didn't know where Jesus was when I couldn't feel Him near. I guessed that the human body would only take so much before protecting itself as well as it can. Great physical pain causes the body to react involuntarily.

The guardsmen repeated the same procedure with the right arm, but, this time, the voice of Christ did not cry out. Both wrists were fastened to the crucifix. Only the nailing of my feet remained.

My head was still rolled to the right, with only my left eye open. The blood from the thorns on my head had spilled into my right eye, completely shutting it. Using my one eye, I tried to witness the guards below me, positioned at my feet. One of them sat on my legs, blocking what little view I had. I could, however, see the blacksmith once again preparing to thrust deeply.

I remembered God's prophecy from Genesis, Chapter 3, "And he shall crush His heels."

"This is it," I said, "the first and final prophecy combined." I took solace in remembering that Satan's head will be crushed in the end--

"Father," Jesus cried out again involuntarily.

I felt Jesus' pain strongly; my body was still very much alive and Jesus was certainly with me. Jesus was still the buffer and, when He was needed, He was there for me.

The blacksmith drove a fifteen-inch spike through the top and heel of my right foot, as well as through the top and heel of my left foot. The second strike drove the spike through the platform and into the vertical beam.

My body convulsed violently. Jesus was in control of my body, but, after the severe pain from the last spike, I wasn't sure if my body had completely expired, or if the convulsions meant that I was still alive.

I focused on trying to feel for a heartbeat. I tried listening to my body. I couldn't even determine if my lungs were still inhaling and exhaling. I reckoned that each spike driven into my body caused such severe pain that Jesus would be shocked into momentary consciousness, then sudden unconsciousness, practically at the same time.

Although I couldn't feel the actual pain to my body, the sorrow beating through my heart made up for it. Feeling the involuntary reactions as a result from each torment I remembered His words. Now, I prayed for the hills to fall on me. Dying would be better then watching the Son of God go through this for me.

"Lord, why are you showing me all of this?" I asked. "Why are you tormenting me this way? What have I done in my life that was so bad? Didn't I feed the hungry? Didn't I visit the sick? Haven't I hungered for knowledge and understanding? Have I not taught enough? Why must I watch your Son suffer this way? Did I miss something? Who do you think I am? Am I your enemy? I don't think I deserve this punishment. I thought you loved me."

Was I becoming delusional again? Father Shelly's stories said that this dream was a reward for all my days of service on earth. Why did I refuse to accept that, leaving me dangerously close to blaming God for causing my suffering? Instead of remembering how God feels for servants that suffer for His sake, I asked why I had to suffer. Instead of viewing this dream as a reward, I saw it as a punishment.

I had no way to know that all Immortal Keepers experience these same feelings during their night of initiation. I had plenty of questions for God and, as with all of God's Immortal Keepers, my questions would be answered the morning after. However, the fragile stability of the Immortals lay in jeopardy. For the first time since the year 33 AD, one of God's Immortal Keepers might not awaken the morning after. The completion of my initiation, transformation, and my very life hung in the balance.

Episode Fifteen
December 31 and 33 AD

While lying on my back, brutally tortured, my only sign of comfort came from the person injuring me. I couldn't see the crowd of people now, though I could hear them. I sensed some civility from the spectators and, from the sounds of their voices, I could tell that there was something unexpected about Jesus' execution. Completely dumbfounded, they still knew what came next and waited in anticipation.

I watched as the blacksmith and the guardsmen positioned one of the carts to carry my body to the top of the hill. The large crucifix needed two carts. With my head lying toward the left side of my body, I could see the blacksmith readying the team of mules to pull the lead cart up the winding pathway. The guardsmen then positioned a second cart to carry the tail end of the crucifix. Four of the guards arranged themselves to carry my body and the crucifix, parallel to the ground but high enough to load me onto the front cart.

I could tell by the way the guards formed up that they were about to move out. It reminded me of a military funeral procession. As my head turned toward the right side, I saw the captain of the guards walk past me. The blacksmith seemed to be waiting for him to take the lead. From what I could tell, there were two guards in the rear, two guards on both sides of the cart, the blacksmith at the front driving the four-mule team, and the captain walking in front of the whole formation.

"Stand back," shouted the rear guards to the bystanders as they continued marshalling.

Episode Fifteen

"Move out," commanded the captain of the guards.

It reminded me of when I was younger. Vanessa and I watched the nightly news together, counting the number of flag draped coffins returning from Vietnam. I thought about the funeral procession for President John F. Kennedy and how honorable it was. For a moment, I thought that this had the same sense of honor. Then the lack of pomp and circumstance reminded me that dying on the cross was shameful. There was nothing honorable about dying this way.

It would be different for the Son of God. He would make it more than honorable. It would be glorious, victorious even. It would bring salvation to the world. I tried to focus on that.

I wanted to thank God for this experience; but still emotionally battered by the abuse that Christ had to endure for me, I felt the shame and guilt that any convicted criminal would feel while being crucified. While I wasn't guilty of any crime worthy of such an ignominious death, I would rather die than to hear Jesus' anguished cries.

"Yaw" said the blacksmith as the procession moved out. I readied myself for what I expected to be a very time consuming journey.

While ascending to the hilltop, I noticed there had been no words, no deep sighs, and no signs of life from my body. However I could hear the shoes of each mule trudging against the pavement.

"What could be going through the mind of Christ during this time?" I wondered.

I figured that God would soon offer His only begotten Son as the Passover Lamb and Savior of the world. Initiation or not, no one could share that spotlight with Jesus. I was convinced that my role in this saga would come to an end sooner rather than later.

"God has to send me back before it's too late. There's just no way I can be...I'm a wretched sinner...there's just no way."

I felt a moment of fleeting comfort as we arrived at the top of the hill without incident. "That wasn't much of a trek at all," I said.

My eyes had been closed during the march up the hill. My left eye seemed to be forcing its way open, while my right eye, open as wide as it would go, was swollen into a bloodied slit in my face. My eyes had become so hard and crusted that they no longer blinked when blood dripped in them. My eyes remained open, but there were no other physical signs that my body was still alive. As far as I could tell, my body could have died with both eyes remaining partially open.

Attempting to determine if I was alive or dead, I tried to sense everything that was going on around me. I could hear the soldiers working diligently to erect the cross and decided to pay as close attention as possible, given what my body would allow.

Assisted by the guards, the blacksmith set up a frame that attached to the back of the front cart. Two slots, one on each side, held sixteen-foot tall wooden columns, supporting a horizontal wooden roll beam. Guardsmen positioned two twelve-foot ladders on each side of the cart, while others rolled the second cart away. The captain inspected the four-foot hole that would hold the crucifix for any debris that would prevent the crucifix from seating properly.

"This must be the gateway to hell," I said, thinking of the climatic scene yet to come.

With one way in and no way out, the archway on the cart appeared to be the doorway to another dimension, just as enormous and frightening as the crucifix. I figured that it would be used somehow to help fix the crucifix in its place.

Focusing on the overhead beam, I watched as it seemed to fall slowly toward me, coming closer and closer. Then I realized that the top end of the cross, with me attached to it, was being lifted higher. The hellish doorway wasn't coming toward me, I was heading closer to it.

One of the guards had thrown a rope over the top of the beam, raising the cart bed and the crucifix, like a truck dumping its contents onto a hill. As the bottom end of the crucifix was carefully lined up with the deep hole in the ground, the blacksmith adjusted the mule team accordingly. When the guards in front of the beam pulled the rope towards them, the front end of the cart bed rose higher. The two guards guided the crucifix upward from the sides of the cart bed while the two remaining guards guided the bottom edge of the vertical end into the ground.

The towering structure seated itself with a percussion so forceful that it seemed to sway the hill's top.

My body shook violently, then feeling as if it was about to take an eighteen-foot plunge to the ground, jolted forward over my feet and knees. As my body collapsed under me, both of my shoulders immediately pulled out of joint.

I spat a mouth full of blood as the voice of Jesus cried out loudly, "Father."

Hearing the voice of Jesus cry out in excruciating pain caused a thundering in my brain. In my mind, I continued to say no, but my body involuntarily complied with my Savior's pain. Jesus' cries for His Father triggered an emotional outpouring in me; I couldn't stop weeping.

Episode Fifteen

"God, help me," I cried, "help us."

"Why, Lord, why did Jesus have to go through so much? How could you have asked Him to suffer through this? How could you stand by and watch? What kind of father would allow this to happen to his son?"

During my ministry, whenever students would ask these very same questions I would always have plenty of answers for them. But now none of those answers made any sense. It wasn't just a Bible story anymore, and there seemed to be no plausible answers.

I begged, "I'm sorry, Father. Please, please forgive me for my sins."

The crucifix was so large that it swayed, creaking and groaning audibly. I felt like I was falling whenever the cross swayed. The guards worked quickly as they freed the cross from the equipment used to raise it. I was able to see the blacksmith as he waited. He prayed, seeming to ask God to forgive him for the part he was forced to play in this treachery. He did not take his equipment far; he would be needed again to remove the remains from the top of the hill.

I watched as hundreds of people gathered in a half-moon shape around me. I estimated that my feet were nailed at least six feet above the ground, putting my head close to twelve feet high.

As my chest and stomach hung past my knees, I felt signs that my body was still alive. The initial shock from the cross plunging into the ground caused my compressed lungs to suck air hysterically, while my chest, stomach, and neck strained violently. I felt like my body wasn't breathing, then remembered that, in crucifixions, suffocation was the official cause of death. Eventually my body would become accustomed to less air, until it finally expired from exhaustion, lack of circulation, and oxygen. Death on the cross was like one never-ending asthma attack.

I tried to calm my body down, but my oxygen-starved brain propelled my thoughts back home to Detroit. Once again, I imagined the chiming of the church bells. The sixth hour rang in as I counted; the church bell tolled twelve times. With each bell my body convulsed as it fought for air.

I wondered if I would be here until the ninth hour. What would happen to me once Jesus died? Where would I go then? Would I be able to return to my own life?

I watched as the crowd made way for the high priest and the rest of the clergy. They seemed dissatisfied about something. I remembered that they complained about the sign above Jesus' head. Supposed to mock Jesus' claim to being the king of the Jews, to their dismay, it read that He was the king of Israel. Some of them complained to the guards, while another priest mocked Jesus.

"He said that He was the Son of God; well let's see Him prove it then."

One of the others said, "He healed others, why doesn't He heal himself? Come down from the cross, Son of God."

I remembered that Jesus prophesied that they would say this about Him. In the book of Luke He said; "Ye will surely say unto me this proverb, Physician, heal thyself: whatsoever we have heard done in Capernaum, do also here in thy country".

I taught that, for most people, if Jesus had come down from the cross then, it might have been proof enough that He was God's son. They should not have needed proof at all. The children of God should have simply been taught the truth about Christ and the testament of His first advent. They should have known by the works that He did and the words that He spoke that He was the Son of God.

I knew that this would also be true in the future. People will be fooled by the seemingly miraculous works of the false Christ and convinced that he is the true one. I used to teach this with a passion, but now, as my body hung so desperately ill from the cross, everything I ever learned or understood about the first and second comings of Christ seemed futile. When the time of persecution was upon me, I didn't care about the future. I didn't care about false teachings or true teachings. I only cared about my next breath. I just wanted to use my arms and legs again. I thought about how people take the simplest things for granted and how normal, effortless, everyday tasks were now impossible. I couldn't do something as simple as wipe the blood from my eyes. I couldn't take medicine to stop the pounding in my head. I felt exposed as hundreds of people stared at me, barely clothed. I just wanted to go home or to wake up. I would accept anything if it meant coming down from the cross.

I felt my body pushing upward as it attempted to stand. My feet had found a way to balance my body despite the spike driving into them. I felt my lower back edging its way up the vertical column of the cross. My body would be able to breathe easier for a few minutes — until all energy escaped me and I collapsed to the hanging position again.

For the first time I was able to look around me. I realized that I was not suffering alone. I wasn't the only condemned criminal being put to death. I saw two men, one to the left and one to the right. "Yes," I recalled, although my memories were beginning to fade, "there were two others crucified with Christ that day."

"I don't believe this! No, I can't believe this. How can this be happening? This is exactly the way it's described in the Holy Bible."

Episode Fifteen

I noticed something familiar about the man on my left and as my head turned I definitely recognized the man at my right as the surgeon who operated on me in Saigon. It was true; I had seen them both in the O.R.

"Those are the two surgeons who tried to save my life," I said. "Well, if they are here with me, then I must be dead already."

I wanted to apologize to them, but couldn't utter a word. I regretted that they had been forced into my dream, and hoped it wasn't as real for them as it was for me.

Then I remembered that one of them had been very sarcastic during the surgery.

"It was cruel of him to joke about me like that," I said, "but I wouldn't wish this nightmare on my worst enemy."

The other surgeon had been compassionate and sincere. I wanted to thank him for doing his best. My throat began to gurgle. More blood spat from my mouth as I overheard the two men yelling back and forth to each other about the plight of Jesus.

"Today, you will be with me in paradise," said the voice of Jesus, struggling for air.

I loved those compassionate words of Christ. As far as I was concerned, it proved that, upon dying, a person is immediately with the Father in heaven, and not stuck in some hole in the ground waiting for the return of Christ. I found it unfortunate that so many Christians argued this point when Jesus specifically said, albeit without any explanation, that their souls would enter heaven that day after death. Although Christ spent time with His disciples after His resurrection, His soul had to go somewhere after His final breath was taken. I hoped the same would happen with me when I exhaled for the last time.

As far as I could tell, their wrists were only tied to their crosses. Realizing that they had not been nailed to the crosses, I understood what all the commotion had been about earlier, at the bottom of the hill. The priests had demanded the ultimate punishment for Christ.

In my head, I once again heard the distorted, frightening sound of the bell as it tolled only one time. It was one o'clock in the afternoon, the seventh hour of the day. I knew that there wasn't much time left and that, if God were going to save me, He would have to do it soon.

"Two more hours and it will all be over," I said, hoping that God was listening.

My body could not stand erect anymore. It collapsed again over my knees, ripping and tearing through the holes in my wrists and feet.

"Ah!" cried the suffering voice of Jesus, "My God, my God why have you forsaken me? Why art thou so far from helping me, and from the words of my roaring?"

I had found myself longing to hear those words. They were finally spoken as my body gave way to their passion. For years, I taught that Jesus quoted the complete Psalm 22 while dying on the cross. God proved again how much He loved us. The Holy Bible doesn't record Jesus reciting the whole psalm, but referencing it. That alone is a lesson for followers of Christ. I would tell my students that he who has ears, let him hear. Jesus wanted everyone to know that He was fulfilling that prophecy while dying on the cross. That message was directed to God's elect.

Traditionally, some churches taught that Jesus was abandoned while He was dying on the cross, that he had become sin and so God had to forsake Him on the cross. I would gently explain how the verses meant that Jesus became the sin offering, not the sin, and how it was impossible to become the Passover Lamb and be a sinner. I explained that God would never leave nor forsake anyone who remained faithfully obedient, and that Jesus' obedience persisted unto death. I would clarify that it was impossible to forsake His Son, when, technically, His Son was God with us. He and the Son are the same.

I wished my thoughts, which now seemed like wasted energy, would desert me. I felt abandoned, unloved, and definitely forsaken. The obsessive methodology I fanatically clung to my whole life seemed futile. As passionate as I was about Christ's final words from the cross, I no longer cared what I believed or what others failed to understand.

The haunting bells tolled only twice this time as I continued to hesitantly count down to my death. It now seemed only minutes away. It was the eighth hour, two o'clock in the afternoon.

As my body attempted to stand again, I noticed that the priests headed back down the hill to the city, in preparation for the afternoon oblation. Instantly, I felt a calm come over the crowd. They were relieved that the priests had decided to leave. Now they could mourn the loss of the man they followed for three years. I heard much weeping from the sorrowful bystanders.

The middle of the crowd began to open from the rear. Someone moved from the rear of the crowd to the front without any resistance. I hoped to see the men from my team. I remembered that Jesus' disciples abandoned Him during the trial and execution, but I hoped that things would be different. I hoped to see the men from First Squad.

Episode Fifteen

Even though they were standing in for Jesus' disciples, maybe they would find enough courage to come out of hiding. After all, they were proven, fearless warriors. I knew that, had this occurred to me while we were on patrol in Vietnam, they would have never deserted me. I knew that, had the enemy tried to abduct me as Christ had been abducted, the confrontation would have ended in a bloody battle. But their absence further proved that nothing about this reenactment could be changed from its original account.

I felt the attitude of the crowd become warm and compassionate. I could see a small group of people moving within the center of the crowd, toward an opening. The crowd seemed gentle, like the hand of a gentleman assisting a lady. Someone important was coming toward the crucifix and this small group of people caused a brutal swarm to become generously companionate. I counted four genuinely sympathetic bodies hurrying toward me.

I remembered that Jesus' mother and a few others witnessed the crucifixion. They mournfully approached the foot of the cross. I felt sure that the sight of Jesus' mother must have eased some of His pain. After all, who better to embrace their own dying son than the one that brought him into the world?

I felt a sudden chill come over my body. The closer she came, the more intense it became. I watched as Jesus' mother fell to her knees in anguish. That was hard to watch, and it made me think about how my own mother would feel, had she witnessed me dying in Vietnam. I wanted to look closer, but my vision was still blurred. My body seemed to intentionally sag on the cross, falling forward as much as possible, as if reaching forward for companionship. My body dropped so quickly that I felt the foundation of the cross giving away a little. Gasping for air, I felt my eyes straining to see detail in the face of the woman whose passionate tears had moved hundreds of people aside.

My heart jumped sporadically in my chest, either from falling forward too fast or because my vision began to clear. I wanted to see the face of Jesus' mother more than anything, but wasn't sure why my body complied. Normally, what my mind wanted to say or do had nothing to do with what my body did. I figured that, since Jesus had control over my body, He must be just as desperate to see her. However, as my vision cleared further, I noticed something very familiar about this woman's face.

"Mom!" I shouted at the top of my voice. "Mom, is that really you?" No one could hear my shouts, but I knew that God heard me loud and clear. "Thank you, Father. I love you, Mom."

Seeing my mother eased my torment. I no longer felt alone. My mother's presence would make dying much easier. I thought about the irony. She was here in Jerusalem, but unable to be in Vietnam where I was actually dying. Thinking of my own death made me feel remorseful once again. I realized, whether in Vietnam or in Jerusalem, I would never feel my mother's arms around me again. I would never get to kiss her cheek and say hello again. I would never get the chance to take care of her as she took care of me.

Did she even know it was me? I wanted to let her know that this was all a just a really bad dream, that she would be okay, and that I was so sorry for dragging her into this nightmare.

Even with most of her head covered, I could still see her dark brown hair just below her scarf. Her eyes, tears streaming, squinted the way they always did when she had to focus on something far away. She held the scarf just below her nose, enabling me to see the light brown freckles on her right cheek. She wore black again, even though the last time she wore black was at my father's funeral. Afterward, she vowed never to wear all black ever again.

How horribly sad this was. It must have felt the same for Christ two thousand years ago. Jesus probably felt physically abandoned by His friends and followers. He must have felt as if He hadn't a friend in the world, until seeing His mother gave Him hope and strength. Her presence gave Him dignity in death.

I tried identifying the three others that were with my mother. A very large black man stood and helped my mother to her feet. I watched the man assist her as she halfway crawled closer to the foot of the cross. Unable to touch my feet she settled for hugging the bottom of the cross and fell once again to her knees. With my eyes now focused on my weeping mother, I saw a large hand carefully reach forward to gently caress my hideously mangled feet.

"Isaac," I said softly. My eyes shifted toward Lump's face. "This is truly worth dying for," I said, desperately trying to breathe. I realized that the longer I stayed slumped over, the harder it was to breathe. I knew that my body would attempt to stand erect again.

"Please watch over my mom as you have watched over me," I said to Lump, knowing that I need not ask.

Just as I thought, my body began to push on the platform, and through my upper and lower back, braced itself to stand. I felt my body struggle as it took a deep breath.

"Not many of those left in me," I said as my head and chin dropped to my chest.

Episode Fifteen

From the top of the cross, I saw a second woman approach to assist my grieving mother. I could only see that she was wearing all black as she ran forward to kneel next to my mother. Her face was hidden on one side, but I could see her speaking. Something about her gestures seemed familiar. The way she moved when she spoke relieved my mother, but it comforted me also. I felt that we were somehow connecting. Other than my mother, I only felt connected to one woman no matter how far apart we were.

"Is she going to do what I think she's going to do?" The lady used her right hand to move the scarf from the side of her face. As she looked up and smiled, I saw her face clearly. It was that same beautiful smile from years ago. It was the same smile that made patiently waiting, seem so worth it, especially when I knew it was coming.

"Vanessa," I said as my body fell forward again.

Each time my body fell, every ounce of air was expelled from my lungs with a loud thudding sound, almost like a car colliding with a densely fitted rubber wall. It was so loud that the people in the crowd would fall backwards, startled. Vanessa didn't budge. She held her scarf away from her face so I would never have to wait to see it again. I remembered how hard it was in the past for her to freely show her full face in public, but now she showed it to me as if to grant my dying wish. Seeing her face now was a gift from God.

I had so much to ask her. I wanted to know everything she had done with her life since leaving college. I wanted to know why her name wasn't on any of the rosters in Vietnam. I wanted to know why I couldn't find her when I first arrived. Seeing her face again brought back all the best memories of my childhood, ones that she had a lot to do with, and the choices I made later in life. I studied the Holy Bible more because she motivated me. I suffered through playing hockey because she treated me like a victorious gladiator when I came home. I enjoyed music because we sang all the Motown songs during the summer block club parties. With her soft smile, she encouraged my patriotism and inspired my drive to save the world.

Now that Vanessa was in Jerusalem I was confused. After seeing her again, I certainly didn't want this to be the last time. I wished that I could come down from the cross, if only for a moment.

"Why now?" I said. "It's too late, why?"

I looked at the fourth person, who seemed to be hiding behind Vanessa. It was a young boy; he just didn't want to look. It was Dino. He was too hurt to look at my body hanging there, so close to death. He never wanted me to go to Vietnam anyway. I recalled how he talked

190

about people going to Vietnam to meet Jesus, and only parts of them coming back home.

"I'm so sorry, Dino," I said. "I wish you could hear me, but I will always be with you, no matter what." I imagined that my father would have told me the same thing given the chance.

My head turned upright, eyes looking toward heaven. I felt sorry unto death and welcomed it now. I didn't know what was worse, hearing Jesus cry out in agony or watching my mother begging God to spare the life of her son. Being rendered unable to relieve my mother's torment was punishing, but being helpless to comfort my mother as she cried was even more agonizing for me. It brought back memories of hearing her crying herself to sleep at night after my father died. I would hear her weeping softly from across the hallway and run to her side. During those lonely nights, the sight of me standing by her bed gave her all the comfort she needed, but that comfort wasn't here now. I could feel her pain all over again. I wished I could stand by her now instead of watching her mourn her son's death.

"Dino, you be a good boy. Behave, and take care of Mommy," I said as I felt the voice of Jesus about to speak.

"Woman, behold thy son, brother behold thy mother."

I heard the words and realized that, for one time in this nightmare, my actions and words mirrored Jesus' actions and words.

Before this dream, I thought for sure that I only needed faith to follow in the path of Christ. A person like me could overcome Satan with just knowledge and understanding combined with faith. I had thought about how easy it would be to die when facing the adversary, but I never really considered how difficult it would be for those who loved me, those I would be leaving behind.

My body had struggled to get those last words out; now it used what might be my last ounce of energy to stand tall against the tree of death at my back.

As my body pushed and pulled to stand once more, I realized that, since the last time I heard the church bell toll, it had been getting gradually darker. Now the darkness was nearly complete. I listened sorrowfully as the bell tolled three. I knew it was the final hour.

Episode Sixteen
December 31 — January 1

By three o'clock in the afternoon, the daylight had turned pitch-black. Silence extended from the hilltop of Golgotha to the bowels of the city of Jerusalem. The wind stopped blowing. In the silence, the crowd hushed in unison, seeming comatose. I wondered if death always felt so determined to win, and if the hunger of the spectators fed into its personification.

I felt like I had been funneled into the black cloud from earlier, but even it paled in comparison as silent anticipation engulfed the atmosphere. The mule team appeared to be frozen in place. The guards looked skyward, toward me, but remained motionless. Everyone on the hilltop seemed suspended in timelessness.

Standing high upon the cross, my body struggled for its last breath. I felt my throat swell and my lips quiver. I knew that the final bell had announced my death, but I was still in Jerusalem. I had no lesson to teach and no more comparisons to make. Any knowledge or deeper understanding of the death of Christ on the cross and how it applied to the future was beyond anything I could imagine.

I waited to hear Jesus' final words, but I didn't want to say goodbye. I didn't want to go to heaven. My heart was torn. Did I really love God over my own life on earth? In the back of my mind, I still thought there might be a minuscule chance that God would whisk me away at any moment—before I died and before Christ took His dying breath.

Once those last words were spoken, I would never see my friends and family again on this side of heaven.

Would I be here in Jerusalem when Jesus pronounces His last words? If so what would be my fate, and could it be worse than death? In this crucial last moment, my unwilling mind turned to Jesus' final words on the cross; they reminded me of a discussion I had after the Christmas sermon.

No, I don't want to remember anymore, I thought, convinced that dying would bring the complete rest my body needed. Still, my mind wandered back to that Christmas day in Vietnam.

"I'm not saying that Jesus wasn't asking God to forgive those who conspired to kill Him but I am saying I don't agree," I said, addressing the audience waiting for me to continue teaching.

"I don't have a problem at all with people who believe that—in fact, believing that theory probably helps those who find themselves wrongly accused. But I believe that His last words were intended to transcend time. Their main purpose was to give hope to those who will be misled by the false Christ prior to His return. If Christ's dying words were addressing the future then He was asking God to forgive us and accept Him as an offering for the greatest of all sins."

People often misunderstood my focus on the bottom line, especially when it came to His final words, the words Jesus was about to utter, that I now hoped not to witness.

Standing erect on the cross, I felt my body struggle for another breath, quite possibly its last breath. The muscles in my upper thighs burned beyond exhaustion. The fierce contact with the vertical beam tormented my skin, shredded by the scourging. My triceps and biceps burned with tension while my neck muscles were taut, involuntarily holding my head upright. My mouth, completely parched from trying to suck in dry air, now hung open.

Looking toward heaven, I felt the final words leaving my mouth. "Father, forgive them," began the voice of Jesus, gasping for my final breath and spewing internal blood, "for they know not what they do. Into thy hands I commit my spirit. It is finished."

I immediately felt the time shifting again; I found myself traveling toward Vietnam.

"No, this can't be it," I said. "I can't be dead. What happened? The last time I was here… I mean…I wasn't in great shape, but at least I was recovering."

Episode Sixteen

I watched from the dimly lit tent in Vietnam as the surgeon made his last desperate attempt to revive me. I saw the futility of his efforts. Apparently, while I lay in bed, unconscious, an infection had set in and caused my heart to stop beating. It looked as if my body had been dissected, as the surgeon tried to manually massage life back into my damaged heart. I could see it lying lifeless in the palms of the mournfully eager surgeon. Looking at the surgeon's tools, among them I saw that same shiny piece of metal resembling a crucifix, the one that caused my head wound. Ironically the head wound had not ended my life.

I thought about the death of Christ in Jerusalem and compared my own death in Vietnam. In a way, I had died twice that day. A crucifix figured largely in both deaths.

"There's no pulse doctor. There's no blood pressure, sir. He's dead! We lost him. You can't bring him back, sir," said the assistant while the surgeon continued manually compressing my heart in his hands.

"Where does that leave me now?" I asked. "Why am I still here? Shouldn't I be in heaven? Why do I have to watch my own death?"

Watching my family disappear as the life left my body was hard enough; I would never recover from experiencing the pain and suffering that Jesus went through. Forced to feel Christ take His last breath before dying made me wish that I were dying instead of Him. Yet my torment continued; I felt as if I was being punished for something.

I never fully accepted the experience of Christ's ministry as a gift, which according to Father Shelly wasn't unusual for the Immortal Keepers. During the initiation phase, none of them ever realized that the dream was God's gift, a sort of compensation for being rejected from heaven later on.

Before sunrise the next morning, the remainder of First Squad brought the villagers into the camp while most of the platoons were finishing their morning P.T. The rear administrative attachment took over responsibility for the villagers, while First Squad, joined by Colonel Harris, stood in formation. He congratulated the team on their successful extraction of the villagers, but was clearly saddened by the loss of three squad members during the mission. On December 31, twelve men had gone out on the mission, but only nine had returned to the base camp. Three of their buddies had died on a mission that was supposed to be nonviolent. Before departing on the mission, most of them were looking forward to a few days off and some leisure time in Nah Trang when they returned. They had planned to kick off the day with a surprise birthday party for me, then head into town, but now Saez, Bart, and myself were dead.

With my death on their minds, they made different plans. They only had one thing on their minds now—remembering Chaplain Vincent Christopher. Dismissed, they headed to the infirmary. Seeing that I wasn't there, they decided to spend some time in the chapel. I had spent most of my time there planning my next Bible study lesson.

The men of First Squad gathered in the chapel, as if trying to hear my voice. The chapel was quiet and the chairs, filled with the whole company when I taught, were now empty. Each man went to the front and stood where I stood during my sermons. They told story after story about Jesus and how I would explain the second coming of Christ. It was their way of honoring me, their fallen comrade.

Peterson and Jinx had decided not to join the rest of the squad. Peterson rushed over to the medical unit with First Squad, but didn't leave with them when they left. He stayed behind in the infirmary, standing at the side of the only empty bed. He knew I was dead, but wanted to check for himself. Feeling like he had let me down in the field, he wanted to see me. He blamed himself for my death.

Peterson heard a voice behind him, saying that the person he was looking for wasn't here anymore.

"Sir, I'm looking for—" began Peterson.

"I know who you're looking for, soldier, but he's not here. He didn't make it," said the surgeon. "He survived the surgery, but his heart suddenly stopped beating a few hours before your squad returned. We did all we could for him, corporal."

"I know, sir. They told us in formation. But where is he now?" he asked. "Where is the preacher? I just want to see him before they ship him out."

"We sent him to the morgue already. Head over to the airfield and check with Sergeant Tobias," said the surgeon. "They should be loading him onto the ramp any minute now; if you hurry you might catch him."

"Yes, sir, thank you, sir," said Peterson, still unable to force himself to move from the place where my body had been.

Before the surgeon left he asked Peterson, "Were you close, corporal?"

"I like to think so, sir," said Peterson

The surgeon took his left hand. "Here, maybe you should have this. I kept it from his personal effects."

Episode Sixteen

Peterson paused before looking at the object in his palm, but then the reflection caught his attention. It was the piece of shrapnel from my head wound. The surgeon had done exactly what the assistant suggested, polished it, drilled a hole and laced it with a lanyard from an old parachute extension cord and I.D. tag chain, perfect for wearing around the neck.

In the barracks area, Jinx rushed to his quarters and his private stash. Searching for his works, he lifted the bedpost off the ground and removed the plug from the end. He was in such a hurry to get rid of his pain that he didn't care if anyone else saw him.

He grabbed his works and double-timed to the latrine. He preferred the end booth, which didn't have a door, but was partially blocked from view. While sitting on the commode he only had one thing on his mind. He had his works, his junk, and his private booth and planned to be feeling fine in a few minutes. Jinx, who never took responsibility for his addiction, blamed the war.

"This damn war's got my mind all messed up. T'ain't my fault the holy man got blowed-up. Told him not to come in the first place," grumbled Jinx, tightening his belt around his forearm.

My death affected him, too, and, although he would never admit it, it left him emotionally unstable.

"Yeah, yeah, oh yeah, that's nice. Yeah baby, take me home. Come on now… take… me… home. Take me anywhere, just take me from this place," he said as his head nodded.

After a few moments he was alert enough to prepare another injection.

"A little more might just take me where I need to go. Yeah. Sho' will. Just might make me forget all about him."

As he injected his second dose the dimly lit latrine became totally dark. It felt like the tent-covered wooden outhouse shook furiously. For Jinx, it seemed like a six hundred pound bomb had exploded, violently rocking the latrine and causing the lights under the tent to flicker sporadically. He wasn't sure if the drugs caused him to hallucinate or if someone outside was playing a trick on him.

"Hey," shouted Jinx "somebody in here? Quit yo' jiving, man."

Unable to see in the darkness, he waved his hand as if someone stood in front of him. He tried to see through the darkness, but he was so messed up from the heroine that he couldn't hold his head up anymore. Fumbling for his flashlight, he heard it hit the ground in front of his feet. As he reached down to pick it up, the lights flashed on, then off again for a second just as he opened his eyes.

"Why you messing wit' me?" said Jinx, "I'm tellin you, t' ain't my fault you dead. Go on from here, leave me, man. You dead—I know you dead. I tried to tell you. Everybody in da' Nam goin' ta hell."

Through his closed eyes Jinx saw the lights flash on again. He opened them just in time for the lights to flash off. This time he was sure he saw someone standing in front of him. In what was surely an act of contrition, he poured his guilt over my death while his body leaned against the partition. He held his head in his hands as if it might burst apart through his ears.

"What did they give me?" he said, referring to his drug dealer from Nah Trang. His eyes rolled; vomit began to spill from his mouth. The weight of his body slumped him over his knees and forward into the stall.

"What. You a ghost? It wasn't my f...f...falt...I... I'm sorry," he said, falling to the floor of the latrine, choking on his own vomit.

That was hard to watch, I thought as Jinx's body faded from view, leaving me wondering why I witnessed that. If I were officially dead, there was no reason for me to be on earth at all, and especially still in Vietnam.

After receiving permission from the surgeon to visit my body, Peterson ran over to the morgue. He hurried since my body was already bagged and crated for the flight back to the States.

The dead were stored in a dreary, creepy part of camp, where none of the soldiers would ever think of visiting. They joked about it, "You don't want to get caught dead in that place," and "That's the last place I'd ever visit." Peterson didn't want to visit it that day, but was driven to.

He handed the slip with the crate number to the morgue specialist who looked through his logbook, then left for the rear of the cooled tent. It was winter in Vietnam; the morgue tent felt like an iceberg. The specialist returned and walked straight past Peterson without acknowledging him. He headed for the NCO in charge of returning the fallen soldiers to the states.

"Yo. Sarge," shouted the specialist over the sound of the generators. "There ain't no body on this shelf, look here, the tag says A-4. And there ain't no body at A-4," he said, clearing his throat. "I know that body didn't just get up and walk away, but it sure ain't there."

Peterson watched as the sergeant took the deceased tag receipt from the specialist.

"That's not A-4, Specialist," said Sergeant Tobias. "It's H-7. Can't you read? Go to H-7 and check, you'll recognize it. It's a silver crate with a red crucifix painted on it."

"Red crucifix on a silver coffin—um, you know what? This sounds a little too spooky to me, Sarge. Besides, I got to get his personal gear and all of his issued equipment inspected and tagged for the return. How about you get the body and I'll get his personal effects ready?"

Peterson noticed that the specialist didn't give Sergeant Tobias a chance to answer, but hurried out of the tent.

Sergeant Tobias looked at his watch as he heard the C-147 air cargo plane start its engines. The plane's on-loading crew marched to the side entrance of the tent and stood in formation, waiting for the first pallet of coffins.

Peterson, clutching the ornament in his hand, watched the forklift driver carefully position one of the pallets, stacked with coffins, and drive backwards toward the morgue's side entrance. As the first detail escorted the forklift toward the plane's cargo ramp, he figured that my body would probably be leaving soon.

Sergeant Tobias was suddenly called back to the front desk. Peterson watched as he passed through the side entrance. There was a problem; the coffin manifest holding numbers didn't match the shipping numbers. Peterson knew that meant trouble, and that he might not get to see me until it was straightened out, and that could take hours. Carefully watching for Sergeant Tobias, Peterson slipped into the back storage room to search for me, but didn't have a clue where to look first.

"Where are you, my friend?" said Peterson, looking up and down each row as quickly as possible. He heard the second forklift driver enter into the side entrance of the tent while Tobias and the on-loading team sorted the coffins again. They had to carry one of the coffins into the storage area and replace it with the one matching the outgoing manifest.

Peterson wasn't having any luck finding H-7, though he had no problem finding rows numbered G and I.

"How can row H not be here?" he said. "This is impossible."

He heard the team enter the outgoing area of the morgue and exchange coffins. It took four men to switch and then carry the correct coffin to the pallet area, where they lifted it to the top of the stack.

Peterson had gotten so turned around in the storage area that he was now lost. He was so lost that he ran into the specialist that helped him earlier.

"What are you doing way back here?" he asked Peterson. "This area is off limits."

"I'm looking for my friend," said Peterson, squeezing the shrapnel tighter. "He's supposed to be in row H, number 7, but I can't find row H."

"I'm not surprised," said the specialist. "There is no row H. H is a special area used for high ranking brass, medics and chaplains. Around here, we call it H or heaven—Hell's way over at the other end. Get it?" joked the specialist as he took a puff and blew smoke from the cigarette dangling in his mouth.

"My friend is… or was… a chaplain," said Peterson.

"Right, well let me show you where it is," said the specialist, putting out his cigarette. "I'm telling you… there was something spooky about that whole chaplain thing from the get-go."

The specialist passed through rows of silver coffins stacked in threes on top of wooden pallets as Peterson eagerly followed. He had high hopes of getting the chance to say goodbye after all. They passed through the out-going storage room and straight to H, looking for number 7. It was clear on the other side of the warehouse tent, but when they got there, there was no coffin number H-7.

"The surgeon said that he should still be here. What do you mean he's not here?" said Peterson. "It's not like he rose from the dead and just walked out of here on his own, so he has to be here, right?"

"Sorry about that," said the specialist. "I don't know what to tell you, except he must have already been loaded onto the plane or he got shipped out earlier."

Peterson felt a little eerie as well. Something here seemed more like a supernatural occurrence, than human error.

"No, no way," he said. "Come on, Specialist, I'm sure the surgeon knows what he's talking about. If he said my friend should be here, then he should be here."

"Well, like I said, I don't see him, do you? Guess you just can't trust doctors, huh? Besides we got dissatisfied customers leaving the Nam 'bout every thirty minutes."

The first pallet driver was halfway to the cargo plane when Peterson made it back to the front of the tent warehouse.

"You still here?" asked Sergeant Tobias, "Did you get a chance to say goodbye to your preacher friend?"

Episode Sixteen

"No, I didn't," said Peterson. "I couldn't find his body." He finally said the words. He referred to me as "the body" and I'm sure it hurt to hear it for the first time. He didn't want to accept that I was dead, but now he had no choice.

"What do you mean, you couldn't find him? What do you think that whole confusion was about half an hour ago? We had the wrong coffin. My crew thought A-9 was supposed to be shipping out but it was supposed to be H-7. We made the exchange, but I didn't see you. I thought you had paid your respects and headed back to your company by now."

Sergeant Tobias noticed the cargo plane starting to raise the rear ramp. He pointed out the side entrance.

"If you hurry, you just might catch him."

Peterson sprinted down the walkway toward the runway, passing by the returning forklift driver, and making it to the back of the ramp just as it began lifting from the ground. The rear ramp officer released the hydraulic lever, halting the ramp in place as Peterson jumped aboard. He immediately saw the red crucifix standing out among fifty or so coffins lining the inside of the plane's belly and carefully stepped over to it.

"I just want to say goodbye to my friend," shouted Peterson to the ramp officer.

"Go ahead, corporal. You got about three mics."

Peterson traced his hand along the red crucifix with great care and affection. He had thought about saying so much, but, in that moment, he couldn't think of anything to say.

He leaned in toward my coffin. "Thank you," he whispered, pausing for a moment, taking hold of his emotions.

"Well, holy man," he said, "There was certainly something special about you. I'm sure I'm not the only one who noticed it. Guess you thought you would come over here and save us all, but ended up giving your own life instead. Well, if no one else is, I'm certainly grateful for what you did. I believe you were clearly in touch with the Lord. It was something about your vision. You helped me. I'm prepared now. I understand what you were talking about and, even if I'm not here in the end, I'll make sure my friends and family understand the difference between the true Christ and the false one. I'll warn them to watch for the false one, be prepared to stand against him, and to continue waiting for the true Christ. Wherever I go from now on, they're going to know about you, they're all going to remember you. You have a safe trip home, lieutenant."

The engines roared; he rushed his last few words, and then jumped from the ramp as it began to rise again. From the rear of the cargo plane he could feel the heat from the propeller blasts. He watched as the plane turned to line up for take off. He didn't feel guilty anymore; in fact, it felt as if he had been part of something extraordinary.

As the cargo plane left the runway, Peterson thought about the weeks he had spent listening to my understanding of the end times. All of his questions had been answered. He remembered something that happened to him a year before he joined the army. One day in church, he heard a voice from behind him asking if he knew what it meant to be born again, and if there were more to it, would he like to know? As he turned around to answer yes, there was no one there, but the answer to that question had been bugging him ever since.

He finally found the answer in a place that was thousands of miles from home, and from a person he probably never would have met in a thousand years. Peterson felt that meeting me was fate. He was determined to carry on, to be held accountable for the knowledge he had acquired.

Peterson knew that, although my death was untimely, my life had been full of purpose. I had presented the world with an understanding that was more important than life on earth. I presented people with unanswered questions concerning eternal life, with the hope of spiritual fulfillment, and knowledge, mostly contrary to popular theories. Peterson knew that I had helped others who felt that there must be more to God's words than lifestyle, values, and prosperity. I had answers to the conflicts and controversies concerning the return of Christ for people who needed to hear more than, "make sure you're among the first taken" or "don't be left behind."

Peterson didn't know that I accomplished all of that without ever completing my initiation into the realm of Immortal Keepers; due to my untimely demise, my real work had never begun. Now, there were twenty-three hundred ninety-nine curious Immortal Keepers whose minds quivered with the unresolved question: would this one unique Immortal Keeper get the chance to live again or had my two thousand year mission finally come to an end?

Episode Seventeen

December 31 — January 1

Lieutenant Chaplain Vincent J. Christopher's life came to an end on the night of this twenty-first birthday. For most young people, their twenty-first birthday is supposed to be the most important day of their life. Vince's expectations were no different. He anticipated waking up the next day with all of life's questions answered. He would come to the full realization of his purpose in life.

As an Immortal Keeper, he was supposed to join their ranks and work tirelessly, marking and sealing God's elect, preparing them for the battle prior to the return of Christ. He was the first Immortal Keeper to not complete each of the phases. His existence hovered in limbo. What would happen now? Would he return to heaven and stay there? Would he return to earth and live a normal life as a mortal, then return to heaven when that life ended? Would he return to earth and live a normal life until he turned twenty-one again, only to become re-initiated as an Immortal Keeper?

The whole realm of the Immortal Keepers intently awaited an answer. They intended to see the final resolution through to the end, no matter how long it took.

On that same night in the city of Detroit, although he was thousands of miles away from home, Vince's family had planned a sort of party to celebrate his birthday. They celebrated the happy day as if he were there with them. Vince's mother, Lump, Dino and other church members had gathered at the Christopher house. Unaware of his death, they hoped that he was celebrating as well. His mother knew that Vince would be happiest spending his birthday teaching lessons about Jesus, God, and end time events. She was at peace believing that he was doing exactly that.

Pictures all over the house showed Vincent, mostly teaching, being content in his calling. Isaac had taken the picture of the football bible and had it blown up to the size of a poster and framed. They had found the negatives; it turned out that Vince's dad had taken about twenty pictures in a row. Isaac had the rest of them developed and stood next to them, telling the whole story.

In the midst of their celebration, the phone rang. Whenever the phone rang in the evening, in the home of someone serving in Vietnam, the whole house would go quiet with silent prayers for the best. Everyone would pray that it wasn't the office of the President of the United States regretfully informing them of the death of their heroic son, daughter, or father, and then thanking them for the patriotic service to their country.

Mrs. Christopher answered the phone while everyone in the room held their breath. Everyone watched as her countenance sank. After hanging up the phone, she called for a taxi, excusing herself from the party. She assured everyone that the party should still go on; there was plenty of fried chicken that needed to be eaten before the night ended. She insisted that her trip was urgent, but she would only be gone for a short while. She asked Lump and Dino to travel with her.

"Where are we going?" Dino kept asking.

Lump wasted no time in putting on his boots, coat, and hat; he leaned on his cane. He stood by the front door without saying a word, his heart stuck in his throat. He hoped that they weren't taking a trip to the airfield or the funeral home. He patiently waited for the cab to pull up in front of the house, while Mrs. Christopher continued assuring her guests that they didn't need to worry.

"The taxi's here, ma'am," said Lump as he and Dino waited by the door.

"Mom, where we going?" Dino asked, "Is it good or bad?"

"You'll see when we get there, baby," said Mrs. Christopher as she got into the back seat of the taxi. She seemed happy, but behaved suspiciously as Dino and Isaac piled into the backseat with her.

"So, Miss Lilly, you want to tell us who was on the phone and what this is all about?" asked Lump.

"I can't," said Mrs. Christopher. "The man on the phone said it was urgent, that it had to do with my son and not to speak a word about it to

Episode Seventeen

anyone. He said that no one would understand it but me—and he said to bring Isaac and Dino with me."

"Understand what? Wait! The man mentioned us by name?" Lump continued to question.

"Yes, he gave me the number to the cab service and told me where to go. He said not to say a word and that the cab driver would already know where we're going." She repeated, "He said that I'm the only one who would understand."

"Is that why you didn't tell the taxi driver where to go—he already knows?" asked Lump while peering at the driver in the rearview mirror. "So, can you tell us now?"

"He told us to go to Detroit General Hospital and that there would be news about Vincent," said Mrs. Christopher.

"Is Vince back home?" asked Dino. "Did he come home, you know, like they show on the TV?"

"I don't rightly know, son. Maybe, but I don't think so."

Lump knew that, whatever the phone call was about and whoever it came from, must have been extremely important for Mrs. Christopher to leave in such a hurry. He had never seen her in such a calm, but quietly panicked state of mind. He never, ever saw her feeling rushed about anything.

Since it was the dead of winter in Detroit, the cab driver could not drive as fast as she wanted him to. The hospital was fifteen miles from her home and the side streets, which would have avoided the slowly changing traffic lights on Livernois Avenue, were packed with ice and snow. The traffic on the main road moved, bumper-to-bumper, at twenty miles per hour. The heaviest snowfall of the season blanketed the roads, making for a nerve-racking trip.

Lump had an instinctive feeling that this was no ordinary taxi driver. He figured that, whoever placed that incoming phone call must have already arranged for this particular driver, making Mrs. Christopher's phone call to the cab service a formality. As he looked out the back window on the driver's side, he saw a police car approaching at a high rate of speed, considering the hazardous road conditions. The police car moved past their cab, but slowed down as it maneuvered in front of them. He looked into the rearview mirror again and saw the flash of headlights following closely behind as well. He turned around to look through the rear windshield and recognized a second patrol car.

Given his nearly fatal run-in with the law, he contemplated every type of suspicious scenario. He anticipated getting pulled over and stopped by the police for 'driving-while-black in a snowstorm,' cab or no cab. He looked up as the traffic light turned from red to green. He began counting the number of lights they passed; to his surprise, they did not stop for a single one.

That's it—they're going to stop us for running red lights, he thought as another traffic light turned green.

Lump calmed down when he realized that the police officers seemed more like an escort than a threat. Mrs. Christopher thought nothing of the two tag-along patrol cars. She was too focused on getting to the hospital and finding out about Vince.

The snowfall grew heavier, the windshield wipers working overtime to clear the driver's view. Soon Lump couldn't see the rear lights on the patrol car ahead of them, though he kept his eye on the road as if to serve as a surrogate driver. The driver reached into his glove box and removed three pairs of sunglasses, handing a pair to each of his inquisitive passengers.

"Wow!" exclaimed Dino, looking through the glasses. "It stopped snowing just like that." He snapped his fingers.

In contrast to Dino's excitement, Lump became even more suspicious. While wearing the sunglasses, he could see clearly, as if it weren't snowing at all. He watched as another traffic light turned from red to green just as the cab pulled up to the intersection.

Looking through the sunglasses was like peeping into a strange and unexpected dimension. With the glasses on, Lump could see something peculiar about the driver's complexion. Then he noticed that it wasn't only the driver. The inside of the cab took on a futuristic, iridescent glow. Lump nodded to the driver, as if to acknowledge his new insight. However, his eyes remained riveted to the road as his mind raced at a furious pace in an attempt to decipher these bizarre events.

The cab swerved and fishtailed, though the driver remained in control, as a mysterious van frantically pulled adjacent to them on the driver's side. The Ford cargo van had its windows painted black, making it impossible to see the driver. The cab driver slowed down, then sped up in an attempt to regain control of his steering. As he did, a second black van approached on the passenger side, just as threatening as the first one.

From the reaction of the cab driver, Lump guessed that these two strange vans were not there to accompany them to the hospital. In fact, it appeared as if the two vans were attempting to sandwich their cab between them. Lump could tell that the cab driver was engaging his best defensive driving techniques. The cab driver figured out how to evade the menacing vans and, without any signals Lump could identify, the escorting patrol cars followed his lead.

The cabbie skillfully accelerated to thirty, then forty, and finally up to fifty miles per hour on the slippery avenue. The patrol cars to the front and back matched the cab's every increase. The two vans appeared to take the bait, trying to keep up with the cab and paying no attention to the two patrol cars. They only seemed interested in preventing the cab from reaching its destination.

Everyone was quiet except Dino.

"They don't want us to see Vince," he said, panicking at the strange turn of events. His mother reached over to hold him in her arms, but kept looking forward, toward the hospital.

After reaching its maximum speed, and without any warning, the cab driver hit the brakes, skidding straight ahead without fishtailing at all.

"Alright!" shouted Lump, impressed by the driver's skill.

Dino nodded in approval, adding a relieved, "Way to go!"

The front patrol car veered to the right, hit its brakes and steered into a fishtail, cutting off the front end of the van on the cab's passenger side. The rear police escort steered to its left and continued to accelerate as the van on the left attempted to slow down. The patrol car hit its rear bumper, causing it to fishtail out of control. To Lump, it looked like a play taken straight out of his old high school football playbook.

He watched as the next traffic light turned from red to green right on cue. He turned to look behind him. Two enormous, fully loaded fire engines were parked engine-to-engine across the road, strategically positioned to block the flow of traffic from every direction on Livernois Avenue.

"About five more lights to go?" asked Lump, looking at the cab driver in the rearview mirror, while wondering why he hadn't seen the fire engines coming.

The driver, never speaking, robotically nodded his head yes.

"Wow!" shouted Dino, "That was some really great driving. We're almost to the hospital now."

This inexplicable trip had become a magical journey. The strange sunglasses and the cooperating traffic lights made it seem as if they had been transported into a different dimension. Lump added up everything in his mind and concluded that there must be some supernatural interference.

Mrs. Christopher seemed already aware of it. Since she hung up the phone, she had seemed to be in a trancelike state, never once reacting to the police escort, the threatening vans, or the fire engines. She never mentioned anything about the glow inside the cab, the glasses, or the conveniently changing traffic lights. She seemed to anticipate each obstacle, expecting them to be resolved instantly. Dino was convinced that Vince had come to town for his birthday, even though he was thousands of miles on the other side of earth, fighting for his country.

"I don't know, but I think Vince has come home for his birthday, and I don't mean like on the TV either," he said again, referring to the flag-draped coffins seen on the news.

The cab driver pulled into the hospital area, straight up to the emergency entrance. There was a convenient patient drop-off area with a circular drive. Mrs. Christopher, holding Dino's hand, got out of the car on the passenger side while Lump exited on the driver's side. He felt the blast of subzero weather hit his face before he covered it with his scarf. As both car doors slammed shut, and before they could thank him or pay him, the driver drove off. Lump was the only one who noticed, as Mrs. Christopher and Dino were already walking toward the entrance. Still looking through the sunglasses, Lump had a feeling that he had not seen the last of that cab driver.

Lump's emotions stirred fearfully, and he was curious about what they would find. Dino acted hyper, his breathing erratic, probably because he didn't know what he felt. But Mrs. Christopher seemed a bit more at ease now that they were at the hospital. She remained focused on nothing but getting to the bottom of it all.

As the outer doors to the emergency entrance swung open, they heard what sounded like an alarm ringing. As they headed for the second row of doors, crowds of people ran toward them. Mrs. Christopher felt Dino's hand yanked from hers as the hallway between the doors became full of panicked patients, visitors, and staff.

Lump and Mrs. Christopher found themselves surrounded by a mob of people running for safety. Lump could hear a few people shouting, "Fire! Fire!"

"I think it's the fire alarm," he shouted.

"Dino, where are you, baby?" shouted Mrs. Christopher as she searched the area, trying without success to locate Dino.

Lump's first instinct was to use his body as a bulldozer and push his way through the entrance, but he couldn't risk leaving Mrs. Christopher alone. He surveyed the perimeter, spying five men dressed in identical black wool overcoats, black dress hats, and scarves. They all wore the same type of sunglasses that the driver had given him. One of the men walked away from the others.

"Let's go this way, Ms. Lilly," said Lump, giving her his arm and walking against the crowd. He was tall enough to see over them and kept his eye on the man leaving. Lump noticed that the man's right arm stretched downward as if he carried something or held onto someone next to him, but he couldn't see what or who it was. The man had the same peculiar glow around him that he remembered from inside the cab, making him easy to follow.

"What about Dino?" she asked.

"I think I know where he is," said Lump, confident that he had an idea what was happening.

He held her hand tighter, maneuvering his way through the flow of people. As they reached the outer edge, he lost track of the glow and the man he was following. Once they reached the edge, Isaac stopped walking. He realized that he was now walking in the wrong direction. Somehow the force of the crowd had turned them around. He was facing a man in black, but it wasn't the same one.

"What? How did that happen?" asked Lump.

As if getting off of a merry-go-round, they turned around and started walking in the original direction again. Looking over the crowd, he saw Dino standing with the man in black, waving them on, but when they reached the edge of the crowd again, they lost sight of them. For the second time, they found that they had somehow been turned around and were on the other side of the crowd. Something kept them from escaping the swarm of people.

Lump looked at the crowd in all four directions and noticed a man in black positioned at each end. They all stared intently at the center of the crowd. It opened from the middle and, as it did, he and Mrs. Christopher walked clear through to the other side, finding themselves completely free. Once again he looked for Dino and the man he had been standing with, but they had vanished from sight. Out of nowhere, but in the same spot that he last saw Dino standing, another man in black appeared just long enough to be recognized, then dashed around the corner from the emergency entrance. He vanished just as quickly as he appeared.

Lump followed his lead as he and Mrs. Christopher darted around the same corner, then into a small maintenance entrance. He held the door open for her, then took the lead as they started pressing forward.

This time, Mrs. Christopher stopped him and took charge. "This way!" she whispered, "He's on the third floor."

As they passed the information desk Lump noticed that the sign for the third floor said, 'Maternity/Pediatrics'.

"Maternity?" he wondered. "Why are we going to the pediatrics floor to find Vince?"

Mrs. Christopher now led confidently, heading toward the elevator as Lump overheard the loudspeaker issuing instructions about which exit doors to use to evacuate the bottom floors. He noticed three to four security teams assisting the elderly, but forcibly removing those who refused to leave. While they waited for the elevator, one of the teams headed straight for them. The men gestured as if telling them to leave the area. They ignored the instructions, as Mrs. Christopher waited intently for the elevator doors to open. The ceiling lights flickered on and off as the alarm siren continued blaring, but Mrs. Christopher seemed deaf to everything around her. She only responded to whoever or whatever was calling to her.

A second security team turned the corner. They were practically within arm's reach when the elevator door opened.

Lump and Mrs. Christopher hurried into the empty elevator; the doors closed immediately behind them.

"There's no third floor button," Lump said to Mrs. Christopher as he looked on the other side of the door.

"We're on the wrong one," said Mrs. Christopher. "This is the express elevator."

Taking the elevator to the twelfth floor, they had to ride back down to the emergency room floor, the scene of the initial chaos. As the elevator doors opened, Isaac noticed that the dim emergency lights lit the E.R. The sirens still wailed; fire fighters ran through the corridors surrounding the elevators. He could see the elevator they needed across from them, the doors open for them to board. However, a security team stood by the doors, ready to escort any stragglers immediately out of the building.

"No, we can't leave yet," said Mrs. Christopher, "We have to find Dino and Vincent."

The four security officers took positions around them. Lump looked toward the exit doors as they were being escorted out, then behind him. One of the guards was missing. A second one had vanished as he looked for the first; and then the third and fourth disappeared. It was as if they were being targeted and picked off, one by one. It happened so fast that he couldn't tell where they were being taken. By the time they reached the exit, there was no trace of them.

Episode Seventeen

Three men wearing sunglasses blocked the exit to the street. Lump reached into his pocket to pull out his own glasses. When he put them on, he had no problem seeing what was happening. The lights were still hazy, but, turning to look toward the elevators behind them, he saw ten men dressed in black and wearing sunglasses. Their glow created a brightly lit path from the exit doors all the way to the elevator corridor. Lump raised his sunglasses to see if it looked any different without them. The glow was there, but did not have the same strong presence.

The men never said a word, or even acknowledged them, as they walked toward the elevator. The path led them to the open doors of the third floor elevator. Once the doors closed behind them, the elevator rose without hesitation.

As the doors opened, they saw Dino waiting for them.

"Mommy" he said, flinging his arms around her.

"Dino," she replied, "Thank God. Son, don't you ever run off and leave me like that again. Do you hear me?"

"Yes, ma'am," he said, "But the cab driver brought me here."

She hugged him as Lump looked down the corridor to the left and into the adjoining hallway. The third floor corridor glowed like the one from the E.R. floor. He counted eight men dressed in black, then four more in the maternity ward.

They had all surrendered to what was happening, saving their questions for later. The supernatural had taken over and was in control. From the moment they left the house, something had been drawing them here, but something else had tried to prevent them from arriving. As this surreal scene unfolded, the unsuspecting trio followed the path of light to Room 310 and entered.

Lump couldn't believe his eyes. Overwhelmed with joy, Mrs. Christopher took one look at the woman lying in bed and the child cradled in her arms and knew that this woman had gone through the same thing she experienced twenty-one years ago today. This wasn't the first time she had seen the mysterious men and their guiding light. Mrs. Christopher remembered the honor of the nine months she spent carrying a special soul in her womb, and how it had changed her. She knew that this new soul had been to earth many times before as well. There was something very different and special about him. She knew, too, that it was no coincidence that they were all in this room together. She looked into the woman's familiar face.

"Vanessa," she said softly. "Oh my baby girl, I'm so happy for you."

"Momma, this is—" began Vanessa.

"You don't have to tell me," Mrs. Christopher said. "I know who this is. Well, hello there, little Vincey." She touched his foot with motherly love. "Welcome home, little man."

Lump took Dino's hand as he tried to figure out what Mrs. Christopher was talking about. Is this the Vince that the phone call was about? he thought. He still didn't know what was going on, and probably never would. Whatever was happening, he was sure it was well beyond normal.

"Isaac, do you remember me?" Vanessa asked, calling him by his given name.

"Yes… Yes, of course I remember you, Vanessa," he said, stammering, "So… so you're here, and we're here, and you have a brand new baby boy. Con… congratulations."

Lump did the math in his head. She was ten years older than he was, making her at least thirty-one years old.

"Thank you, Isaac. I named him after Vincent. I hope you don't mind, Miss Lilly," said Vanessa.

"I don't mind at all," Mrs. Christopher said, "And, from the looks of things around here, and the welcome committee, it doesn't seem like you had much of a choice."

"How did you know to come?" asked Vanessa.

"That's quite a long story, and I'll have to share it with you one day soon. Where are you living?" Mrs. Christopher asked.

"Well, I just arrived back in the country earlier today. My husband is a medic in the Army. He is scheduled to come back from Vietnam soon, but I had to come straight to the hospital. I didn't expect this to happen tonight…so…I don't…"

"Don't say another word, honey. I still have a room for you and little Vincent. Both of you are welcome to it just as soon as the doctors release the two of you. Rest now, I'll come back tomorrow to help you as you need."

As they left the hospital, each absorbed in their own thoughts about what happened that night. The ride back to the Christopher house was normal. The traffic lights changed every thirty seconds; they had to stop at every single one. The cab driver had to drive at twenty miles per hour because of the drifting snow.

Lump considered letting the driver use his sunglasses, but decided that he needed to protect them. He just might want them again. He felt that whatever happened tonight might not be over yet. It might not be the last time he saw those mysterious men in the vans, police cars and hospital.

Episode Seventeen

Lump would never understand who the men were, or how they orchestrated the whole evening, beginning with the telephone call to the Christopher house. However, his intuition was correct. A supernatural force had orchestrated the evening's events. The Immortal Keepers, drawn into the same eventful journey as Lump, Dino, and Mrs. Christopher, were very interested in the implications of Vince's death in Vietnam that night, the birth of a newborn child, and why they were so closely related.

Curious, they wanted to find out if the circumstances surrounding Vince's death would allow him to return to heaven. They all hoped so. However, if this newborn child contained the soul of their fallen comrade, then part of their question has been answered. They knew that Vince did not complete his initiation before succumbing to his wounds, yet another soon-to-be Immortal Keeper had been born while all others were accounted for.

They knew that this child, like all of the others, would go through the initiation when he reaches the acceptable age. But their question still lingered unanswered. When this Vince's life ends, will he return to heaven and remain there forever, or return to earth and continue to wait for the second coming of Christ?

For now, it appears that the Immortal Keepers must watch and wait a whole lifetime for that final answer.

Arriving back at the house without incident, Mrs. Christopher and Dino thanked Lump for accompanying them to the hospital. Since their dinner had been interrupted, she fixed him a heaping plate, hugged and said good night. The evening had been eventful and exhausting.

Settling in, Mrs. Christopher sat on the couch in front of the television. Dino went over to turn up the volume and then returned to sit next to her. She looked at the end table and noticed that next to the telephone there was a hand-written note from her friend.

"The phone kept ringing while you were out, but we decided not to answer it. Hope everything is okay, see you tomorrow. Love, Willa."

Staring at the telephone Mrs. Christopher folded the note and left it on the table.

"Look, Mom, they're showing the soldiers coming home again, see?" said Dino as he pointed to the black and white footage on the news.

"You can change that channel, Son. We don't need to watch it anymore."

Her attention was diverted as the telephone began to ring. She sat on the couch, motionless. Dino looked into her now-serene face, wondering why she was not moving to answer the persistent ringing.

"Mom, said Dino after the third ring. "Want me to answer it?"

"No, Son," she said with a sound of knowing comfort in her voice. "It's okay. They'll call back. Besides, we don't need to hear what we already know."

THE END

About the Author

Tony Scott Macauley, ordained Christian Minister, Non Denomination, is a former U.S. Army Ranger, serving with 1/75, 3/75 Ranger Battalions, and finally for the Department of the Army Ranger School as instructor/trainer.

His love for the word of God, the military, and sharing knowledge that provokes and inspires followers and non-followers of Christ to think deeper/simpler, is profoundly embedded and continues to be his life long personal passion.

He believes that whatever is emphasized from the word of God, be it Christian lifestyle, prosperity, or Christian values, the bottom line, the return of Christ should be well understood and hidden messages revealed.

"The word of God should be made easy, taught simply with emphasis on training, chapter by chapter and verse by verse, revealing each prominent example and how it can be applied to the second coming of Christ."

His focus is driven by 1 Corinthians 10:11. "Now all these things happened unto them for examples: and they are written for our admonition, upon whom the ends of the world are come."

Most of all, learning the word of God should be fun and made easy, the characters brought to life and made familiar and the complete plan understood. For Christians, teaching the word of God is one of the most responsible jobs on earth, for how will people learn unless they have a teacher.

Since resigning from the U.S. Army he has been teaching ballroom dancing for over ten years and owns a small ballroom dance studio in historic West End Atlanta Ga. His next book — *The Immortal Dance: The Preparation* — highlights ballroom dancing and answers many questions about the Holy Bible and the Second Coming of Christ.

www.adreambeforedying.com
Email Tony: TonyMacauley@att.net

Published by
Dancing House Publishing
PO Box 10566, Atlanta, Georgia 30310

$16.95
ISBN 978-0-9830881-2-7

CPSIA information can be obtained at www.ICGtesting.com
227167LV00002B/7/P